WITHDRAWN

The Night Fishers of Antibes

By the same author

BLOOD AND GUTS IS GOING NUTS
CASABLACK
LOONEYHIME

The Night Fishers of Antibes

Christopher Leopold

HAMISH HAMILTON
LONDON

First published in Great Britain 1981
by Hamish Hamilton Limited
Garden House 57-59 Long Acre London WC2E 9JZ

British Library Cataloguing in Publication Data

Leopold, Christopher
'The Night Fishers of Antibes'
I. Title
823'.9'1F
ISBN 0-241-10413-0

Printed and bound in Great Britain by
Redwood Burn Limited
Trowbridge & Esher

For Jenny and Olive

CONTENTS

The Dead Casino

1

The Riviera coastline was cleaner in the late 1930s. The only flotsam was the new tide of people who flowed down to the Côte d'Azur. Sun-seekers, card-sharpers, ruined Russian aristocrats, bogus artists, counterfeit old Etonians, war-scared industrialists and lesser crooks, together with a hotch-potch of refugees from the dynamited playgrounds of Europe, began to crowd on to a blue shoreline which was destined to become, gradually, a little more grey.

It was the people the tide of events brought in who left the slick on the beaches.

But there was one refugee who arrived on that coast (in the year 1936, to be precise) whose humanity and genius were as expansive as the sun at noon-day over Cap d'Antibes. He was running from the horror of war and the grotesque things that could happen to a peaceful Basque town like Guernica. But instead of keeping his talent locked up tight in his getaway suitcase, he spent it wildly, like Prince Baccarat, the craziest Russian in the Nice casino. And the miracle was that the more he spent his genius, the richer he became. *'Faites vos jeux,'* the god of creativity cried. And again and again Pablo Picasso collected.

He didn't know about people who were really frightened, frightened to the depths of their souls. He didn't understand about people like Michel André: young and handsome, urbane and apparently inexhaustibly rich, with his invariable morning glass of champagne at the poolside; but in reality as sick as democracy itself in a world that had become all stamping feet and high-stepping jackboots.

Oh yes, Picasso could appreciate a joke with the best of them. He could play the matador or the bull at a party at Hélène Colmar's studio, and smilingly sketch a centaur on a door behind which two couples were locked in love-making. He survived, and so he reasoned he was alive. And life was crude jokes as well as masterful brush strokes.

So, when one drunken evening in his studio in Antibes Michel André threw down this wild and impertinent challenge, he accepted it in good part.

'I have an inspiration, a magnificent, luminous concept which puts your talent in the shade,' he had cried.

From his old rival Matisse, Picasso might not have taken such a taunt lightly. Michel André was young and rich and also very drunk, and the master who loved youth and was not averse to money was prepared to be indulgent.

'Listen to my brainwave, and see if you can compete with it on canvas,' André had said. And then, although they were alone, his voice had dropped to a whisper as he outlined the brilliant idea he claimed outshone the genius of Picasso.

Picasso had been drinking a good deal too, which was fairly unusual for him, although he was always prepared to give any facet of Life's comedy or catastrophe a whirl. And so he had accepted an impossible challenge and, as Michel André talked, his brush had started to go to work. Fractured faces, artificially lamplit, began to appear on the canvas, peering into the depths of an opaque sea.

'You can try Pablo, but you can't better my masterpiece,' Michel André had laughed tipsily. 'My inspiration is worth millions to the people who will know how to use it. Your daub will fetch a million at the most!'

While Michel André talked, the first sketch of Pablo Picasso's major painting of the period, *Night Fishing at Antibes,* began to appear on the canvas.

'There is a natural menace about harbours after sundown,' he said to himself, because he was sober enough to realise that his guest was too drunk for intelligent conversation.

'Daub away, old master!' André shouted. 'I'm selling to the highest bidder. However hard you try you'll never touch my price.'

A young man shouting how he would astound the world, and an ageing master approaching another masterpiece, as time slowly ran out for Europe, like sand through an hourglass.

2

The man in the kiosk that sold *glaces au chocolat* thought at first it was the biplane which pulled the Michelin publicity streamer down low over the bay and the harbour round about this time in the season. He expected at any moment to see it appear from behind the steep incline of the château, to come shooting along the Promenade des Anglais just a hundred or so feet up. And he craned his neck accordingly.

The machine-gunner dozing on a sandbag in the June sun on the top of the Casino didn't quite know what to think of it. With its bulbous nose and hump-backed cockpit, it resembled no silhouette of any French or British plane he'd ever been shown.

From the beach opposite the Hôtel Negresco a little boy in a sun-hat pointed at it excitedly. His modish mother, slumped deep in her deckchair, gave it one incurious glance and twisted her body round to catch the setting sun. She turned her back on the interloper in the sky, and gave just one thought to her husband cut off on the Maginot Line.

Three grandiloquent storeys beneath the slumbering sentry reservist atop the Casino, things were getting a shade more fraught. Jerome's problem was that he was an instinctive gambler, in other words he operated by some kind of feline Italian empathy allied with frequent communion with the soul of his saintly dead grandmother. It was also true he always seemed to win at Nice. Whereas this Englishman, Dominick Craufurd, was all systems and grey matter. It was hinted Dominick Craufurd brought luck to no one but himself. Some sensed that, behind his conventionally British appearance, his Thirties forehead with the thin black hair brushed back from a parting precisely dead centre, the blank blue eyes, there lurked a memory as deadly as that of Nikolas Zographos; of whom it was rumoured he could remember individually each and every one of the 312 cards played in a show of baccarat.

But if Craufurd was trying hard today it wasn't just because Nice usually jinxed him. Also the stakes were rather special. Jerome di Cavazza had put his faith in eight seemingly arbitrary numbers called Les Orphelins (not surprisingly – he had been one himself). But today he was not 'feeling' the numbers. Not that anyone else was exactly breaking the bank. Only Dominick Craufurd seemed to be doing any good at all: you could tell by his habit of drawing in the breath quickly so that it whistled through a gap between two upper molars. By the way he nonchalantly twisted one fist in his dinner-jacket pocket, cut in a style set by the Duke of Windsor when Prince of Wales; the black tie manhandled into the tiniest of black knots, the red buttonhole. *'Numéro vingt-et-un,'* droned the croupier. And Jerome di Cavazza's dwindling stake was depleted by a further two hundred francs. Missing the vital 20 of his brood of Orphelins by a hair's-breadth. He had just two hundred francs left.

'I take a rest,' he muttered, and strolled past a makeshift footman in an ill-fitting periwig into the fresher air of the antechamber.

He stood on the balcony with the sea air flapping the heavy red and gold curtains, and sighed.

It was unwise to leave the table. While he stood here, Dominick might be clinching it. He only needed another thirteen hundred . . . .

But, also, Jerome guessed that he'd inch towards it, get there by half-sou bits. When you'd played that trick for *that prize,* you didn't throw it away. But there was also the character of the man to consider, and the thought enabled Jerome di Cavazza to take in the smoke from his Gauloise in long slow lungfuls. Craufurd would want his best friend and rival physically there when he made the winning coup. Just so he could flash him that quizzical look, as if to say, 'see, I've beaten my jinx.'

Meanwhile there were things to take the eye. The gentle movement of fishing boats and a few last yachts on a sea of china blue, the opulent Rolls owned by one of the richest and weirdest men in the world as it nosed its way down the almost empty Promenade des Anglais, an anti-aircraft battery up there by the château, just by the exit from the *ascenseur*, projecting its ugly snout just above a line of palm trees.

A flotilla of destroyers hooting their way out to sea mixed in his mind with the smell of garlic and fried langoustines, the voice of Jean Sablon behind a third-floor shutter. And something else, a drone which was also a cough. But a cough that stayed in the throat and wouldn't give up. A burring up there in the sky.

'Hopeless,' said squat Monsieur Labiche, another refugee from the killing game. 'Impossible. On such a day, what can one do?' Jerome di Cavazza put a comforting arm round the shoulder of the little man. 'My friend, there are days like this,' he murmured in his impeccable French. 'We learn to treat them like....'

The drone had become a dot. The dot lost height and began to twist around in the distance. It did an awkward turn and began a slow run in towards the *plage*.

'It's a Potez,' said Jerome almost to himself, wondering again at the sheer clumsiness of this obsolete French fighter. 'With such planes ...' he gave his charming shrug, a Cavazza hallmark.

'Of course there is a sleeper,' said Monsieur Labiche, 'but unfortunately in my case....' He made the gesture of turning out his pockets. On closer sight it wasn't a Potez at all. It was something even further down the evolutionary scale.... 'A sleeper, eh,' he remarked to Monsieur Labiche. 'I hadn't noticed.'

'Numéro Twenty-three. When I left the table it hadn't shown up for one hundred and thirty-one throws.'

Now as every gambler knows, a 'Sleeper' is a number that obstinately refuses to turn up. But it was odd the number should be Twenty-three. Of all the possible numbers; and people still insisted they didn't believe in Fate. Mind you, it wouldn't strike Dominick Craufurd in quite the same way. It was a very private secret of Jerome, that the most dangerous woman in Nice had only last week celebrated her twenty-third birthday.

'Do you know what,' he murmured, turning to Monsieur Labiche. 'I think that thing's going to attack us.'

The snub-nosed, hump-backed Fiat G-50 Frescia Fighter might be a good advertisement for Mussolini's Regia Aeronautica, but Jerome distrusted its intentions. He preferred to let his mind lollop delightfully over the figure of the Sleeper on 23; preferred to filter out the whine of the engine and the stammer of the guns, to remember a voice as soft and voluptuous as a flesh tone by Bonnard. Rat-tat-tat went the guns, as the Frescia lazily sprayed a group of bathers. Rat-tat-tat again, and a man abandoned his telescope on the Promenade and made for the shuttered-up Tea Rooms. Behind him, Jerome heard that well-known thin whistle.

'Isn't it one of your lot, Tenante?' Dominick Craufurd enquired.

Jerome, eyes still on the Fiat Frescia, mind still on the Sleeper at 23, gave him a very Italian shrug, two white hands emerging from tight cuffs and performing their eloquent spider's dance.

'Well, you've got your war, Tenente . . .' the Englishman said, but the rest of his words were blocked by the Fiat as it came zooming close above them and saluted the Promenade des Anglais with a trailer of lead.

They heard the anti-aircraft gun open up from the promontory. They heard the machine-gun post on the Casino three storeys above them join in. They saw, too, the garrulous deckchair man make a dash for the beach huts. Saw him stumble, writhe, collapse and lie still. Saw the raked sand turn a delicate pinkish red.

'First blood to Il Duce,' remarked Dominick Craufurd. Then with a roar that seemed about four times louder than the Fiat, a prehistoric seaplane rose from behind the jetty in the port and prepared to do battle with the intruder. Unlike the Frescia it wasn't on anyone's current list of military aircraft, in fact it was hardly military at all, a species of coastal patrol plane that happened to have two machine-guns perversely placed aft and stern. It had hardly fluttered beyond the promontory when the Fiat pounced. Again that almost inaudible rat-tat-tat-tat.

The French plane lurched drunkenly then slowly turned on its side and started dropping towards the sea, smoke pouring from one of its two engines. Finally it belly-flopped into Mussolini's Mare Nostrum.

It was the 11th of June, 1940 and Italy had just declared war.

A war had started, but there was another one to finish. Jerome di Cavazza turned to the worst friend a man ever had in the world and made a gesture backwards and inwards – in the direction of the Salon Privé.

These were the rules. Each man took to the table a thousand francs' worth of chips. There was no time limit. You won by being the first to make ten thousand francs. You lost when your stack of chips was demolished. In your bid to be the first to reach that ten thousand figure you might take risks. You could lose the lot – and the Lady. The game was roulette, pure uncomplicated roulette, with no frills attached. You played until you won or you lost or you dropped. Of course the rules of the game demanded total absorption. The only problem now being that the croupier's attention, not surprisingly, was elsewhere. A crack had appeared in one of the Empire mirrors which, for a century of seasons, had reflected back impartially so many distorted faces. Most of the diehards who had kept the Establishment going, had left the tables. Herr Zumfayrer from Zurich alone held on, his beady eyes still on the wheel, his pockets stuffed with scribbled lines and numbers. 'I am sorry, messieurs. The house is closing,' the manager informed them. 'It is no longer possible to play. It is a farce,' gesturing to the great chandelier wobbling above them to the rhythm of the French gunfire. 'Nonsense, Gaston,' remonstrated Dominick Craufurd. 'Stuff and nonsense. You can't stop when I'm winning.' 'Besides, it is illegal to close now,' muttered Herr Zumfayrer gloomily. 'I will report you to the Maire.'

'It would be very kind, very obliging, most delicate if even under these circumstances you could contrive . . .' offered Jerome, turning on the full power of his Italian charm. 'I don't think it will take too long.'

'Come on, Gaston . . . just five more turns of the wheel, that's all we ask,' urged Dominick. 'You can't lose your neck on that.'

The manager bowed curtly and nodded to the head croupier. Bets were laid. Jerome dumped all his collection of chips on Red. Dominick, pursuing his cautious addiction to contreAlemberg, put 500 on Impair. Both won. By the end of the third throw, Dominick had amassed some 8600 francs. Jerome had lost over three thousand. 'The chap who ends with the most chips wins, agreed, old chap?' suggested Dominick as they went into the final throw. 'I'm sorry, old boy, but I'm simply not sticking my neck out any more today.'

Dominick had waited till the white ball was in play, and until just before the croupier intoned *'rien ne va plus'*. Then he took all his chips off the board and quietly pocketed them as if to say, my case rests. Jerome was left with only one hope – to win on a number. When he placed his few thousand on 23 it was less a nod to mathematics, more a response to a voice which had said the word in that outrageous little love tent they'd shared. A revelation about an age, for his ears only. . . .

'You are lucky, my friend,' Dominick told him as they strolled onto the Promenade. 'Don't think I didn't notice that naughty Sleeper on Twenty-three – the harlot. Nothing for one hundred and thirty-three moves, wasn't it? By the way,' he added, watching the footmen prepare to seal the massive doors of the Casino for the duration, 'I hate to interfere with anyone's pleasure, but if I were you I'd get along to Villa pretty smart, the jolly old camping-site rather. I mean, you are an enemy alien, aren't you? They might just get the idea of sending some stupid *flic* to arrest you.'

3

'How can the Government order it?' the Commissioner for Police shouted. 'The Government is not in Paris!'

'The cable has the signature of the Minister himself,' the young Inspector said.

'The Minister is a refugee,' the Commissioner snarled. A plump hand grabbed and crunched an empty packet of Gitanes. 'The whole damned Government are refugees. How can refugees give orders?'

The Inspector was a young man in his mid twenties from Normandy. The Commissioner was a fat, sallow-faced official in his fifties who hailed from Cagnes.

The two men looked at each other across this distance of age and background.

'The Government has left Paris; but they will be in Bordeaux tomorrow,' the Inspector answered coolly.

'You're still insane if you think this Department has time to round up every Italian in the region,' Commissioner Lazzaron growled like a Provençal farmer over his evening glass of *marc*. 'We have our hands full of enough refugees without a refugee Government ordering us to round up more refugees!'

'We are in contact with General Montagne's headquarters, sir. The army has promised full co-operation.'

'The army!' Strong peasant teeth tore the lid off a new mutilated packet of Gitanes. I wouldn't put any faith in the army if I were you. Well, look what they've done for your province,' he added with a malevolent gleam, 'I understand it's crawling with Boche. The army should be fighting the Boche instead of sitting on their backsides down here.'

'We are at war with Italy now, sir.'

'They should be fighting like they're supposed to fight instead of rounding up aliens.' The Commissioner sucked at his Gitanes pack, which he had now rolled into a cigar shape. 'Do you know how many Italians there are living in the region?' he demanded, and added with an extra snarl of prejudice, 'Didn't they teach you anything in the North?'

'The order is from Monsieur Mandel's office, sir,' Inspector Clément replied evenly.

'I said, do you know how many Italians there are living in the region? Do you know? I'll tell you. It's every other waiter, every croupier, every other grocer, hairdresser, hotelier, gambler, pastry cook, pickpocket, banker, gigolo, and priest on this coast!'

'They are enemy aliens now, sir. It is a necessary precaution in war....'

A raucous ringing interrupted him. The Commissioner was banging on a primitive desk bell. 'You want to know, I'll tell,' he shouted, as a greying sergeant with a cigarette in his mouth came in. 'I want the files,' the Commissioner rasped at him, 'The files on aliens – Italian. And bring me a packet of cigarettes.'

'You see what I mean,' Commissioner Lazzaron grimaced as the sergeant eventually began to unload a heap of sepia files on to his desk. 'Aberoni, Abuzzi, Acelli, Augustini . . . it goes on forever. You want to know why, since they obviously didn't teach you at school? Nice used to be an Italian town. Here we go again ... Canuzi, Cavazza, Cavetti, Cavour. Look, you can see the problem for yourself!' He pushed the files across the desk. News had come through that the German 6th Army had reached the Seine. Everyone's nerves were jagged. Some files tipped over and spilled their contents on the brown linoleum floor.

'Go ahead and arrest that lot,' the Commissioner waved, 'it'll take you longer than the duration of this war!'

Inspector Clément was not proud, only dedicated to efficiency. He knelt down on the floor and began to reassemble the spilled files as if, almost single-handed, or so it seemed to him, he was trying to pick up the pieces of France. The classically austere notepaper of the Hôtel Westminster caught his eye. He did not associate Italian citizens with the Hôtel Westminster. He thought of grey-moustached, elongated individuals, panama-hatted in blazers and fawn trousers, walking on the Promenade des Anglais with dumpy wives wearing pearls. The letter was from Count Jerome di Cavazza requesting an extension of his residential permit in France. He turned the letter over. The file on Jerome di Cavazza did not add up to an extensive correspondence. There were further letters from impressive hotels and villas at Cap d'Antibes, requesting further extensions of his residence permit. But there was also a confidential memo from the Sûreté dated 27 July, 1936, notifying the Department that di Cavazza had been removed from surveillance, and another dated May, 1936 to the effect that he had been placed under it.

Inspector Clément knew how he would begin.

'You realise Mussolini and his boys will be here in two days!' the Commissioner called after him. 'They won't thank you for your trouble.'

Up to a point the Commissioner was right. There were not the resources to arrest the entire Italian population in Nice in one afternoon. But he could make a start. This morning he had seen a column of armoured cars in the Rue Gambetta trying to move towards the Italian frontier against a flood of refugee traffic from Menton. It would take only a handful of fascist saboteurs to play havoc with the army's narrow supply lines. He needed, in fact, another file – the Sûreté's records of individuals who at one time or another in the last ten years had been under surveillance. Then, by cross-checking with his own card-index system, he would arrest the Italian nationals who featured on this list.

Three hours later, his shirt glued to his back by sweat, Inspector Clément and his assistants had completed the process. Again Jerome di Cavazza's name had come out on top, like some lucky, or unlucky, card.

4

Jerome di Cavazza took the country road that threaded among the hillsides of orange and pink summer houses behind the deep blue sea. It should have been the road to the frontier. This was alien territory now, an odd fact to come to terms with for a man who knew every twist and turn of it, but as certain as the crash of the French seaplane he had seen spiralling out of the sky.

He should have been headed east as fast as his flashy Ferrari could carry him, but here he was rounding a bend in the twilight and seeing the harbour of Antibes come into view behind Fort Carré – watching the furtive lights, beyond the harbour walls, of a couple of night fishing-boats at work in defiance of the black-out regulations.

He should have been racing home to King, Duce and country. Instead, he was putting even more distance between himself and what would have to be his ultimate destination. He cruised around the outskirts of the old town and along the herb-fragrant shoreline deep into fashionable villa country.

The old concierge sullenly creaked open the gates, and Cavazza's pointed, two-tone shoe went gently down on the pedal. He had almost forgotten how acutely the driveway corkscrewed through a forest of scented shrubs up to the villa of Les Ombres. But, then, it had been designed by that unpredictable genius of the French cinema, Georges Bizet, protégé of Jean Renoir and Marcel Carné and inventive friend and architect to the dead owner, Michel André. Bizet had swung the driveway around in a series of hairpin bends quite alien to the villa's stately and monumental portals. The effect was trompe l'oeil, and it truly deceived.

Cavazza's headlamps picked out a wraith-like clump of pine

saplings and hibiscus, then round the bend and slap into something resembling a black metallic hearse. The next second he was mowing down the saplings, his car crazily swerving on three wheels, finally to brake in a grotto dedicated to the Goddess Minerva whose statue, fresh from a factory in Nice, now lay shattered underneath his chassis.

'Christ, turn those lights out,' came a voice from the drive. 'Do you want every Wop bomber dropping its load on us?'

A figure came through the failing light, a short figure in a tight-fitting tweed suit with a waistcoast which, as far as Jerome knew, only one Englishman was crazy enough to wear at the height of a Côte d'Azur summer. It was Philip Hickson-Smith, British vice-consul in Nice. His Old Hurstpierpoint tie gleamed in the dusk.

'Excuse me,' Jerome enquired. 'Your head lights – don't you use them any more?'

'Some of us obey the black-out regulation. My God, it's Cavazza!' The little Englishman peered up at him. 'What on earth are you doing here?'

'I am on my way to present my compliments to Mademoiselle Colmar.' He didn't explain that he had won her at the Nice Casino; Hickson-Smith was an Englishman of the old school.

'I mean to say, what are you doing in France – at least what are you doing out of internment? Aren't you an enemy alien now?'

'Couldn't I ask the same question of you?' Jerome smiled in the gathering darkness. 'At least I can ask what your business is with Mademoiselle Colmar?'

'Just making one of my many parish calls,' Hickson-Smith sighed. 'Quite frankly, we've been worked off our feet recently, and this news today isn't going to make things any easier. Oh yes, didn't you know the Consulate has a fatherly interest in Miss Colmar's welfare? Apparently, she has a mother of English extraction. Everyone seems to have discovered an English mother down here this summer. In Miss Colmar's case, we're prepared not to be too sceptical. I daresay she's only imagining things,' he added, 'we're all feeling a little highly strung just now.'

'What things does she imagine?'

'She's got the idea that someone is trying to gain access to the villa, could even have got hold of a key. Some sort of menacing presence. Of course, the place has been completely deserted since André died, though there are some pretty queer people wandering around these days. This infernal war! Anyway, I think I managed to reassure her.'

'Hélène is a very pleasant lady to reassure,' Jerome said, with a sarcastic edge. 'Now you must excuse me. I am in rather a hurry.'

'But, Cavazza, wait,' Hickson-Smith shrilled. 'The car. The damage.'

'Oh, take this.' Jerome flung him one of the wads of notes he had earned that afternoon at the roulette wheel.

'No, this is too much, much too much. You've only bashed in one wing. My Riley is built like a tank.'

'It's just paper – alien's paper,' Jerome sneered, turning back towards the villa.

He was surprised to find Hickson-Smith was trying to shake him by the hand. 'Whatever the news bulletins say, I've always had a tremendous respect for your country and in a way your Prime Minister or . . . er, dictator. At least he made your trains run on time. I'm sure if we could all get round a table and talk sensibly . . . well, I must be flying.' The voice sank an octave. 'We have some *truly important* guests down here on the Cap. A charming couple not unconnected with Buckingham Palace, I must drop in on the way home.'

'The Duke and Duchess of Windsor at their villa?'

Hickson-Smith whistled softly, cautioning silence. 'It's absolutely confidential. I hope you'll treat what I said as absolutely confidential.'

Jerome got back into his car, thinking it was a funny kind of confidence to bestow on an enemy alien.

In Cap d'Antibes did Michel André a stately pleasure dome decree . . . .

Not that he was around to enjoy it. His body lay somewhere up there in the Bavarian mountains in a grave of ice. So talented. So much to live for; but that was another story.

Of course, it wasn't all that stately really, rather a piece of frippery to please a lady. Michel André had inherited more money than was good for him, along with a chemical plant near Lille. But his love had been moving pictures. He had been attracted not just by the French cinema during its golden age, but by something even more exotic, its hot-house offshoot growing so voluptuously in the Côte d'Azur. Nice had become a kind of Hollywood, devoid of the ballyhoo but with something rarer to commend it: a realism, an artistic integrity, and a star called Hélène Colmar.

Hélène. For her he had thrown together the whole jerry-built villa, a palace of concrete glinting skeleton-white under the arch of two searchlights chasing each other across the sky. Of course, she wouldn't be in the big place itself. She'd always hated it. Like Marie Antoinette, she'd sought something simpler, if you could describe Le Bijou as simpler, and indeed if you could find it.

Jerome got out of the car and walked towards what he imagined to be a woodland path, and blundered straight into a fence. Peering through the wire mesh he recognised it for what it was, a prisoner-of-war compound, empty as yet and without guards.

Then he blinked again and made out the wooden posts inside; the tennis court at Les Ombres had been quite something. Le Bijou was a joke, but it was also a sanctuary. Her joke, her sanctuary. It stood on the highest terrace in the Les Ombres estate. It looked east and was cut on a narrow vista down that fabled coast which terminated in the grey bastions of Cap Ferrat. It was a log cabin, such as early American settlers might have built in Arizona. It still smelt of pitch and newly-varnished chestnut, mingling with the faded nostalgia of Revenir, a scent specially designed for the exclusive use of Hélène Colmar, and a few of her friends. The furniture, the bed, like a crude four-poster, was all New Frontier. From the exposed planks in the ceiling fluttered an old Confederate flag.

That was Le Bijou, and Jerome, moving towards it, forgot one more obstacle, until his left foot slipped neatly in and twisted round with excruciating pain. It was the ninth hole of that other prevailing passion of the *jeunesse* of the Riviera – 'Le Clock Golf'.

With a stifled groan, he dragged his feet across the long grass meadow which only last year had been the trimmest piece of lawn east of Cannes.

A squeak of the door.

Tip-toeing over the buffalo skins, dodging the great white American bearskin, the well-oiled pine planks creaking under his feet; making for the wigwam, searching for La Belle Squaw (she had been known to dye her face redskin red) snuggling up there without a stitch of a nightdress, a squaw in a million.

Another two steps and he heard closer deep breathing, then a snore, but a snore that was music to his ears.

The Sleeper at 23, now at most favourable odds, was about to be gently awakened. The white ivory ball had click-aclacked across the numbers on the wheel, and now she was his for seven nights, if the French authorities would leave him in peace. It sounded sordid, even arbitrary, but seriously was there a better way to settle an affair of honour among gentlemen? A duel perhaps. But when one was a Cavazza one didn't kill one's best friend, even though among the Fascist aristocracy in Italy the duel had become once more fashionable.

Her bed was a heap of huge bearskins lumped together on the brand new pine. And, above, a canopy, a flapping of canvases, a chic Parisian game of wigwams.

A matter of seconds to lose his suit of lightest turquoise blue, to unbutton his silk shirt, and to climb in beside the prettiest squaw east of the Rockies. To feel her body snuggle around him like an animal pleasurably stirring in its sleep.

And something else stirring too. A hand running through his hair and feeling his cheek, but still the hand of a Beauty not yet awakened. A hand that was ruffling through the hairs on his chest. All his for a week, he thought, as one finger tickled his navel. And then the breathing lightened, and the voice which was always husky as if she was starting a perpetual cold in the throat.

'Ah, Dominick,' she breathed, 'Nicky, Nicky. My poor little Nicky. But, wait – this is not Nicky. This is ... ah, this is better, darling Jerome, better than I had ever hoped ....'

5

Life had been slipping away from Dominick Craufurd for some years now. You could pin-point the moment it started to a night in the officers' mess, and the hysterical spoilt boy of a subaltern who laboured under the illusion he had an uncanny touch at backgammon. Unfortunately, he was also in Captain Craufurd's C Company, which made things a bit difficult. It had been a shaming experience for Dominick. His personal definition of a 'gentleman' was someone who could keep the killer instinct buried well below the surface, so that not a hint of a fang was revealed. That night he had overdone the whisky decanter and upped his stakes. The colonel had come in at the precise moment when Dominick was engaged in transferring the unearned thousands that idled in the boy's bank account into his own more needy custody. Cashiering was probably correct (he did seem to remember some regimental edict against wagering large sums), but the colonel had done it nastily, with an imputation of cheating. Of course the thought hadn't been further from Craufurd's brain.

Captain Dominick Craufurd's casual façade of a 'gentleman' was stripped from him in one throw. Of course he had not even been allowed to hang on to the boy's money, though God knew why.

Suddenly life began to look bleak for a Craufurd who was no longer a gentleman. It was the mid-Thirties, a time of massive unemployment, and even the old-boy network didn't want to help. Nor did it take long for his delightful and entirely cold-blooded wife to run off with a Conservative MP called Sandy Pennard, who just happened to own Grampington Place in Oxfordshire with two thousand acres thrown in, quite enough to guarantee the respectability and future security of that cad Craufurd's ex-wife.

He could not really blame her, but over the next few years he kept on asking himself why he and not the Pennards had taken custody of the two children, Niall and Oriana. Of course, he was glad to be alive and to possess still a reasonable gentleman's wardrobe. But he had to admit that, on this sunny June day, there wasn't much barrel left to scrape.

Not that he could explain any of this to Dalio, the swarthy old fisherman, as they sat at a table outside the café and shared a few Pernods (a drink which in fact Dominick Craufurd cordially detested).

'Les salauds, les cochons,' Dalio was shouting, gesticulating out past the bay, where brightly coloured boats bobbed in the soft evening light.

Dominick nodded sympathetically and turned round to flick a finger at Alphonse the waiter, conscripted back into café service now that his son was at the front.

'Two more Pernods,' he told him. 'And by the way, has my call come through yet – the one to Dieppe?'

'Dieppe, Monsieur Craufurd,' echoed Alphonse, with his most tragic expression. Of course only a madman of an Englishman would want to telephone a place like that. Wasn't it common knowledge that the German Panzers had occupied the town days ago?

Craufurd wondered why Dalio was so angry at the prospect of an armada of Italian fishing boats sailing in from Ventimiglia and beyond to pinch his catch. Loup de mer was a pretty commonplace fish, and anyway Dalio was probably basically Italian himself like so many so-called Frenchmen around here.

When would that blasted call to Dieppe come through? That was what was really niggling at Dominick Craufurd.

'You understand, eh?' spat out Dalio, perhaps noticing a vacant look on Craufurd's face. *'Les cochons. Nous sommes foutus ....'*

'I wouldn't be too worried about Mussolini if I were you,' Dominick told him. Which led his thoughts back to a certain Tenente Jerome di Cavazza. Normally it would have made Dominick Craufurd's loins ache excruciatingly to think of his Italian rival fondling the limbs of the most beddable woman on the Riviera. But today it didn't. Jerome had won. Hélène Colmar's body was his for the next week – or at least until the French police or Italian call-up papers caught up with him.

There were problems nearer home. For instance, though he had been clever enough to leave the tables today when he was still up (though not as far up as Jerome), his collection of bills far outnumbered any cash he could put in the field against them. And this Italian invasion was inconvenient. It spelt the end of Dominick's precarious survival as agent and go-between, dealing in anything from renting villas and yachts, to disposing of other people's antiques, fakes and works of art in a reasonably civilized and discreet way. With Mussolini's armies thumping their way up the Corniche road nobody was likely to be in the market for anything other than a fast car or an air-raid shelter. Which left in the balance all those bills littering the front-door mat of his apartment. Unless of course he decided to do a midnight flit.... But, then, how could that prim young governess he had hired, Miss Audrey Hopkirk from Godalming, Surrey, reach him with those two brats of his? Would she have had the presence of mind to whisk them away from Dieppe before the Panzers moved in? His money was on No. So where the hell could they be? It was quite a revelation to Dominick Craufurd, now very much the confirmed bachelor, to realise that he actually missed their confounded chirruping. He had a vision of Niall down here waving a shrimping net, Oriana with her hair blowing in the mistral and a cheeky grin on her freckled face, and that curiously proper young lady, Audrey Hopkirk.

Christ, just to hear their voices, to know they were alive and kicking. Phone connections between here and the lycée in Dieppe had not been that good even in peacetime. Which was why, when Alphonse started shouting from the café door in his execrable Marseillais patois, 'Monsieur Craufurd, Monsieur Craufurd – the telephone ... Dieppe – it's through,' he turned on him one of those famous Craufurd blank stares.

For a second his heart had raced with joy, but today of all days pleasure clearly was not made to last. All he got from Dieppe was some concierge or other with the information that the Germans were here, the school shut down, and all the children dispersed.

He returned thoughtfully to swap Pernods with the fisherman Dalio.

6

Hélène Colmar was talking in her sleep. Not the voluptuous whispers, the rich cadences of pleasure that had issued from her an hour or so ago — she was muttering disconnected names and uncompleted sentences, punctuated by little moans and, from time to time, childish cries of alarm.

Listening, Jerome felt a tinge of apprehension and also of guilt. It was so tempting to think of Hélène as a spoiled animal, a golden squaw, a scented and bejewelled courtesan.

He had forgotten that Michel André had left her a sizeable fortune in debts and that opportunities for starring parts were scarce in the French cinema industry in 1940. He failed to take account of the fact that golden Hélène, like most other people on the Riviera this season, was pressed for currency. Perhaps the occasional winnings he and Craufurd tossed onto her dressing-table were her only source of income, apart from any other commissions she picked up – and he did not want to think about those.

Hélène was talking incoherently about shops and banks and credit and the rising price of butter. Awake, she had been a glorious tigress, but asleep she was a nervous little girl. And as Jerome listened he discovered another source of anxiety. In among the grocery bills and the overdrafts and the disconnected names of various creditors, an imprecise fear was emerging concerning faceless intruders and unidentified visitors with keys – the fear Hickson-Smith said he had reassured her about.

'They're coming, they're coming – don't please let them in!' The gibberish was suddenly a piercing scream.

And now she was awake and staring with popping eyes through the drawn-up flaps of the sham wigwam.

'*Chérie, cara* – there is no one here, only me, and you want me, don't you? Look – ' he picked up a flashlight by the bed and played it around the cabin. There was nothing there except a yellowing photograph of Sitting Bull and the horns of a bison, and a picture.

For a moment or two he kept the flashlight on the picture. It was the only incongruous thing in this cabin dedicated to Wild Western culture, and it was perhaps the only thing among the entire heap of bric-à-brac of genuine value. Under dim castle walls two shadowy fishermen were peering into an oily sea lit by a giant torch. He could not see at this distance, but knew that one of the fishermen had skewered an outsize fish, because of course he had seen the picture before, and half remembered the story Michel André had told him one night before he fell to his death in the mountains – a boast to the effect that he was the only man in Europe ever to have persuaded the old genius to do a painting to order.

He turned off the flashlight and buried his mouth in Hélène's neck. 'There is no one here. No one is coming, except your Jerome.'

But in this he was mistaken. It was the sound of feet on the gravel and crossing the piles of old heaped fir-cones that awoke him to the danger. The night was so still you could hear a whispered command; the click of the safety-catch on a revolver.

Of course, his pursuers did not quite know the lie of the land – this crazy land of Le Bijou. No one could, except for a certain unemployed film technician called Georges Bizet. This early log cabin was a more perfect facsimile than anyone could have guessed. The original in Denver Museum had an unusual feature – an escape hatch at the rear in case of Injun attack. It took Jerome di Cavazza very few seconds indeed to put on his clothes and crawl out into the thick grass behind, reflecting wryly as he went on other uses Hélène might have put this to, and how many lovers had tumbled like him into the moist long grass. Peering round the cabin he could see what he had to deal with. Converging on the cabin from all points of the compass, except behind, was a group of Inspector Clément's gendarmes, most of them armed.

For a moment, one thought troubled him – Hélène. Was it a point of honour for him to declare himself, stay and fight it out with the posse of gendarmes? But Jerome was more than an impetuous young aristrocrat. He came also from a subtle race, the seed of Machiavelli. In his heart he knew that a distraught young woman could put a policeman to flight faster than ever he could, and that besides he must live to fight another day.

The police van at the entrance by the extinguished flambeaux started at once, and soon Jerome was manipulating its stupidly thick wheels round the twisty bends that led down along the Cap d'Antibes coast road.

7

'It's been nice talking with you,' the US State Department official had said as the Lisbon Clipper flying boat had cruised to its moorings. 'Most Americans I know are travelling the other way this summer.'

'I'm not "most Americans",' Marvin Huntingdon had answered confidently.

Yet the State Department official had put his finger on it. Most people were cashing their savings, selling their jewellery or bribing travel clerks with their wives to get out of Europe this summer, but one thing Marvin Huntingdon never did was to move with the trend.

The trend said Europe was finished. For the next decade, maybe even the next century, the New York art world would have to do without its regular imports of genius from the studios of Paris and the Côte d'Azur. The trend said that, for the foreseeable future, there was going to be a terminal shortage of fresh Matisses, Picassos, Légers, and Rouaults. The business would have to live on its fat, or try to discover another Jackson Pollock or Ben Shahn.

Who cared what other people said!

Marvin Huntingdon was by profession an art dealer. You might have said he was an artist among dealers. He shared with the truly great minds a total contempt for current fashions and fads, and in the long term it tended to pay off. Marvin Huntingdon was, if you like, a man whose delight in the rare and the beautiful went hand in hand with a shrewd business instinct.

His journey was not strictly for art's sake. On commercial grounds there were reasons for thinking that, as Europe fell, so would picture prices. With the Panzers beating a path to their studio doors, even the most expensive French painters would be tempted to deal at knock-down prices. All this had entered into Huntingdon's practical calculations. And yet there was another tug that had impelled him back to Europe at a moment when it was collapsing like a house of cards, and this was his reverence for genius, in particular the genius of Pablo Picasso.

What Picasso was doing, what he was thinking and most of all how he was painting mattered vitally to this little New Yorker, who in so many ways temperamentally was a world apart from the confident, life-loving Andalusian. Painters were Huntingdon's bread and butter, but Picasso was food and drink to his soul. In fact, Marvin Huntingdon just could not bear the thought of a world without the works of Pablo Ruiz Picasso.

Hence this fantastic journey in the one direction no one else wanted to take; those arguments at Lisbon airport with those sallow officials who had suspected him of lunacy; that everlasting hell of a train journey across a Spain shattered by civil war; that small difference of opinion at the French frontier with two *gardes mobiles* who wanted to shoot him as a spy. It only made sense if you loved Picasso even more than the prices he fetched.

And this is why it made sense that, at ten o'clock at night in the old town of Antibes, when most Americans were home, or dining out on their Blitzkrieg experiences aboard some illuminated neutral ocean liner, a small man wearing a dapper, double-breasted, sky-blue pin-striped suit, and a straw hat to disguise a premature spot of baldness, should have been knocking at an unlit door.

There was no answer. At the same time Marvin Huntingdon knew there could be no mistake. He had never visited Picasso in Antibes, but his research had been precise down to the last curb-stone. You did not travel over three thousand miles without making sure you had an exact description of Picasso's Antibes hideway.

And you did not come over three thousand miles to take no for an answer. Not if you were a dedicated pilgrim like Huntingdon.

A quick look around the street, an art expert's job with a sensitive strip of metal, and, hey presto, he was in the magician's cave. Yes, he felt a twinge of guilt; but he had come a long way and Picasso's spirit was, he felt sure, generous enough to understand.

It felt right. It smelled right. As far as he could see, it looked right, even down to the absence of pictures on the walls. You got to know about great painters' houses, you knew that one of the distinguishing features was the lack of hung paintings. So you did not look at the walls, which in this case seemed to be as naked as Adam and Eve, you looked for the canvases filed behind easels, or desks or even under beds. Where was the light switch? There was no electric light switch. You got to expect this too; but if you looked around with your cigarette lighter you usually found an oil lamp somewhere. Yes, it was as he had expected.

When he reached the first floor, Marvin Huntingdon experienced a sort of psychic *frisson.* He somehow *knew* that this was the room where Picasso had painted his last prewar masterpiece – *Night Fishing at Antibes.* It was an awesome, humbling, spine-tingling feeling.

Pablo Picasso had draped three walls with a giant canvas, measuring nearly seven feet high, and waited for inspiration. Then he had gone feverishly to work on one of the walls to produce perhaps the most richly luminous statement of his career, or so the legend went. Afterwards, he had trimmed the painting to its definitive size, and left the canvases on the other walls untouched, so the legend continued. And, hey, Jesus, look, behold!

The oil lamp revealed that the blank canvases were still hanging on two walls, leaving a gap of tacky and torn wallpaper where the paintings had been. Legend was breathing close down Marvin Huntingdon's scrawny neck.

There was another part of the legend which was not so convincing in Marvin Huntingdon's expert view. Picasso had painted *Night Fishing* straight on to the canvas without the help of any preliminary sketches, or so some wiseacres maintained. But Picasso always made at least one preliminary sketch! In most cases he made a gallery-full – look at the number of near masterpieces that had led to *Guernica*! Of course it was just dandy for the Guggenheim Foundation, which had bought the picture, if there *was* no preparatory sketch or painting for *Night Fishing.* It added a lot of exclusivity to their showpiece.

Marvin Huntingdon hitched up his blue pin-stripe trousers and sank on to his knees. Mostly, it was in devout gratitude for the revelation that had been bestowed on him. At the same time Marvin Huntingdon was a businessman. From his knees he slid on to all fours and began to make an exhaustive search of the studio. Somewhere, perhaps only inches away, there had to be a preliminary sketch for *Night Fishing.* At current US prices for Picassos he was prepared to settle for the roughest of drafts.

Sometimes love blinds. A scholar can feel such empathy with his subjects, a dealer such an intuitive understanding of a painter, he overlooks vital little practical details. Huntingdon was confident he knew exactly where Pablo Picasso could be found at any given time in the year, but his confidence was based on outdated information. In the late autumn of 1939, Pablo Picasso had moved, on impulse, to the small fishing village of Royan at the mouth of the Gironde. The studio at Antibes had been empty for more than seven months. And somehow no one had told Marvin Huntingdon.

8

'She's rather fun, isn't she?' Dominick had said, gunning the engine, so that the docile Mediterranean turned into a foaming ocean. He had bought the boat from an American millionaire (correction, ex-millionaire) who had lost a good deal of Nebraska one evening at *chemin de fer;* picked it up for a song from another born loser it had been his good fortune to meet. Hélène had smiled at the explosion of surf the engine had created and turned away from Jerome to call affectionately to Dominick, 'Nicky, you look ridiculous in that yachting cap, but your boat is *tellement puissant!*' And with an airy wave he had placed it at her permanent disposal. For a month or so it had roared across the Riviera seacapes packed to the gunwales with laughing *mondains* and rich bohemians. Then it had been returned like an unwanted toy to the little harbour of Antibes. With luck it was still there, Jerome prayed as he searched in the darkness among a forest of masts without sails.

The chances of getting clean away would be measurably improved if he could get his hands on the wheel of this sleek black surface torpedo, instead of taking his chances on the refugee-choked road to the frontier past Menton. Besides, as chance would have it, he happened to have the key to the black beauty. Hélène was always generous with her unwanted possessions.

'Can I help you, Monsieur?'

He could not see the face clearly, but the silhouette belonged unmistakably to the trenches of Verdun and the Chemins des Dames. A *poilu* was raising a hand to his '14-'18 style helmet, a gesture half respectful and half suspicious. He had been called up for a reserve Division, to guard what it had been supposed was a quiet stretch of coast as far away as possible from the war. In fact they could have done with more veterans like this *poilu* at the Meuse crossings last month.

'I am looking for a boat – Mademoiselle Colmar's boat.'

'A pass is necessary if you are to take out a boat tonight, sir. You are not a fisherman, are you?'

'Mademoiselle Colmar urgently requires her boat,' Jerome announced, and added a little more impressively, 'She is assisting the Prefect with the evacuation of non-combatants to safety further down the coast.'

'A pass will still be necessary, Monsieur.'

'Ah, there it is!'

The slim sensual lines were unmistakable even though its decks were draped in protective canvas.

The old *poilu* followed him with his Lebel rifle slung. Jerome switched on his flashlight, risking an accusation of black-out infringement but at the same time, he calculated, giving the veteran an opportunity to take in his Savile Row blue silk suit and his two-tone brogue shoes, and the fact that he was undoubtedly a person of a certain class.

'You have an authorisation from the Prefect, Monsieur?' the *poilu* asked, half servility and half menace.

'Naturally, but first I need your help.'

At this moment Jerome heard the wail of a police siren rounding the walls of the old town.

'Help me get this canvas off. We cannot keep the Prefect waiting,' he ordered.

The *poilu* did as he was told; he was a soldier of the old school.

'Now, if you could be so kind....'

Three precious jerry cans of petrol from the summer of 1939 were collecting cobwebs in the stern. He handed one of them to the *poilu* on the quay and motioned towards the boat's silver-plated petrol cap. 'She's got to take a full complement to Toulon,' he explained as officiously as he knew how.

The veteran of the trenches poured the contents of the can into the fuel tank, but he took his time about it, examining the trickle of petrol as if it was the essence of some new device invented by the cunning Boche. Jerome had nearly emptied the contents of the second can when the old soldier said, 'Stop. I must ask you to show me your authorisation from the Prefect.'

'Let's get this boat launched first,' Jerome told him, putting down the can and leaping on board.

'Will you be good enough to cast off,' he called breezily.

The *poilu* had obeyed to the extent of releasing the painter; but now he was holding the rope in his hand as if uncertain what to do next.

There were so many keys on this ring he had forgotten what most of them unlocked. There was a married woman in Rome, the wife of a party official . . . perhaps this was her key; God knew what this was, unless it was the key to his locker at the Juan Les Pins golf club. And what was this little tin wedge? Of course, it was the key to Poste Restante box *numéro* 375 in Nice, the place where he was supposed to leave information concerning French military preparations in the Alpes Maritimes. Like the key to his golf locker it had hardly ever been used. And here was another that did not fit into the control panel, perhaps because it was the key to Dominick Craufurd's flat in Antibes which he had won at a game of 'Liaisons' one evening in the period when he had suspected his friend of cheating in the arrangement they had about Hélène. But where was the ignition key?

The boat rocked unexpectedly. The old soldier, holding his rifle at the port, had jumped into the stern.

'Do you know what I think? I think you are a spy,' he muttered as he advanced down the boat. Behind him a police siren wailed on the Avenue de Verdun, as if in confirmation.

The engine sprang into life. Jerome had finally found the right key. However, there was a new obstacle. The old *poilu* had locked his hands around Jerome's throat. His warrior's moustache was rubbing against his chin. The night was full of the scent of Marc and black tobacco. The boat idled out into the harbour as the two men danced cheek-to-cheek in the wheel house. Then it seemed as if one of the dancers tripped. In fact, Jerome had stamped viciously on his partner's boot. It took a lot of shoving to get him into the water.

But now he could hammer the engine so that it roared like a seaplane entered for the Schneider Trophy. The yachts and fishing boats lying around the harbour suddenly picked up speed and rushed past him into the night. He was out in the bay, accelerating fast under the medieval walls of the Fort Carré. In no time he was cruising past the blacked-out hills of Nice and watching the tree-lined silhouette of Cap Ferrat knifing towards his bows.

There was another thing Dominick Craufurd did not know about his boat. One June morning when Jerome and Hélène were out for a joy ride, and she was still thrilled by the power of her new toy, there had been this unspoken dare between them. The rules of this game, never repeated, were unformalised but simple. You left the wheel spinning and kissed Hélène as seriously as if you were in bed with her. Then, while a blue-sailed little yacht full of screaming passengers lurched across your bows and the pink rocks of Cap Ferrat came almost into hailing distance, you pulled her down on to the floor of the wheel house and rushed through the preliminary motions of love. It was cheating if you looked over your shoulder and saw that the rocks had doubled in size since you last looked at them. The aim of the game was fulfilment before the zigzagging boat exploded into Cap Ferrat. They had won by a whisker. He remembered leaping back naked to the wheel, yanking it hard to port, as an isolated rock dashed past to starboard, and Hélène lay naked on the deck, as golden as Venus, laughing near to hysteria. That was an afternoon in the sun in the summer of 1939. Now it was dark and there was only a half-moon.

Jerome di Cavazza was a Christian, not a pagan; otherwise he might have decided that what he was looking at in the moonlight was the hand of Neptune on the deck-rail. The thing, in any case, turned his face whiter than the moonlight. He watched, letting the engine slow, as another hand swung out of the darkness and fastened on the deck-rail. And then, very slowly, a head began to appear – black, shiny locks, a dripping moustache as long as a triton's. It took a little more time to recognise the outraged eyes of the old *poilu*. Truly a soldier of the old school, he had clung to his adversary even though it had been necessary to travel like a sack of fish in the wake of the speedboat. Now at last, as the boat slowed he had found the leverage he needed, and a dripping khaki shoulder and half a khaki torso came into view by the deck-rail. It was at this point that Jerome noticed he had left his Lebel rifle on board. If he had not been so panicked by the other worldly nature of the apparition, he would not have brought the butt of the Lebel down so hard on the Frenchman's hands, striking, again and again, at what seemed two shifting unnatural objects, giving the old *poilu* no chance to save himself from sliding back into the black water.

We are not so far from shore, if he can swim at all he will soon have his feet on terra firma, Jerome prayed as he bounded around Cap Ferrat. 'That peasant Mussolini. I could kill him for starting this war!' he shouted at the moon.

The lights of Monte Carlo were out too. Although the Principality was officially neutral, no one was taking any chances. To risk a light anywhere in Europe was a sucker's bet in the summer of 1940. Nor were there any lights around Cap Martin. He had expected a shower of Verey lights, a myriad gun-flashes – a proper firework show at the very least because he was now approaching Menton and the Casino where he always lost and what must presumably be the front line. If it was the front, it was all quiet here.

He remembered that Dominick's speedboat drank petrol like a drunkard who had lost at cards. The engine was starting to cough, he slammed on full speed, desperately anxious to clear the shoreline of French Menton. And then it stopped, and he was floating in no-man's sea where, if he had been able to be objective, he probably belonged.

In a pastel-grey morning promising another gorgeous Riviera day, Dominick Craufurd's outrageous speedboat finally drifted in to shore. What shore? Jerome di Cavazza climbed reluctantly out of the boat not only because he was suspicious of his landfall but because it seemed a shame to stick a pair of two-tone brogues into the sea. But when the bullets started to fly over his head he remembered he was a reserve officer and refused to panic. He methodically took a blue and white spotted handkerchief from his breast pocket and waved it in greeting. He only allowed himself to sink with relief on to the sand when he was surrounded by a small crowd of chattering Neapolitans in green-grey uniforms. Certainly, they were glad to see him. The men of the 21st Regiment of the 2nd Infantry Division of the Italian Army's XV Corps had captured their first prisoner of the war.

9

'If a British expeditionary force were to be landed here to support our French allies, and Mr Churchill were to require a commander, or at least a figurehead who could help to rally . . . ' the slow Hanoverian drawl died away. Four years of exile had taught the Duke to be careful not to court rejection too enthusiastically.

'I will naturally keep you closely informed,' Hickson-Smith promised his ex-monarch as he rose from his chair. 'In the meantime I can assure you we are leaving no stones unturned to find suitable transport for your safe evacuation.' He bowed to the Duke and gave the Duchess the little nod that protocol prescribed for someone who had not been honoured with the title of 'Royal Highness'.

The Duke and Duchess accompanied him to his car. She was dressed in a summer frock. The Duke wore an open-neck shirt and casual trousers. Hickson-Smith was sweating, discreetly, under his three-piece grey tweed suit.

The drone of distant aircraft was coming off the sea. By screwing your eyes against the sun, you could have seen a number of specks in the hazy sky above the water, which were in reality a squadron of Maschetti-Savoie bombers en route to bomb the dockyards of Marseilles.

'You're not worried about security, I take it, Sir,' Hickson-Smith said from the driving seat. 'Obviously we are urging the local police to redouble their efforts. We'd like to do more ourselves, if we weren't so appallingly short-handed.'

'Please don't worry yourself on our account,' the Duke said, shutting the Riley's door.

Hickson-Smith drove back to Nice against a seemingly non-stop stream of little black cars with strapped-on mattresses, all eager to overtake one another in the rush westwards. He cursed savagely, but quite respectably, under his breath. This endless exodus was making his job as roving representative for the British Consul at Nice that much more impossible. As he hooted his way eastwards, against the traffic stream, he wondered what exactly was the official line on the Windsors? Was one really meant to move heaven and earth for them? And would there be a title at the end of it if one did? Or did one somehow run the risk of courting the disapproval of the new occupants of Buckingham Palace? There was a maddening shortage of clear directions or even hints from Whitehall.

One thing was certain, he would give the town of Antibes a wide berth. Antibes had unpleasant associations with the impossible 'Captain' Dominick Craufurd (what extraordinary nerve to call oneself 'Captain' in such circumstance!) who, only that morning had been yelling at him, unprintably, down the telephone about a couple of bairns and a governess stranded in Dieppe, as if Dieppe were his province!

10

He was going for her neck, but it was not quite as obvious as that. Just more bizarre.

He was in the process of fitting a gigantic pendant around it, and he had to prop her head up to do so.

She said, 'Ouch, you're hurting.' He quietly laughed.

She said, 'It's getting worse.'

She said, 'Stop it.' He had been fiddling with the clasp. Now his fingers had slid down to her windpipe. They exerted a gentle pressure.

He smiled at her with those eyes of his. Like stained glass windows – blue, fragmented with salmon pink.

Oh, God!

She awoke. She realised that the lace of her nightdress was soaked with sweat. Beside her was a crumpled pillow, abandoned in some haste. Jerome, the beautiful, was always boasting. And yet he was so charming she had to try to hide her later disappointment. She glanced up. She saw a wooden effigy of Big Chief Geronimo grinning down at her. He was all right, he made her smile. Not so the big oil canvas with those grotesque fishermen that stood near her bed. Even the complimentary inclusion of Hélène Colmar herself, her green tongue flicking over a double cone of ice-cream, did not make her like it.

She threw off her nightdress and got under the shower, the cool water draining off the night, its pleasures and its terrors. A couple of aspirin and her head was beginning to clear. With a smile she raised both breasts before the ten-foot mirror in a kind of coquettish salutation to the dawn.

Then she settled luxuriously back on to her bearskin couch and cradled the telephone in her hand.

His voice came through very clearly, with that slightly bored edge to it.

'Nicky?'

'Good morning, dear lady. And how can I help today?'

'Oh, Nicky.'

'No, seriously, darling, I was under the strict apprehension I might just be *de trop.* At least until the new moon, whenever that is.'

He was playing his super-bitch role, the one that often made her giggle, but not this morning.

'Look, darling,' she started, 'I need money.'

'Congratulations,' the voice purred, *'Moi aussi.'*

'Look, he left me so much. Just sell something.'

'Bad taste. No market.'

'But I've got a collection.'

'My darling, the buyers have buggered off. My contacts are not favouring the Côte d'Azur this particular summer, and frankly I don't blame them.'

'Look, Nicky,' she sobbed, 'I'm desperate, you don't understand, I've been having nightmares.'

She felt a softening in the voice the other end of the line.

'You must eat, you know,' Dominick urged. 'A woman as pretty as you should never let herself get skinny. Yes, surely, there must be something we can do. Forget the furniture, even Michel André admitted most of it was fake. Forget the trimmings. Georges Bizet I fear at his most inarticulate. Now let's think a bit. What about that Picasso Michel left you?'

'I hate it, I loathe it,' she screamed, giving it a dainty kick with her toe. 'Nicky, *cher* Nicky, can you get rid of it for me?'

Dominick was musing. 'Somewhere there must be somebody who loves Pablo enough to risk his skin for him.'

'And will it bring money?'

'Oh yes, money, plenty of money. If authenticated, that is.'

'Nicky, will you help and then maybe we can ignore ... well, Jerome is an enemy now ... strictly, isn't he? And already I miss my Nicky so much.'

'I promise nothing,' said Dominick Craufurd crisply. 'I suppose there's no harm in putting out a few feelers.'

11

'It was lucky running into you,' Jerome said.

'Yes, it was lucky,' the young naval Commander agreed. 'Saved you from a firing squad.'

'Really?' Jerome tried to look nonchalant.

'Your Neapolitan friends were quite determined to shoot you as a spy.'

'And of course I'm not a spy.'

'Not an enemy spy,' the Commander assented.

Jerome gestured towards the bottle of Napoleon brandy that had been set down on the sooty, stained table cloth (the Hôtel Cavour had an unrivalled view of the marshalling yards of Ventimiglia).

'Please help yourself,' the Commander motioned back. 'We'll soon be floating in this stuff. At least if you believe our propaganda people.'

'It's very pleasant to meet you again, my dear friend,' Jerome said, raising his glass. 'You've done splendidly, I must say – a fully fledged naval Commander.'

'Everyone has to have a uniform in wartime. This one opens the doors that I require to be opened.'

'Tell me, how is Betina? I always envied you Betina.'

'I don't know any Betina,' the Commander smiled. 'I never did.'

'Surely she was madly in love with you that summer at Rapallo . . . well,' he was halted by a look of total blankness in his old friend's eyes, 'well, it was certainly a coincidence running into you, quite a stroke of luck.'

'We haven't met before,' the Commander told him.

'Surely at the tennis club at Rapallo. Or . . . wait a minute, was it at the Cianos?'

'We've never met before. It depends on you whether we meet again.'

It was Jerome di Cavazza's turn to look blank, in his case with incomprehension.

'Still, as you say, it was coincidence that you turned up just now. You could have saved us a great deal of expense and effort if you had come earlier. Never mind, we can still use you – definitely use you,' the Commander decided.

He had been away from home a long time. He was perhaps out of touch with the way people thought and talked now. He said, 'Obviously I am anxious to rejoin my old regiment as soon as possible.'

A steam engine squealed in the marshalling yards. Another train tugging another consignment of tanks was trying to edge its way into a terminus that was already a camouflage sea of field guns, Autoblinda armoured cars, tanks and machine-gun carriers. A frantic squad of military policemen ran on to the track, trying to wave away this irresistible load of metal, but its rear was already blocked by a screeching freight train from which a fresh draft of infantry was already debouching.

'You're not needed in the army. You can see that for yourself,' the

Commander said. 'Well, look at the chaos down there. You don't really want to add to it, do you?'

In fact, Jerome was half-impressed by this display of national power. The clanking of heavy metal had set up responsive echos from the latent patriot in him. He said, 'All the world laughed at us for Caporetto. They forget the sacrifices we made to hold the line on the Piave. I'm thinking of my father among others. At least they can see we've got some muscles here.'

'It's quite absurd,' the Commander assured him. 'Do you know how many serviceable roads there are into Menton? Just one coast road, the rest is a mountain fortress. Assume we get to Menton, do you know how many serviceable roads there are to Nice? The coast road and the Corniche, if they've not already been detonated. It's madness to suppose you can push a major offensive along this coast. The Duce has been seriously mis-advised.'

'The French have a good deal on their hands at the moment,' Jerome pointed out. 'They've taken a terrible beating in the north.'

'Are you interested in painting?' the Commander asked him. 'You look surprised; but you will perhaps admit it's a potentially more fruitful subject than an army which insists on beating its head against the mountains.'

'Paintings? I like them of course. I can't say they're a consuming passion.' It was true, he did look surprised.

'I only ask because it could be an asset.'

'Not with my regiment, I think,' Jerome tried to humour his eccentric interviewer, 'unless they are the kind of paintings that get passed around after dinner at the officers' mess.'

'For the time being you will only be re-joining your regiment so as to be fitted out and put *en route.*'

'May I ask who says so?'

'With respect, I say so – I have the full authorisation of the war department incidentally.'

'But listen, Commander ... I'm sorry, it's ridiculous, but I've forgotten your name.'

'We never met before. I don't have a name,' the Commander assured him.

Now there were human as well as engine screams coming from the tracks of Ventimiglia station. A posse of tank crew men in leather helmets were in high-pitched argument with the military police. One of the MPs was shaking a red flag in the face of a tank crewman. Perhaps he was a communist in a fascist army, more likely he was an affronted signalman. The tank crewman, who was the larger of the two, grabbed the red flag and pushed it into the pit of the smaller man's stomach. The other MPs moved in, shouting, to make an arrest, but they met a hail of fists from men used to handling 47-mm turret guns.

'You are fortunate,' the Commander commented. 'You will be spared all this degradation. Unlike this cannon fodder, you will have the opportunity to exercise a little artistry in this war. I am inviting you, as a man who I understand enjoys games, to play at chess rather than toy soldiers. Instead of getting yourself killed for a few useless French precipices I am giving you the chance to capture a castle, or, if you like, a king.'

'You want to send me back to France?'

The Commander nodded. 'You will be liaising with a small expedition we have already despatched to Antibes. Of course you've just come from there. That's convenient, isn't it?'

Antibes, Hickson-Smith's murmured indiscretions last evening at Les Ombres, the chess analogy – capture a king. It all suddenly clicked in Jerome's mind. 'You want us to bring back the Duke of Windsor. What a brilliant coup. It would be quite a lark, wouldn't it?'

It was the young Commander's turn to raise an eyebrow. 'What would Italy want with that jaded playboy?' he asked.

'A bargaining counter at the peace conference. A puppet king to put on the English throne. In any case, quite a feather in our caps to snap him up before those German bastards get him.'

The Commander shook his head.

'Your mission will be a little less spectacular, but if it is successful it will be of rather more strategic value to Italy.'

'What is my mission?'

The Commander opened his mouth just as a troop train engine started to whistle like a demented owl.

'What is my mission?' Jerome had to ask again.

Even though the engine had stopped whistling he had to ask a third time. And then he smiled, and then burst out laughing.

'But it's ridiculous. Quite crazy!'

'It is entirely serious.'

'Crazy or serious, if you had only let me know last night I could have brought it with me. Holy Mother, I only had to reach up and take it off the wall.'

'Then go and take it off the wall, for Christ's sake!' The Commander's cool composure had suddenly snapped.

The Night Fishers

12

'Oh, my God,' yelled the fat American woman. 'Another goddam traffic jam.' She could not have known that this was quite usual in Lyons, even in the balmy days of peace.

Audrey Hopkirk, sitting beside her in the great Packard convertible, had been given just one task, to look for signs to Vienne and the road south, but the Michelin on her lap was out of date.

'Oh, my God,' groaned the fat American woman as once again she punched the Packard's horn.

She was right. The traffic snarl-up north of Lyons offered a heaven-sent target for the Stukas. Suddenly everyone in France had seemingly decided the Riviera was the only possible place for an early summer holiday.

The road was full of flotsam and jetsam, Renaults, Citroëns, and the odd British car, not to mention the hordes of pedestrians, push-carts and trolleys with children strapped on tight – all making for the south and the sun.

'It's just a question of getting round this lot,' volunteered Audrey Hopkirk quietly.

'Easier said than done.' exploded the fat American woman. 'Look at the gauge. We're just about to boil over. I daresay your kids are proud drinking all the spare water.'

Although it was only early June, heat records were already being broken. You could not really blame the children if, having gone through their ration of two bottles of lemonade each, they had attacked the reserve water can. Now, miraculously in the boiling noonday sun, they were asleep, curled about each other: Niall and Oriana Craufurd, two children who had already wandered far from their lycée in Dieppe.

'I don't know why I didn't stay put. I'm neutral, at least I figure nobody's going to intentionally blitzkrieg an American citizen.'

It was true. She had no business here in the fume and garlic-ridden air of Lyons. She belonged in the Salon de Thé at Dieppe with her back-numbers of the *Miami Post* and the *American Journal.* It was there Audrey Hopkirk had run into her just a few days back. She had quite unfairly talked her into taking her dead husband's Packard out of mothballs in the small garage nearby and joining the rush to the Riviera. Now, it was not just the Packard which was about to blow a gasket — its owner, panting voluminously, seemed to be heating up too.

'Why don't you drive on the other side of the road?' volunteered Niall, waking up in the back. 'Show them we're British.'

Audrey Hopkirk was becoming aware that, in her need to remove the Craufurd children out of harm's way, she had been a little selfish. Playing on an old widow's fears about Panzers and Stuka bombers was not really very nice. If she ever got her benefactress to the comparative safety of Nice she would have to make amends, spend an afternoon with her, perhaps playing scrabble, or persuade Captain Craufurd to lash out on a shower of orchids.

'Look at that poor gee-gee,' said Oriana. 'The man's beating it to death.'

The horse she was referring to had come to a halt in the road in front of them. Its peasant driver in a light blue smock and dark blue beret had loaded up his cart till the axle scraped along the ground. Now, as the horse struggled to move it, he started to bombard it with his whip.

'You'd better not look,' counselled her brother. 'I wouldn't be surprised if it's on its last legs.'

'It must seem a long way from Coconut Grove, Miami,' remarked Audrey Hopkirk to her perspiring benefactress.

A gendarme who had been attempting to direct the traffic gave up and came over, attracted perhaps by the foreignness of the car.

His French was rich and Lyonnais and as garlic-ridden as some of the local sauces. Soon he took out a notebook and began to shout.

'Oh, go to hell, get lost!' offered the American, turning off the engine as she saw clouds of steam begin to emerge from under the car's bonnet. The gendarme did not understand a word of English, but he knew a slur when he heard it in any language.

His response was to open the door and drag the owner bodily on to the road. Audrey Hopkirk did not know exactly what violation of France's traffic laws they had committed but, as the fat American woman began to counter the gendarme's questioning in querulous slang, she was aware that the little girl in the back seat had started to cry. Oriana Craufurd had good reason. Under the peasant's brutal whipping, the tired old horse, still attached to its overladen cart, had lain down on the road and died. A few driblets of blood issued from its foaming mouth.

'Let's get out of here,' beseeched Audrey Hopkirk. She had already slithered across to the driving seat, and now the Packard's engine boomed into life. There was a sickening judder as the gears clashed and then the car shot forward, only to stall.

'Take the handbrake off,' shouted Niall. 'It's there by your feet!'

Then the Packard was off afresh, plunging across the central barrier to give them one final glimpse of her benefactress shrieking to high heaven, while the gendarme flipped the page of his note-book.

There was very little traffic in the left-hand road, just a military scout car, an abandoned tank and a column of weary *poilus* resting by the ditch. Audrey Hopkirk's determined acceleration took the Packard past these obstacles in one full-throated surge. At first she tried to avoid the oncoming objects, then she realised if she drove straight at them they would get out of the way. Soon the Packard was speeding down to the Riviera on the side of the road that should have led upwards to Paris.

'I thought you couldn't drive,' yelled Niall Craufurd.

'I can't,' laughed Audrey Hopkirk, as she ripped the axle hub off an oncoming cart.

'It's like a switchback at the fair,' giggled Oriana Craufurd, forgetting for a moment the dead horse.

Of course, Audrey Hopkirk knew she could not go on like this. And then again maybe she could, it all lay in the lap of chance. As the poplars, now in open country, waved to her in the breeze against a sky of flawless azure, Audrey Hopkirk saw in her mind the sardonic face of her employer, Captain Craufurd, into whose hands by hook or by crook she was going to dump his children (if dumping was a fair word to describe something she loved). 'Not bad for a *jolie laide,*' he would probably have said.

13

At 3.46 a.m., a small incident occurred just a few miles out beyond the point of visibility in the almost motionless sea.

A motorboat belonging to the Nice customs and scantily armed with two machine-guns encountered a noble silhouette, a classic ocean-going yacht designed by the great firm of Philipson of Maine, one of the now nostalgic glories of the Côte d'Azur. One of the customs boat's powerful searchlights established, to general relief, that it was flying the marine emblem of Monaco. For the *douanier* it was a case of *déjà vu*; even so, remembering his duties, he prepared to hail it, reflecting that this was probably the last time he would be fulfilling this regular peacetime duty.

The *douanier* tilted his searchlight like a panning camera lengthwise along the elegant decking of the yacht he had now established was called *La Belle Bête.* He was half-looking for a pantomime figure he knew of old, a caricature figure with a bent beanpole body and a forked off-white beard, a man known in seagoing circles thereabouts as Prince 'Baccarat'.

He was enjoying the thought of giving the senile old dodderer a bit of a scare. What he in fact saw caused him to jolt the searchlight back from the stern and flick it back again across the deck.

In place of the blazered *raffiné* he had expected, staggering up for a much needed nocturnal breather, he was descrying objects with the metallic consistency of centipedes, shinily dark, scaly figures that flashed in and out of his light as if it might scorch them.

'*Tiens,*' he muttered under his breath as two huge centipedes plopped into the sea. Another he caught, up by the poop, was more human, posed there like an Olympic diving champion, preening itself, shiny black scales bouncing back the flare.

Others on board the customs boat had also registered the insects. The boy, who had never fired his machine-gun before on a job, started to let off sporadic bursts in the general direction of the *Belle Bête*. The head *douanier* was busy at the wireless set trying to contact Nice. He saw too late a pair of slimy grey tentacles attaching themselves to his starboard railings, heard too late the padding of soft feet along the deck, the machine-gun ceasing with a stifled moan, as if it too were human, felt too late the shiny thong that came from behind and attached itself round his neck, the plunging of the fish knife into his guts from behind.

It was a small incident compared with what was going on up there in the mountains. The loss of one customs boat would not be reported, scarcely noted; after all, the subtle probing art of customs and excise was an outmoded game in these more hectic times. Yet this tiny event did have its own significance.

Centurione Pugno took his knife out of the *douanier's* back and wiped it on his uniform trousers with some disgust. He would have preferred more of a fight, his men were still not battle-hardened, their muscles were pappy, they needed the stimulus of blood.

'We sink her, and we go for a little swim, eh?' he commanded Emilio Battaglia, his *capo* – a man, like himself, born deep in Calabria.

'What about him?' asked the *capo*, gesturing towards the sole surviving youth who had manned the machine-gun, now whimpering on the deck, almost licking the salt sea off one of his men's webbed flippers.

'Slit his throat,' said Pugno. 'Use your knife.'

'Can't we . . . ' half-asked Battaglia, his frogman's goggles glistening over his oily black hair.

'Use your knife. No, better, tell Bertucco to use his. The boy needs a little blood. Tell him to stick it in the throat – like a pig.'

A minute later, Battaglia was flailing his flippers and arms in a desperate effort to keep up with his Centurione as they surged back towards the graceful *Belle Bête*. It was an unwritten law that he had to beat Pugno, at least once in three times, otherwise he would be scrubbed down to the ranks. But on this occasion he did not stand an earthly. Pugno was using his mammoth shoulders to cut through the water like a projectile. No man could live with Pugno in this mood.

Pugno had not stopped smiling since they left Genoa the night before (how Battaglia knew that smile!). But now the face was as tight as a mask. Alone among this élite group of frogmen, the *capo* Battaglia could guess the reason why. A coded message had come through just an hour ago. It had caused Pugno to cut the engines and then change direction. It was a badly kept secret, which Pugno himself had hinted at in a restaurant called Mama Leoni's in dockside Genoa, that their orders were to make history by cutting through the submarine nets that protected the French battle fleet at Toulon and then running amok with their limpet mines. In fact they had drunk to success from Mama Leoni's finest Barolo. Now there had been a change in the orders, a change, it seemed, that was bringing out the smiling murderer in Centurione Pugno.

'You lost,' snapped Pugno as he kicked off his flippers. 'Once more and, my dear Battaglia...' Pugno flicked his fingers playfully across his throat.

The *Belle Bête* twisted south-west again and the dim promontory of Antibes slid into vision. Dawn was breaking. The sea was being transformed into a gentle swelling ice-cream orange. On it bobbed the slighter, more intense glow of two yellow lights from simple fishing boats overtaken by the dawn and the war. Centurione Pugno jerked his fist angrily towards these specks. 'Start with them,' he ordered.

14

'I'm a busy man, Captain Craufurd,' Marvin Huntingdon shouted at the windscreen of Dominick's open Lagonda. 'I hope you're not wasting my time.'

They were driving down one of the Cap's narrow, twisting lanes, bordered by high, privacy-seeking villa walls, themselves made higher by rampant wistaria and bougainvillaea. It was a quiet part of the world where you could take corners in broad sweeps without too much risk of hitting a car coming the other way, especially these days when most people who had a car were driving as fast as congestion would allow along the coast road in the direction of Perpignan. So there was some justification for Dominick being mildly curious about the car radiator he could see from time to time in his mirror, and why he should ask the American, 'You're not being followed by anyone, are you?'

'Followed!' The little art dealer craned his neck round and saw nothing but a bend in the road. 'Who the hell would be following me?' he squeaked. His mind anxiously hurried through the possibilities. The Schaeffer Gallery? The Westcott Foundation? The Guggenheim people? Huntingdon's departure for Europe had been a closely guarded secret. But the art world was a small one, and people talked. Who the hell *would* be following him? He reminded himself that he had a heart condition, and he must be careful about getting excited.

Now they were sweeping up the corkscrew drive to Les Ombres.

'Your friend has a nice place here,' Huntingdon said nervously.

'Not here,' Dominick answered curtly as the Lagonda twisted round the château, down a maze of a laurel drive and drew up beside an incongruous timber cabin. 'The owner is not at home, but I have the key,' he explained.

Inside, Marvin Huntingdon looked around him suspiciously. He took in the giant wigwam and the wildly Western décor.

'I didn't come over three miles to buy a lot of Indian junk,' he said eyeing the portrait of Chief Sitting Bull.

'I believe that tomahawk over there is genuine Cherokee,' Dominick observed lazily.

'That's authentic Navajo crap,' Huntingdon snapped, 'they make those things for tourists down on the Reservation. I didn't come....'

'Perhaps you'll join me in a whisky and soda,' Dominick said soothingly. 'It will soon be as scarce as a Modigliani down here.'

'You've got a Modigliani?' Curiosity had won out over suspicion and anxiety.

'Something even more *recherché* in its way,' Dominick murmured, pushing a glass into his visitor's hand.

Huntingdon slipped a tablet on to his tongue before he gargled down the scotch. 'I've come a long way and I haven't got much time,' he said.

Craufurd led him towards a canvas hung between two prints of US Cavalrymen by Remington. 'This may intrigue you and even *interest* you.'

Huntingdon steadied his horn-rimmed spectacles. 'Who's that?'

'The portrait is of Prince Bibesco, a close friend of Marcel Proust. The significant thing is that it's attributed to Jacques-Emile Blanche.'

'That's no Emile Blanche,' the little man said irritably.

Dominick waved his Player's Navy Cut cigarette. 'Before, of course, he had found the style for which he is recognised,' he suggested.

'That's a goddamn weekend painter! The *belle époque* was lousy with them.'

Craufurd pointed to a nude in pastels, explaining that it was by a pupil of Poussin's. Huntingdon said he must have been a lousy pupil.

Then Dominick produced his ace.

'I don't believe it!' Huntingdon whistled.

'Of course you will be familiar with the subject,' Dominick gestured at the figures of two fishermen peering into a lamplit sea. '"A prophetic vision of the impending years of darkness," at least one critic would claim. *Night Fishing at Antibes* is, I understand, the showpiece of the Guggenheim collection in New York. What you're looking at here is a masterpiece in the making.'

'I don't believe it!' Huntingdon whistled a second time, as his fingers groped for his tablet bottle.

'A friend of mine, alas — he's no longer with us — actually watched the old wizard paint it. Apparently it was a revelation – the speed and the precision with which the old boy worked. I doubt if you'll find a more valuable souvenir of Antibes,' Craufurd added, switching from a soft to a harder sell.

'I said I don't believe it, because I don't believe it,' Huntingdon cut in. 'There isn't any record of a preliminary sketch for *Night Fishing.* No such work has been catalogued and, as I understand it, no mention of one has been made of it by the artist himself. I would suggest, Captain Craufurd, that what you and I are looking at is a *fake*!'

'Mr Huntingdon, I have it on first-hand authority that this is an authentic Picasso. Look again at the picture, if you will. The woman with the bicycle, and the ice-cream. Could anyone else paint a picture precisely this way?'

Of course, they couldn't. No one living or dead could have painted a woman that way, except a certain little Spaniard with a godlike talent. Huntingdon was as certain as a Picasso fanatic could be that he was looking at the real thing; but he was also a businessman who drove a hard bargain.

'Besides, the woman in the picture is the owner of this house and the picture. She was, of course, a friend of the painter. You must take my word for it that this is no fake.'

'Your word as an Englishman?' The little American appeared to be grinning sarcastically, although in fact he was biting hard into his lip to prevent himself from breaking into a smile of rapture. 'It's a phoney, Craufurd,' he muttered between his clenched teeth. 'Hell, it's not even signed.'

Dominick stifled his anger, reminding himself that he had insufficient funds to back a punch to this ignoramus's jaw. Instead, he turned on the salesman's pitying look. 'I may say as an art expert you surprise me, Mr Huntingdon. I thought it was common knowledge that Monsieur Picasso is extremely erratic about signing his pictures. As often as not his pictures are unsigned and undated. In this case as you see we have a date, 25.5.39, which is clearly in the master's handwriting.'

'I'll give you five hundred francs for it,' Huntingdon said, seeming to walk casually but, in fact, dragging himself towards the door.

'My dear fellow, are you aware of the prices Picasso is fetching these days?'

Huntingdon turned round at the door and looked at him shrewdly. He thought he saw a fake English gentleman trying to make a few francs in a market he knew peanuts about.

'Six hundred francs is the top price for a Picasso that isn't in any of the catalogues,' he challenged, his hand deep in his jacket pocket, twisting at the cap of his bottle of tablets. 'Okay, six hundred francs,' he seemed to sneer. 'That's got to be the ceiling price for a Picasso phoney.'

He did not expect the Englishman to shake his head as if he had been talking to a kid or a lunatic, and say coolly, 'Mr Huntingdon, I am afraid I have been wasting your time. My client is not interested in such an absurd offer.'

He said to himself, you know you've got to have it, you know you can't live without having it, you've got to give this English stuffed shirt a glimpse of real money. But that was the half of Huntingdon which warmed its hands against the fire of art. The practical side of him drew attention to the fact that, whatever his instinct said, there was no catalogue listing for a preliminary sketch for *Night Fishing.* His two sides wrestled with each other as he hesitated by the door of the cabin.

'Why don't you think it over and give us a ring,' Dominick drawled soothingly. Marvin Huntingdon was a coolheaded businessman but today his indecision was transparent. 'Look, I'll give you a lift back to Antibes.'

'Is anyone living in that château?' Huntingdon asked as they swept past Les Ombres.

'No, the owner died last year.'

That was funny, because the little art dealer thought he had seen a light burning in an upper window, at high noon of all times.

'Hello, I've seen that car before,' Dominick observed, with an eye on his mirror as they drove back towards the main Juan-Les-Pins-Antibes road. 'Are you sure nobody's interested in your movements?'

'Nobody's following me,' Huntingdon piped. Then he leaned out of the car and vomited, so hard he thought he was going to throw up his heart. He knew it better than any doctor could have told him, so much excitement was not doing his heart any good.

'I get sick in automobiles,' he curtly explained.

Dominick dropped the American art dealer at Antibes station and watched him scuttle on to the palm-fringed platform, crowded with the khaki uniforms of reinforcements for the Alpine front.

A few seconds later another car stopped at the station entrance. The driver had no interest in the destination of Marvin Huntingdon. He was watching Dominick Craufurd. As the Lagonda pulled away from the kerb and took the road down to the port, the other car also slipped into gear. It was Craufurd's exposed head and shoulders which seemed to interest the driver.

15

'Cheer up, darling, I think I've found a nibbler for that Picasso scrawl of yours. He's playing hard to get, but methinks the fish will bite!'

'He will have to pay a good price, a very good price,' Hélène said, squeezing Dominick's hand, as they walked together along the quayside.

'Of course he'll have to pay a damned good price. That's our agreement, isn't it?'

'So much money I will be able to get right away from here, perhaps to America. It's no use otherwise.'

'You don't seem particularly thrilled by my efforts on your behalf,' Dominick mildly sulked. They had reached the point on the cobbled quayside where the speedboat was meant to be moored. 'Hello, you have a guest, or rather you had a guest. Someone seems to have helped themselves to your boat.'

Hélène shrugged.

'No prizes for guessing who filched it?' Craufurd icily enquired. 'As far as I am aware, only three people had the key – you and I in the first place, and subsequently *Cavazza*.'

'You gave me the boat. Who can tell how many keys I had made. There were no conditions. So if I say that Philippe took the boat to visit a girl friend in Saint-Raphael I want you to believe me – otherwise I'll think you don't love me.'

'It's of no consequence,' Craufurd said, 'except, confidentially, you and I know that Jerome went to pay a visit to that wop Musso! It's only that it could have been useful – that boat – if I, and you of course, needed to make a fast getaway.'

She started to speak. He raised his hand to cut her short. For the first time ever she thought he looked a beaten man.

It was at moments like this that she felt closest to him — furthest away when he was winning, turning round from the tables with that terrible look of jubilation on his face. She put her hands on his cheeks, and then stroked the back of his head, as she never stroked it when he was winning. 'You're so sad and noble, sometimes,' she whispered to him. 'What did England or the world do to make you so sad and noble – sometimes?'

He suddenly laughed. 'My wife didn't understand me, did she? Pity we had two children who don't understand either of us. I don't think the Army quite understood me either. Still,' he kissed her forehead, nuzzling into her special scent called 'Revenir', 'I'm lucky to have you – at least when my luck is in.'

'You didn't win yesterday, did you?'.

'Who's to say I didn't win?' he murmured, slipping his hand through the back of her matelot blouse and discovering her breasts. 'Jerome is no longer with us.'

'It was Jerome who won yesterday, wasn't it?'

She never pressed it any further, never insisted that either Dominick or Jerome should explain the arrangement they had between them. What woman, even the most desirable woman on the world's most fashionable coast, wanted to depend on the spin of a wheel? The rules of this superficial game were superficially simple: Dominick Craufurd and Jerome di Cavazza were the two closest friends of her fiancé, Michel André, two friends who, after his tragic death on an Alpine holiday, had done their best to console her, notwithstanding the fact that the comforter in question inevitably happened to be that month's lucky number at the Casino.

'Jerome is missing, and so is my boat,' Dominick mumbled, kissing her neck. 'What's to prevent me staking my claim?'

'I do not know he is missing. I do not know he will not be back,' Hélène protested, in strict obedience to the secret rules behind the superficial rules. Her resistance goaded Dominick Craufurd into a flash of inspiration.

'I lost,' he said, 'that's the truth of it, darling. You like me better when I lose, don't you?' And then he added harshly, 'And don't pretend you've never said yes before when I've lost. Last year in the boat's loo, don't you remember? Quite a launching party!'

Strictly speaking, he was breaking the rules. He could touch Hélène; he could peck her politely on the cheek, but no more, so long as the winner still had nights to spend. Jerome had won thirty nights. He had spent one, there were twenty-nine still owing to him. But Jerome was an alien now, and had almost certainly left the country. He thought that even Jerome might have agreed that the rules could be bent in these exceptional circumstances.

'I'm sorry there's no boat left,' he whispered in her ear, 'but we can still have another launching party, can't we, can't we?'

'Monsieur Crawfure! Allo, Monsieur Crawfure!'

The putting of a motor accompanied the friendly shout. A small fishing smack was chugging into view. It was Dalio, returning, in war as in peace, from another day's moderately successful fishing.

'It's good you are still here, I thought you had deserted us.' The old fisherman twisted his sour, tanned face up towards them. 'Pichu, Legrand, they went out last night. And, pffttt. Nothing, not a floating plank. Not a sausage. Out there,' – he gesticulated clumsily to the wide open sea turning to a yet softer shade of blue under the midday sun's bombardment. 'You can't hide out there ... eh?'

'You can't capsize either,' mused Craufurd, 'a schoolboy of eight could float on a raft for a week out there.' Dalio gave him a flip of the hand and, after ejecting a spurt of saliva into the water already packed with the decaying remains of rejected small fish, chugged off towards the end of the port where the customs house stood.

'And another thing,' he shouted as an afterthought. 'Even those buggers there – they seem to have flipped it too. Bloody *douaniers*!'

Then, as Dalio's dirty red sails moved out of view, Craufurd was confronted by a kind of ghost. How could he have missed it before? A schooner was anchored on the far side of the harbour, more a delicate man o'war than a pleasure boat, it was certainly the only craft of its kind on the coast. Or rather it had been until it had disappeared over the horizon in April, apparently never to be seen or heard of again.

'Christ!' Dominick said. 'It's *La Belle Bête*!'

They called him Prince 'Baccarat', which he wasn't. His real name, or rather three of them, was Prince Yaroslav Nikolai Bakaloff, ex-courtier to the Romanovs and ex-divisional commander in the White Army of the Ukraine. Some time in the early Twenties Prince Bakaloff had arrived in Nice with a saddle-bag that contained all his worldly wealth. As the saddle-bag held treasures dating back to Peter the Great and beyond, he could have lived out the rest of his life in moderate style, if, of course, he had not been a compulsive and disastrous gambler.

The Prince adhered to the Alembert theory of roulette. You backed a number and increased your stake every time it did not come up, reasoning that the odds were improving on it coming up. Pretty soon, Prince Baccarat had to leave the Hôtel Negresco. For a number of years he lived, rather apologetically, with a series of decreasingly wealthy widows. Then the rumours started that he was sleeping in a beach cabin, although he always appeared at the Casino in immaculate evening dress. Then, on April 1, 1940, he walked up to the roulette table and said, 'It is the fools day in England, is it not? The day, *n'est-ce pas,* when the idiot is king? You shall see.' And for the whole afternoon he stuck on number eleven, from time to time doubling up while the ivory ball rolled nowhere near it. And then, to everyone's disbelief, the croupier was announcing *'numéro onze'*. They told him for God's sake to take his money and run. But 'Baccarat' put his winnings straight back on number eleven and up it came again. And again. Next day, the Prince was the proud owner of a schooner-sized yacht, *La Belle Bête.* For a week he sailed up and down the coast on a binge that almost succeeded in making the Riviera forget there was a war on.

Then suddenly Prince Baccarat and *La Belle Bête* sailed for points south. 'It's spring in the south,' he said. 'It's no good spring here.' Baccarat's friends, of which he now possessed a fair number, had assembled on the quayside to see him off. He was not alone. By this time he had purchased a small jazz band which played cheerfully among the rigging as the sails flapped and *La Belle Bête* powered swervingly out to sea. Also on board were a number of *demoiselles* of Baccarat's recent acquaintance, or, as one not so charitable new friend described them, plain whores. 'I'll be back in May to break that bloody, damned bank again,' Prince Baccarat had called from the wheel. But he, his crew and his boat had vanished off the map for over eight weeks now.

'Baccy, you old scoundrel,' Dominick called from the quayside, 'where the hell have you been?'

There was no answer.

'He's probably asleep,' Hélène said, 'Russians always sleep in the afternoon. They have such enormous lunches.'

'Perhaps he's dead.'

'Why do you say that?'

'Just an instinct – there's something wrong about this boat.'

On the face of it *La Belle Bête* was as deserted as the *Marie Celeste,* but it was not as silent. The sound of male voices singing had been seeping up from below decks. It only now stopped.

'Shall we have a look around?' Craufurd suggested. He already had a suede shoe on the deck of *La Belle Bête.*

'Darling, do you think the Italians really will rape all the women if they reach here?'

'God knows. Why do you suddenly ask?'

She clasped her arms across her body. 'I don't know, *chéri.* Perhaps because I suddenly feel frightened. So frightened.'

Something was creaking. A door had opened in the hatchway, a gap which seemed to be watching them as closely as they were watching it. This mutual inspection seemed to last a number of seconds. Then suddenly the door was pushed open, and a lugubrious grey-haired man with a goatee beard pulled himself up the steps towards them.

'Baccy, my dear old chap. How are you?'

Dominick's greeting ended in a question mark. If this was Baccy it was not the same Russian prince who had sailed away in the spring, raising a glass of champagne to the stars. This was a ghost of the man who had broken the bank at Nice.

'It's an honour to see you, yes, two old friends, . . . yes, yes, a great honour,' Prince Bakaloff told them, looking down at his two-tone brogues (these at any rate were authentic). 'Look, I promise you we must have a drink at the club sometime soon. We must drink to old times, yes?'

'No time like the present, is there, Baccy?' Craufurd said, glancing round at the deserted deck and noting how shipshape and spruce everything looked in comparison with the evening Prince Bakaloff had put to sea with sails flapping and saxophones playing. 'I suppose we couldn't split a bottle of Pommery now? It's damned hot on the quayside.'

'Yes, old times . . . old times,' Baccarat stammered, looking down at the *La Belle Bête's* scrubbed deck. 'We will have so much old times to talk about,' he added vaguely. 'Better times than these times.'

'Don't say you've lost it all,' Hélène asked directly. 'What happened to the jazz band? And the charming girls? And all the champagne?'

'And incidentally what happened to you, you old rogue?' Dominick tried to ask heartily.

They had not noticed him coming up the hatchway because Prince Bakaloff was standing in front of it. But now a head emerged, and then a pair of shoulders. The swarthy newcomer was twice the man the Prince was. His rough shirt was open to the waist, revealing a gorilla-matted chest, in the midst of which a golden crucifix sparkled faintly. 'My friend, Monsieur . . . my, er, partner,' Baccarat choked by way of an introduction, looking down at his two-tone shoes.

'What's your business?' Dominick asked 'Pleasure cruises along the coast? Not quite the ideal summer, is it? Though they tell me there's a fortune to be made in shipping refugees for Africa.'

'Englishhh?' The human gorilla asked, examining Craufurd with unfriendly olive-green eyes.

Dominick nodded towards his Old Westminster tie.

'Dunkuk,' Baccarat's friend spat out.

'I beg your pardon?'

'Dunkuk! Englishhh sheeet-scared. Run away.'

'Is he trying to tell me something?' Craufurd slid an eyebrow towards Hélène.

'He's telling you that Englishmen are not very reliable. Of course he's right, isn't he, *chéri*?'

'Yes, no friend of France, *perfide,* sheeet-scared,' the muscle of Prince Baccarat's new organisation echoed.

'Perhaps he'd like to tell me what the French army's been doing in this war – if he is French,' Craufurd's fists tautened, 'although with that accent I'm tempted to doubt it.'

'Dunkuk! Sheeet-scared!'

'He's very large, darling,' Hélène cried, 'he is very powerful.'

'To hell with that, he's a bore,' Dominick said, swinging his arm back in a way that caused Baccarat to shrink aside, leaving Craufurd face-to-torso with a vest filled with muscles, and breasts almost as big as a woman's.

And then something went click, and Hélène screamed and a flick-knife was sparkling in the late afternoon sun in Antibes harbour.

'Dunkuk. Sheeet in trousers!' Baccarat's friend grinned.

'Chéri,' Hélène urged, 'if you don't have a knife I think we should leave now.'

'Yes, we must drink soon, to old times, please,' Baccarat called after them as Dominick accepted the inevitability of a personal Dunkirk.

When they were back on the quayside, Dominick said, 'I think I ought to tell the French security people about that boat of Baccarat's. He's found himself a damned odd messmate.'

'Yes, but they must be very busy now,' Hélène said, looking up at the sky. Another squadron of Savoia Machetti bombers was *en route* for the docks at Marseilles. To westward, two little black smudges like the smoke from an expiring steam engine had risen to greet them. It was Cannes's one and only anti-aircraft gun swinging into action. 'I'm so frightened of all this.'

'Don't be too depressed, we could still sell that picture,' Dominick comforted her.

16

'Congratulations,' sneered Colonel Grimaldi. 'Considering the life you've been leading, you really are in excellent shape.'

Jerome di Cavazza was hardly in a state even to hear him. Lacking any other expedient, he was literally sleeping on his feet. At the same time, paradoxically he had the uneasy feeling he was the only man in the entire Italian army who was actually moving.

Turin had been a bad joke. It had not exactly helped that the 121st Regiment of the Line had been shunted back into the junction half an hour after leaving, banners waving and chianti bottles swinging, for Ventimiglia. The decision had been made to transfer the regiment instead due north to General Guzzoni's army, massing on the higher slopes around Monte Viso. 'Is it true you put the regimental silver on a horse?' one officer had asked.

This was not where it was all happening. Rumours were rife about a dramatic breakthrough down the mountainside towards Annecy, a pincer attack destined, so they said, to curl round by Lyons and join up with the Germans in the rear of the Maginot Line. They said, too, that a detachment of Italian frogmen had broken through the barriers into Toulon harbour and immobilized half the French battle fleet. They said, they said.

Not that this comforted Jerome di Cavazza. After five years' absence from the reserves, the pursuit of military glory was suddenly like a deep draught of pure spring water to a man dying of thirst. He yearned to dare the devil, but after less than forty-eight hours of war and France down for the count, time was running out. 'The best one going about is how you concealed a common street whore under the table the night the officers entertained Marshal Graziani.' Mussolini of course was a pathetically inglorious lecher, and yet, as his train finally steamed out of Turin station, Jerome knew he had touched the real Italy: the soldiers with tunics undone and helmets back to front, those dirty priests with crucifixes upraised, and the loudspeakers booming Verdi and fascist songs along with news of departures; those weeping mamas and shrieking bambini, those old ladies sealed up in funereal black, those porters literally running from platform to platform, the whole sweaty mass of it. Was not this La Bella Italia at last, the one Garibaldi had loved?

Then the train rumbled up towards the mountain passes of Cenis, from which, so they said, General Guzzoni's army had leapt to drive the effete French, riddled with communist and fifth-column soft socialists, down from the higher ravines and into the valley of the Rhône.

Lyons had to be the target, what could possibly stand in their way? 'The story that you gambled with your brother officers for the honour of my predecessor the colonel's wife is, I trust, apocryphal....' It was good to be up here in the mountains, good to see that the Alpini still carried themselves well, that there was a sparkle in the eye and the gait of these élite troops. Good to get off that train at the mountain stop of Bardonech and breathe fresh air.

'I didn't expect to find you here,' he had told a baby-faced Tenente Juvenesco. 'I thought by now you'd be eating bouillabaisse in Moutiers.'

Juvenesco was apologetic. For the past month the Alpini had been on a total war footing, but they could not move yet or their flank would be exposed. There had been shameful delays, after the victory they would have their post-mortems, their drumhead courts-martial.

'But at least you must have got your bayonets into a few fat French stomachs,' smiled Tenente Jerome di Cavazza, gesturing towards the wooden huts of the frontier post which was still intact in the snow a mile or so across the valley.

'Help those frogs over there digest their snails a little faster, eh?'

Shamefacedly, the fresh-faced Juvenesco had twisted on his toes and turned away.

'If you don't like it here, you should take a look at Fourth Army headquarters. Guzzoni doesn't know if he's coming or going. The Duce's sudden command to attack caught him completely on the hop. The whole bungle makes Abyssinia look like a blitzkrieg. One of the problems is our people have been getting on so well with the Chasseurs Alpins over there. I've got my work cut out even trying to persuade them to mount a reconnaissance in force.'

'Well, let's see what we can do. That French frontier post is a sitting duck. Let's dash over right now and sling in a few grenades. Look, they've even got their bloody tricolour flying.'

'I'm afraid, as I hinted, you're too precious to lose, my dear Cavazza,' said the Colonel. 'It's my regret that in the coming campaign the regiment will have to go without you. You're destined for higher things. You know, my friend ... politics.'

Immediately after his arrival at the regimental depot in the mountains, Jerome had been subjected to a rapid medical which he had sailed through. He had also sailed through a crate of Spumante with the officers, splashing it into a huge regimental silver toasting bowl.

He had been given a feel of the new 9-mm Beretta automatic by the armoury instructor and had made some neat patterns in the targets in the shooting gallery. The Beretta he had been allowed to keep, but not the beautiful field-grey uniform of the Alpini with its pouches, plus-four trousers and puttees, nor the lapel flashes with the twin stars of Tenente, his rank as a reservist, nor above all the proud huntsman's hat with its bright feather. All of this he had gazed at nostalgically in the store-room. But he was given one thing: a heavy, semi-military, fur-lined white skiing coat, because at this altitude it was still chilly even in June.

Colonel Grimaldi had a simple way of contacting his opposite number commanding the crack regiment of Chasseurs Alpins. He simply lifted the telephone and talked to him.

'*Salute,* mio Colonello,'

'*Bonsoir,* Colonel Grimaldi.'

'I regret to inform you that you are outnumbered.'

'You think so, eh?'

Whatever Mussolini might have intended in his race to get into the war so as to grab French territory in the approaching peace conference, it was going to be difficult to persuade the members of these two fine regiments to start sinking lead into one another's bodies. They had shared too much: the wine, the ski-runs, the gaming tables, the women, the toboggans, the one efficient mountain whore. Not to put too fine a point on it, these two fine bodies of fighting men were on the best of terms. What was worrying Colonel Grimaldi was the realisation that to make them fight he had first to make them hate.

'Look,' he was saying into the telephone, 'in your position I would surrender. Yes, that would be the cleanest solution, and *merde* to their stupid war.'

'My instructions are to the contrary,' clipped back the Frenchman. 'My men are keen to show that down here at least the French army can still fight.'

'But seriously, Colonel, we could come over....'

'Into a storm of well-aimed bullets.'

'No, come to talk.'

'That would be stupid, there would be nothing to say.'

'Maybe a little wine would loosen our tongues. The Spumante as you know is excellent. In fact I am sipping a glass now. Excellent, I assure you, the bottles are nicely chilled – they've been out in the snow for an hour or two. Now it would be a great honour to offer you a glass....'

'But I must warn you, drinking among friends is one thing, capitulation something different. But by all means let us talk.'

The small party that followed the Colonel and ski-ed down the slope towards the French line carried a 'blood wagon' loaded with the regiment's finest Asti Spumante. There was a major there, the Adjutant, the baby-faced lieutenant and, among some other officers, a figure in a heavy white skiing coat.

The parleying party, preceded by a sergeant with a white flag, went through the outposts of the Chasseurs Alpins right up to the huts that acted as battalion HQ. While the two Colonels warmly clasped each other under a thin half-moon, only one man noticed a figure detach itself and go like a bomb down the steepest slope, in the general direction of the distant Col de Larche. Tenente Jerome di Cavazza was *en route* for the French skiing resort of Briancey. It was a gamble, but one backed by the firepower of a 9-mm Beretta and the fact that its owner, in certain circumstances, would not hesitate to use it.

After the Italians had returned to their line the French noticed one of their sentries on a downward slope. He lay frozen in an envelope of red snow.

17

'You look like something out of one of Dickens's more harrowing masterpieces,' Dominick Craufurd said, eyeing the tattered little party in the passageway. 'What the hell have you three been up to?'

'Daddy, Daddy, we saw a Stuka.' Niall Craufurd cried. 'It came down so low you could see the swastika on its tail. It came down so low you could see the flashes on its wings where the machine-guns are. And, Daddy, Daddy, we saw real people falling over dead!'

'Daddy, you've got to teach Miss Hopkirk to reverse. She can do all the gears except reverse,' Oriana Craufurd revealed. 'We could have got away from that police car if we'd known how to reverse.'

'I'm sorry we had to walk some of the way, Captain Craufurd,' Audrey Hopkirk apologised. She was still smarting from the shame of having to abandon the Packard, just when she was beginning to gain complete mastery over the vehicle.

Dominick Craufurd thrust his hands deep into his blazer pockets.

'Why the hell did you hang on in Dieppe? Didn't they tell you about the German breakthrough?' he complained.

'We were waiting for news of Lady Pennard, Captain Craufurd. She was posted to Paris in April. She was anxious to be as close as possible to Lord Pennard,' she explained without undue sensitivity for Craufurd's feelings about his ex-wife's fixation with her new husband.

'Well, what in damnation is the news of Lady Pennard?'

'Lady Pennard drove north to try to contact Lord Pennard. She was worried by the reports about the BEF being encircled. She said they'd both try and join us in Dieppe; but if she didn't turn up we were to take the ferry.'

Dominick Craufurd could well believe it. He could picture his big-eyed, scatty-brained, ludicrously emotional ex-wife in her absurd FANY auxiliaries uniform, which he suspected was just a cover for her insatiable lust, pounding up the shell-torn roads of northern France with great tears running down her face and blotching her make-up. Her pathetic grand passion for a little tin-pot soldier called Sandy Pennard! It would be typical of that randy little prig to get himself cut off in Dunkirk.

He wondered with mild curiosity if his former wife had been run over by a column of Panzers.

'Well, why didn't you catch the ferry in Dieppe, as Lady Pennard told you?' he rounded on the dust-caked governess.

'The Germans were too close. The ferry had stopped running.'
'Then what about Cherbourg, damn it?'
He found this gauche young girl was looking at him pityingly. 'Captain Craufurd, the war is moving rather faster in the north than it is down here.'
'Obviously you've done marvels, Miss Hopkirk,' he conceded, vaguely patting his children's heads. 'I can't say you've chosen the ideal time to look me up, but that's war, I suppose. Of course, what I ought to do is to try and get you and the children to the Spanish frontier. Trouble is, I'm stuck here for the time being. I don't think I can push off just yet....'
Now he was talking more to himself than anybody else.
'We'll be all right,' Audrey Hopkirk assured him, 'the Italians will be easy after the Germans, won't they, children?' Did he detect a look of near scorn in the direct glance she turned on him.?
'Daddy, Daddy, can we go for a bathe, Miss Hopkirk promised us!'
'You'd all better take a shower and I'll have to see what I can do about accommodation.'
'Please, Daddy, all the way here Miss Hopkirk said we could bathe in the sea. She said it's a million times warmer than the Channel!' Niall Craufurd appealed.
'It's true I did promise them,' Audrey Hopkirk said in a tone of voice Dominick decided you did not argue with.

The beach of Antibes is not much to write home about, assuming you have a home to write to, but it was the best thing the Craufurd children had seen that summer. Dominick Craufurd watched his children run down past two empty deckchairs and across a narrow stretch of sand that led splash into the Mediterranean. He also watched Miss Hopkirk striding after them, and noticed that her breasts were surprisingly full and firm.
He thought, Damn her, if she had the initiative to get the children all the way across France, she might have been considerate enough to board a boat in Normandy. On the other hand it was nice to see the blighters alive and kicking.
'Daddy, Daddy, we've found a fish.'
'A huge, huge fish, Daddy, come and see!'
His children were calling from the other side of the small cove by the two outer harbour walls.
Something about the way Oriana was shouting 'an enormous, enormous fish!' made him start to run.
Now he could hear Audrey Hopkirk telling them to keep away.
And then he could hear his daughter screaming.
Dominick Craufurd had never seen anything like it in his life. The thing was man-sized but its feet were webbed like a giant frog's. At

first it seemed that the skin was more shark-like than human, but if you looked closer, which was not altogether easy, you could see that the dead creature was dressed in black rubber, You could also see that the two grotesquely swollen hands were fundamentally human and that the 'beard' of netting the thing was wearing had throttled a human throat . . . .

'I told you, you should have taken a shower and had a nap,' Dominick Craufurd said irritably to his children.

18

'So what price glory?' Marvin Huntingdon whistled to himself as he looked from his high hotel window on to the slate-blue rooftops of Nice, a pleasure city basking in the false benevolence of another cloudless afternoon, another radiant blue sky spread over France's darkest hour.

But Huntingdon's agony was not France's agony. He was experiencing a more private torment. Every man at some time in his life has an appointment with greatness, and Huntingdon had an uneasy, palpitating feeling that his appointment had arrived. Up until now he had been essentially a figure in the background, never a full-length portrait. Imported works of art passed regularly through his hands, but he never left so much as a thumb-print; he was just materially a little richer every time. But, as of this moment, he stood on the threshold of making a piece of art history, a little bit of immortality for himself. He was about to become the man who disproved the experts and demonstrated for all time that there *was* a sketch of *Night Fishing at Antibes* – if his nerves could take it, and he could be one hundred percent certain the painting Craufurd had shown him was authentic.

He had not wanted to ring this number. It connected him to a man called Stephan. Officially, he supplied brushes and materials to the art colony on the coast – Picasso included. He also supplied information to the New York galleries – for a price which could double or even treble if Stephan sensed that big fish were biting. Stephan had to be handled carefully, and preferably not at all.

So Huntingdon gave the voice at the other end of the line a good deal of aimless talk about the weather and the war and how he wasn't buying anything down here on the Côte d'Azur because, as he figured it, the way the war was going he'd be lucky to get out with a washbag.

Besides, in their desperation, a lot of local operators were trying to sell him out-and-out garbage.

'Only yesterday this Englishman, Craufurd, I think the name was, tried to sell me a picture he said was a Picasso sketch for *Night Fishing.* He's got to be crazy, hasn't he, Stephan? There's no sketch for *Night Fishing* listed anywhere in the universe?'

'You are no doubt correct,' the Frenchman answered laconically.

'Sure I'm correct; but, you don't sound one hundred percent convinced.'

'Perhaps there have been a few paintings, sketches which have not been listed.'

'How many?'

'Is this a business call, Monsieur Huntingdon?'

'Listen, Stephan, I just don't like phoney Englishmen trying to sell me fakes. It gives the business a bad smell.'

'If this were a business call I could perhaps be a little more helpful.'

'I'm just asking you to confirm there is no preparatory sketch extant for *Night Fishing at Antibes.* Hell, that's not a business call is it?'

There were some moments of silence at the other end of the line.

'Okay, one business question. Could that painting of Craufurd's just be authentic?'

'Not every sketch Monsieur Picasso made has been catalogued. That's all I can say on the telephone – without a preliminary business discussion.'

'Tell me, why would Picasso want to disown a sketch of a painting like *Night Fishing*? The guy wants to make money, doesn't he?'

'It is possible, just possible, he might have been ashamed of it,' Stephan answered.

'Possible?'

'We will need to meet and talk if I am to be of genuine assistance to you, Monsieur Huntingdon.'

'Okay, we'll meet,' Huntingdon grimaced. And then again, he reflected, maybe you've told me enough.

His heart was starting to race again. He spoke to the hotel operator through a half-masticated pink tablet.

'Hello. May I speak to Captain Craufurd, please?'

'Captain Craufurd is not here. Who is calling, please?' It was a Frenchwoman with a sexy English accent.

So far, so good. He wanted Captain Craufurd not to be there. That was why he had taken the trouble to get his client's number and ring her direct. He preferred, whenever possible, to cut out the middleman.

'My name is Huntingdon, Marvin Huntingdon – it's about a certain seascape he showed me out at your place yesterday.'

'You are talking about the *Night Fishing* by Picasso?'

'Well, I guess that's the problem, Mademoiselle. You say it's by Picasso, Captain Craufurd says it's by Picasso, and I'd like to believe it *is* a Picasso. But the investigations I've made frankly haven't been reassuring.'

'So why please are you ringing?' Hélène Colmar asked with a French directness, which slightly threw the art dealer.

'I'm ringing because I'm prepared to take a gamble on a one-in-a-hundred chance of its being genuine,' he laughed back. The proposition and the laugh were supposed to come later, after he had carefully demolished the Frenchwoman's expectations a whole lot further.

'The picture is not for sale.'

'I beg your pardon?'

'Not at any price, and I am speaking as the owner,' said Hélène Colmar, putting down the telephone.

It was then that Marvin Huntingdon realised that he loved the picture so much he was prepared to steal, perhaps even kill, to acquire it.

19

'You know one thing, darling,' said Hélène Colmar, 'an Englishman always hangs up his suits – even when making love in the afternoon.'

Dominick Craufurd was a man in a hurry, but he knew the respect due to Winterbotham's, one of the more conservative tailors in Savile Row. So he meticulously pinched back the knife edge into the creases of his trousers before carefully folding them over a crude stool. He turned towards the huge bear rug, his spotless silk underpants (from a shop in Albemarle Street) pitch-forked out of shape by desire.

'Would Jerome be too sad to see us here together?'

'He'd be jealous as hell – so would I. I've done him out of his thirty nights.'

'Thirty nights, thirty days, thirty years, it all sounds so arithmetical,' complained Hélène. 'Darling, would you do something for me? I feel just now before we start anything I would like a White Lady. Can you mix me one?'

'A White Lady,' grunted Dominick from deep beneath the rug. 'That stupid yankee concoction. I thought you had some pink champers hidden away somewhere.'

'No, it must be a White Lady – you forget, *chéri,* it's almost the happy hour.'

'Where the blazes do I do it?' he demanded, erupting almost viciously from the love lair, standing there above her, with the extent of his desire all too patent.

It was while he was fiddling with the bottles and the ice over by the fake early American fidelity chest that he first experienced a sense of loss.

'Where is it?' he asked the gin bottle.

She looked up half-innocently.

'The daub, the picture, you know what I mean!'

'So lucky, yet so serious.'

'In our state, my dear, one doesn't joke about valuable works of art.'

'You know *chéri,* one day I woke up and I said to myself, I don't like it at all. Not the least bit. Pablo was so perverse, he knows quite well that I don't lick ices with a forked green tongue. So I said to myself, very well, goodbye, you only kept it here for Michel's sake. Perhaps it will make me rich. And then suddenly I realised I would miss it.'

'Where did you put it?' growled Dominick. 'It could be the last ship you've got left.'

'It's better it should be safe,' she told him with troubled eyes. 'It's not so much the picture, it's....'

'Your lover's final gift?' said Dominick flatly. 'You realise I practically had our little American friend netted?'

'I told him it was not for sale. I have locked it in the villa – it will be safer there,' she explained like a guilty child.

He wondered at the power of this ghost that could make her still clutch tightly to her one ticket to prosperity.

'I must admit I was a bit disappointed in Michel André,' he remarked, climbing in again beside Hélène, a White Lady in each hand, 'his ghost insists that you do yourself out of a new wardrobe, not to mention a fair amount of much-needed financial security for some sentimental attachment to a second-class daub by a randy old picador.'

'And you lose your commission, my poor Nicky!'

'That's got nothing to do with it,' he flushed.

'Well, my little loser,' she whispered, her long painted fingernails crab-crawling over his fleshy but hairless chest. 'Unlucky at play but, who knows, maybe a little more lucky in love?'

'My feelings have nothing to do with it,' gasped Dominick as her fingers cupped him below.

'Unlucky at play ...' whispered Hélène, her fingers commencing a sliding motion. 'Unlucky at love ... and then again maybe lucky....'

Hélène Colmar had one characteristic that could be considered charming or not according to one's innate animalism: she snored. Not that the satisfied lady's delightfully porcine grunting was needed to wake up Dominick. True, he was a light sleeper, but on this occasion he had not gone to sleep. He had lain awake in Hélène's modish tent pondering a throw roulette addicts might call a 'martingale': if you have a winner, leave your winnings on the same number and aim to double up.

The first half of that elusive martingale he had already pulled off. The sweet tingle of well-satisfied nerve-ends, the mellow, even thumping of his heart, a certain languid ease that flowed about his body, proved that.

The second half of the martingale was a bit more desperate. It touched more than the delicate matter of a breach of honour among gamblers, it touched robbery, the kind of thing that had almost got him expelled from Westminster – even though it was for the girl's own good. Hell, she needed to find a buyer more than she admitted. The first steps were easy: to detach himself from the lady and creep through the tent flaps, to wander out into the glaring hangover of a late June afternoon with a quick glance to take in the jollily painted *bateaux* bobbing around the Cap. Easy also to neutralise the burglar alarm system of André's vulgar villa – Dominick had snaffled the key. Harder to discover where, in this ramshackle piece of perverted film-set design, the lady had placed the picture. In the salon or the ante-salon? In the Mandarin Room or the Vikings' banqueting hall – or upstairs in Marie Antoinette's cavernous boudoir? As he walked up the ample stairway in his supple pair of two-toned shoes, a step gave way beneath his tread. The whole edifice stank of jerrydom. Halfway up he paused to study a Derain. Now that was really quite something – an *oeuvre* that our friend the painter-picador could not have got near in a million oil-clogged bull fights. For a moment Dominick was sorely tempted.

But one thing distinguished the angelic super-whore: the tightness with which her pretty little hand clasped the moneybags. Besides, he had a shrewd guess Derain had painted no such picture. All of which did not help to find that damned Picasso daub. And then he remembered there was only one place tarts put things – unless tucked up their knickers. Up a further flight of stairs, round that piece of pseudo Epstein rubbish, turn left by the fake Salvador Dali and glide through a hung piece of rich (and genuine) Flemish tapestry that hid a doorway with a concealed latch. The Borgia strong-room.

Dominick's eyes were on the *trompe l'oeil* hinge which was uncovered by just one sliding panel of old oak. His pointed toes met something furry and soft. The dog was a Golden Labrador with a difference — it was about half as large again as the commoner species.

It was also dead, otherwise it would be pawing its way up Dominick's keen-edged trouser leg, nuzzling inwards towards his crotch – a greeting Bobo only accorded his late master's very best friends. Whoever had done it was a rotten shot. He had had to fire four or five times into the huge body before Bobo had salivated his life out against a tapestry gloriously depicting the Death of Adonis.

Dominick Craufurd bent down and examined the dog, which was dumped sack-like against the door; the huge mastiff's collar encrusted with semi-precious stones surprisingly still around his neck. Bobo had died as he had lived, guarding Michel André's deposit room, his unique collection of fakes. For it was here that his friend had crept when really down on his luck, to snaffle out some early Léger, some fancy of the adolescent Bonnard, wave it before the eyes of his creditors and somehow get back into the game. That was Michel André – he had used art as gambling stakes. It was just left to determine who else was seated at his table in a gamble of robbery and death. Huntingdon? Of course, the bugger had botched it up. He had slain the dog, but he did not know that the strong-room key was recovered by an expedient as simple as pressing the left tit of an early nineteenth-century statue of Lucrezia Borgia. Her head fell forward revealing the key in her body.

When Dominick had finally admitted himself to Michel André's Borgia strong-room he found nothing much more than a dirty floor and a good deal of string and discarded brown wrapping paper. The major masterpieces in the Michel André Collection, as Dominick well knew, had over ten months ago taken flight. Propped up against the walls were just a few daubs, mostly valueless. And one brown paper parcel, tied loosely with bits of string. It looked like a bit of dirty washing. And yet it was a part of history! Picasso's toe-first dip into that nocturnal water of Antibes, which was to be so luminously haunted by his *Night Fishers.*

Well, Huntingdon or some other crook had thought it worth killing a dog for. Until he found a respectable buyer he decided the picture would be safer with him.

20

Niall and Oriana Craufurd had managed to give their governess, Audrey Hopkirk, the slip. It was nice to sit out here in the evening in a peasanty quayside café, licking a giant ice-cream.

'You think she'll find us?' asked Oriana.

'Hardly matters really,' observed her brother. 'We're all doomed anyway. Talk about Stukas and Panzers – they haven't even started yet.'

'You mean there's worse to come,' shrilled Oriana, eyes goggling, lips smeared with vanilla.

'Of course, silly, haven't you read about them? Nerve gases for instance. And things they grow in test-tubes that give you diseases like mumps and measles only far worse. And powders they sprinkle from aeroplanes that will stick on to everything and destroy all known forms of life, a bit like the stuff they squirt out of rose-sprays. But that's nothing — have you heard of the death ray?'

'The death ray?' echoed his sister, letting a huge chunk of *glace à la framboise* dribble down the cone and settle on her fingers.

'It's all very hush-hush, of course. If they told us about it we'd all surrender, that's why they're keeping it secret. It's a bit like a gun firing infra-red beams at you, if you know what I mean. It just passes through the body, you wouldn't stand an earthly.'

'Golly,' said Oriana Craufurd, her mouth an ice-cream oval of horror. And then the look of horror intensified still more.

'Niall,' she stammered, 'It's . . . Dad.'

The son twisted round to see his father, black as thunder, a large paper parcel under his arm, staring at them from the dark street outside.

21

He knew that animal look of content on her sleeping lips. The pleasure had to be very recent.

'Now I have opened my eyes and I can see that it's you,' she whispered.

Of course, it had not been too hard for her to guess. Only three people had a clue about Le Bijou, and one of them was dead. So it had to be Jerome di Cavazza who had slid open the canvas flap and whispered 'guess who's here'. It had to be him, or Dominick Craufurd again.

'Has Dominick been here?' Jerome asked, kissing her shoulder.

'Only to look for pictures that aren't here. My darling, you won me for thirty nights, didn't you? And you and Dominick are both gentlemen, aren't you? Your word is your bond,' she smiled with a trace of bitterness. She added, 'I suppose you also won my boat.' She looked at him closer, 'My darling, you look different somehow. It's hard to believe you've only been away for a few days. Mostly, I think the change is exciting. You've been outdoors in boats, in wars, I don't know, but you look very lean and manly. And, of course, Jerome *chéri*, I love you when you are winning.'

'I am always winning,' he smiled, putting his mouth to her lips like a tired traveller to a water tap.

Later, not too much later, she said, 'I wonder if you are winning. It was very nice, but it was very short and sweet. You are a little restless and anxious, aren't you, darling?'

He lit a cigarette and tried to look totally relaxed as he lay back on the pillows in Hélène's love tent. 'The *Night Fishers* has gone,' he seemed to remark casually. 'You say Dominick was looking for it?'

'Chéri, you keep looking at that wall. If I thought that Picasso was so important to you I would have kept it here. Would you be happier and more relaxed if I told you where it was?'

He thought how absurd it was to sneak like a thief into this villa of follies when he could have been so much better employed leading a charge into the French positions in Menton, or skiing down a slope in the Alps with a Beretta blazing, or at least equipped with a whistle and officer's stars, doing something to sort out the chaos at Ventimiglia.

They needed him at Menton, they needed a breakthrough in the French Alps. They needed to sort out the traffic jam of armour at Ventimiglia. Did they really need a sketch by Picasso? What did you do in the Second Great War, *caro* Papa? I stole a sketch by a famous artist.

'I shall show you it – anything to stop you looking so worried. Just so long as you don't take it away. Nicky tells me it's my only cashable asset.'

'Where is it?' he asked more roughly, playfully twisting her fragile white wrist, which seemed to be overpowered by a gold and diamond bracelet as large and tight as a handcuff.

'Sshhh,' she purred, brushing her fingers in a feathery caution across his lips.

She led him out of the vulgarity they called Le Bijou, across the sloping lawn that had been so colourfully floodlit by that young lighting impresario, Georges Bizet, into the villa proper and up the ornamental staircase.

Rounding a corner they stopped in their tracks, just staring.

'I can't believe it,' she sobbed. 'Bobo.'

'A dead dog,' whistled Tenente di Cavazza. 'It was wise to put it in the safe.'

'Oh, Bobo ... Bobo,' she was sobbing, down there on the carpet, cradling the huge smashed head in her lap.

'Well and truly dead, I'd say,' said Cavazza. 'It's already stiff,' feeling for the nipple on the statue, turning the huge brass key in the lock.

'My God,' he muttered. 'Somebody's grabbed it.'

She glanced up quickly from the floor, a new hardness shaping her face so that the tears seemed suddenly an anachronism. A moment later she had clean vanished.

He rushed down the way she must have gone. A door creaked and somewhere footsteps seemed to be audible. Perhaps the villa was haunted. Perhaps that was what had frightened Hélène away. It would have been typical of Michel André to have owned a haunted villa, providing of course the ghost was sufficiently aristocratic. It would have appealed to his sense of humour – an aristocratic ghost roaming his corridors. He would answer its moans with that wild demoniacal laughter which had sometimes made Jerome wonder if he was not perhaps just a little mad.

But this dog lying in its own dried blood would not have amused Michel André. Hélène had told Jerome the animal would not leave the villa after his master's death. The old concierge at the gate came in twice daily to feed and presumably exercise it. Perhaps that door opening behind him in the upstairs corridor was the old concierge going about her chores. Then again perhaps it was not.

Michel André had loved mirrors. Every square foot of wall space which was not occupied by a painting or some drawing sacred or profane, was covered by a mirror. There was one in front of him now, a *trompe l'oeil* in effect, because it gave the impression the corridor was extending into infinity when in fact it was taking a sharp right turn.

Although it was dark in the corridor, it was possible to see the reflections of a man about fifteen yards in front of him. He did not look like an old concierge – or a ghost. He was a short man with a monklike tonsure. He was scurrying along with fast agitated steps. Jerome had never seen his like among Michel André's perverse collection of regulars. He looked like a man who could fire four or five bullets at point-blank range at a superb pedigree hound and even then miss with some. He inspired almost instinctive loathing.

Jerome di Cavazza followed noiselessly after him along this corridor of twisted mirrors, at the same time drawing the Beretta from his pocket. His soft whistle was enough to stop the man in his tracks and twist him round in Jerome's direction. As Jerome was weighting whether to shoot him there and then or question him (which unfortunately meant speaking to him), he felt his gun spontaneously jerking out of his hand. The mirror in front of him suddenly became all fractured shapes, like the most contorted Picasso, and a revolver shot thundered down the corridor.

A harsh voice from behind shouted, 'Put your hands up and stay right where you are!' He saw a criss-cross reflection of a man built like an all-in wrestler and crushed into a chocolate brown suit.

He was being prodded at the point of an automatic into the Marie Antoinette room, and told to sit down on a dubious Louis Quinze sofa. It was probably not genuine. Jerome remembered that Michel André had bought the Trianon set as a job lot.

'Goddamn it. He tried to plug me . . .' the little American cried, no longer a reflection in a looking-glass.

'It's an Italian called Cavazza,' his companion spoke. 'Quite a local celebrity hereabouts!'

Jerome noticed something about the American. His hands were gesticulating with a pillbox he had just pulled from his pocket, but his eyes were feverish with excitement. A few seconds later, leaning back on the genuine or fake Louis Quinze sofa rubbing his jaw, he thought he would have done better to observe the swinging movement of the companion's fist.

'You're under arrest, Cavazza!' the American art dealer cried. 'Inspector Bazain here is going to have you shot as an alien and a spy, but first you're telling Inspector Bazain what the hell you're doing snooping around this villa!'

He started to explain he was there at the invitation of the owner, then realised the stupidity of telling the truth to madmen. Instead, he pushed back hard against the Louis Quinze sofa, the object being to up-end it and make a getaway in the resulting confusion. But the back of the sofa snapped off, as if it had been put together with matchsticks (after all, it was just a theatrical prop), so that all Inspector Bazain had to do was to lean down and haul Jerome up by the collar with one indecently large fist.

'What do you know about modern art, Cavazza?' Marvin Huntingdon demanded, gulping down a pink tablet.

'Some say it began with Manet's *Déjeuner sur 1'herbe,* others prefer to see the seeds of modernity earlier, in the paintings of Delacroix for instance. Others, perhaps the more *avant garde* critics, insist that it was born out of the apocalypse of the last war. It depends what you mean by modern art,' Jerome choked, as Inspector Bazain's fist tightened its grip around his throat.

'I notice you deliberately avoid any mention of the surrealist phase of Pablo Picasso.' Huntingdon's voice was menacing. 'I guess you wouldn't be interested in Fauvism, would you, Cavazza? Or the prices even certain off-the-cuff sketches are fetching among the art world's cognoscenti since last year's retrospective exhibition in New York?'

'I consider Picasso a talented but much overrated painter,' Jerome answered honestly, before Inspector Bazain's free hand flipped like a whale's fin across his face.

A plump, pink Venus by Boucher was looking down from the ceiling in seeming sympathy. Jerome was sure she was an impostor.

'Don't try and deceive me, Cavazza! You can't bluff your way round a missing Picasso,' The little American betrayed as much anxiety as anger.

'If I am under arrest, why don't you take me to a police station?' Jerome asked.

The question seemed to anger Inspector Bazain. The whale's fin chopped into his cheekbone, filling the Italian's eyes with tears.

'When did you last see Pablo Picasso?' Marvin Huntingdon was shouting at him. The pain and the absurdity of the question provoked Jerome into an unfortunate answer.

'Night fishing at Antibes in the nude. But I couldn't be sure because it was dark.'

The American art dealer was about to launch into another tirade of questions. He abruptly stopped. His jaw dropped open and his eyes bulged. 'And you say you're not interested in Picassos,' he breathed thickly.

The eyes of a ram were staring at Jerome from above the powder-pink Marie Antoinette-style bed, an esoteric allusion on the part of the dead decorator, Michel André, to the Bourbon court's alleged dabblings in the occult. This time there was no hint of sympathy. Why should one goat worry about another? Jerome thought bitterly.

'I warn you, Cavazza, Inspector Bazain is an experienced French police interrogator,' Marvin Huntingdon was shouting. 'He's going to probe you, question you in depth like the professional he is, till you start talking facts about what happened to a certain sketch for a certain major modern painting which I am acquiring from its *rightful* owners, the Michel André Trust.'

'You know there are a lot of fakes in this room, but the biggest of them is Inspector Bazain,' Jerome panted. 'If he were a genuine policeman he would take me to the Préfecture and have me interned as an alien. What does a real policeman know or care about Pablo Picasso?'

'Question him, Inspector. There's no Geneva Convention for spies and thieves! Where have you hidden the picture you stole from that safe?'

In fact, Inspector Bazain needed no encouragement. He had already lifted Jerome off the remains of the fake Louis Quinze sofa and thrown him across the room so that he landed like a sack against the foot of the powder-pink Marie Antoinette bed. Now he was going in with the boot, except he was not wearing boots. Inspector Bazain was wearing a pair of size ninety, or thereabouts, patent leather shoes. A novel fashion feature about these shoes was that they had sharply pointed black steel toecaps. These he was now aiming at Jerome's wriggling abdomen.

The pink coverlet came off with a tug and draped nicely around the Inspector's pudgy head. Of course he tore it away, but Jerome, who had scrambled on to the bed, now had a flower-patterned eiderdown ready to replace it with the purest silk, or linen, depending on its authenticity. For another few vital seconds the Inspector was blind, rolling around at the bottom of the bed, breaking its springs and crumbling its gold-leafed feet.

'Get your hulk out of the way so I can shoot,' Marvin Huntingdon was yelling. That was the original reason why Jerome pulled down the black and gold sculptured ram's head – as a useless kind of protection against bullets. But the Inspector had got rid of the genuine, or fake, eighteenth-century eiderdown and was now panting into Jerome's face with a breath that was not unreminiscent of the sewers of Toulon. He had also got a knife out, which, as far as Jerome knew, was not regulation police issue. So the ram's head came down on Inspector Bazain's head. If it was a fake, it was not so cheap a fake that it splintered on impact. What happened was that the golden horns tore two trenches down the sides of the Inspector's face and embedded themselves in his bull-like neck.

Inspector Clément was an obstinate young man. Although he was desperately short of police officers he had insisted on keeping an observer on the Michel André mansion since the evening of Jerome's escape. His observer suddenly had any amount of suspicious activity to report. The inevitable refugees and frontier-bound army trucks had forced Clément's police Citroën to take to the country roads causing an unavoidable delay. But he now had one unsuspected advantage. Bazain was hollering so much that Clément and his raiding party were half-way up the main stairs before Marvin Huntingdon shouted, 'Christ, it's the police!'

The person this news seemed most to distress was, oddly enough, Inspector Bazain. His eyes rolled with anxiety as he struggled to lever the ram's horns out of the rhino-hard tissues of his neck.

For Jerome, of course, the word 'police' had to mean flight. There was another door to the Marie Antoinette chamber which did not lead directly back into the corridor, but which could give access by way of a fin-de-siècle drawing room and a neo-medieval armoury to a spiral flight of stairs the servants had once used. He knew because, when he and Hélène were not supposed to be lovers by any rule of any game ... Never mind, this was the direction he now took, with Marvin Huntingdon his eager follower, no longer his pursuer. Inspector Bazain made a desperate attempt to accompany them. He managed to pump himself on to his feet and make a lunge at the second door; but he was giddy from his battle with Michel André's satirical little *objet d'art.* So at least Inspector Clément was able to make one immediate arrest, a notorious local racketeer and thug called Vaselli who seemed to have been attacked by a sculptured animal.

22

'You take the bed,' he said, 'such as it is – and sorry about the lack of clean sheets – the geyser at the local laundry seems to have blown up.'

Audrey Hopkirk had wanted to say something about being used to roughing it, that was the acceptable kind of chat to an employer. But he halted her.

'I'll camp out next door on the floor, and come to think of it there's not a bad bed up the road.'

She should have fallen asleep almost instantly, but when you have not slept for five days it is not that easy. Dominick Craufurd's old First Empire bed which creaked and threatened any minute to collapse under even her light weight, the unusual almost oppressive smell of the heavy linen sheets, which had the general effect of making her nostrils twitch, the sound of the tide lapping against the harbour walls, the glint of moonlight through the tattered curtains which had seen better days – all these things stopped her eyelids from closing.

It was a new and different world to Audrey Hopkirk, a world of gentlemen and gentlemen's gentlemen, a smart yet tatty world that exuded a vague, threatening, intriguing ambiance of masculinity.

Audrey Hopkirk twisted her head round towards the wall and away from the window with its ripplings of moonlit waves, and, finding the pillow too high and too hard for her, took out a bundle from beneath it.

It was her employer's pyjamas neatly folded. They were boldly striped in the colours of a well-known old school tie.

Her last conscious resolve was to tiptoe in and see how Niall and Oriana were coping on their mattress in the box room. It was not ideal. If they lingered here, Captain Craufurd would have to find a larger place. These colourful 'digs' over a bar called the 'Artiste Assoiffé' was all too bohemian; though certainly it was nice to be in the old town opposite the port with its gently bobbing yachts and speed-boats, mostly abandoned for 'the duration.' But the children needed room to play and decent clean beds to rest in, and regular meals, and respectable places to be educated at.

She wondered where her employer had gone. She thought she had heard him leave about eleven, sauntering through the deserted bar, the heavy key jingling on his ring. Stepping out onto the promenade below her bedroom, a pause to light a cigarette, then setting off with his quick military gait, whistling something under his breath. He had referred to that other 'not bad bed'. Audrey Hopkirk had a sudden spasm of irrational jealousy or regret.

He had gone gaily into the night to join those other nocturnal animals that hung around the harbour of Antibes.

There were the fishermen in their boats with their lanterns beaming down to attract and dazzle the fish into their nets. Others, she had noticed, who could not afford even a small boat, cast a line hopefully instead from the steep quay into the murk of the Mediterranean. Still others crouched low over the waves, a crude harpoon in their hands, waiting to spear surfacing fish.

Finally she entered water, rather than sleep, drifted out into the oily brine, heard the fishermen's curious bird-like calls from boat to boat, peered with them into the choppy blackness and seemed to discover, with them, strange shapes. Underneath the flat, crudely painted boats, dark sinuosities flitted, unrecognisable from the gaily painted fishy things of all shapes and sizes she had seen strewn out in the market that morning.

One in particular caught her attention. It was a clammy black and it steered itself with an ominous waggle of its giant flippers, cruising easily under the boat, a deep-sea killer. She sensed its purpose, but for some reason could not summon the breath to speak, to warn the others.

Peering down she caught it again, its evil great beady magnified eyes glinting upwards towards her. Her throat was choking in an attempt to deliver the scream. And then it sprang. With a sharp crack it fractured the water's surface as if it were glass.

She awoke in horror, amazed that fragments of fractured water could so shatter and fall to the ground like broken splinters of glass. And then the thing was on top of her, its black rubber flippers from which protruded damp white hands and fingers reaching for her windpipe to stifle the scream which was still unarticulated in her throat.

Her last memory was of rubber black as hell, sinuous as eelskin.

'At least we can give him one thing,' commented Dominick Craufurd opening his last remaining packet of John Player Navy Cut. 'He didn't take advantage of a defenceless lady in distress.'

Audrey Hopkirk was propped up on the bed, a cup of steaming black coffee in her hand, a little shaken, a bruise over her forehead and a stretch-mark on her neck, but otherwise unharmed.

'May I recommend a small addition,' said Dominick Craufurd, advancing with a bottle of Napoleon cognac which he tipped into

Audrey's cup. 'Even though it is a bit early in the morning for café-cognac.'

'Look what I've found!' shouted Niall, holding up a pair of black goggles with thick glass lenses.

'Part of the property of the Italian Navy, I daresay,' drily observed his father.

'Not a bad souvenir. I've read about them in *War Illustrated*.' Niall Craufurd was beginning to enjoy his war. 'Smashing. They say the frogmen are Mussolini's secret weapon.'

'Just now it was the death ray,' mocked his sister.

'They certainly made merry hell with my window,' sighed Dominick, eyeing the vast hole in the glass through which the frogman had dived. 'If only they knew how difficult it is to get that kind of thing repaired these days.'

'Can I keep the goggles, Dad? I could wear them in the school swimming pool, when we get back to England, that is.'

'They're too big for you, stupid. Besides, the Italians might come back and catch you with them,' warned Oriana.

The coffee laced thickly with brandy was bringing Audrey Hopkirk round.

'Feeling better?' asked Dominick with unusual kindness, and for a moment she luxuriated deliciously in a warm glow that seemed to travel so slowly up her body. Then she noticed that her employer's eyes were not quite as generous as his voice. Hastily, she pulled a shawl down and over the cleft which had opened up between her breasts.

Dominick was saying, 'Yet it all sounds a rather tall story when you think about it. An Italian gentleman surging in from the deep blue yonder with seemingly the single purpose of trying to strangle a young English governess. I wonder what the hell he thought he was playing at. All he seems to have pinched is that marine lamp I took off my old boat. Odd thing to take, don't you think? Anyway he's missed the Big Fish.'

Curled up again with his sister on the mattress on the box-room floor and covered with just one smelly army blanket, Niall Craufurd could not forget that he was the proud possessor of an Italian frogman's goggles. He put them on and got a strangely magnified view of the bare bulb swinging from the ceiling, the strips of peeling flake and a moth circling in and out of the half-drawn curtains. A frogman's view. He did not hear the door open, he did not sense the soft tread on the bare floorboards, he did not even smell the whiff of a Gauloise. Like a huge round-faced jolly sea monster with a moustache as big as a walrus's, a thing came gliding into his aquarium water tank, distorted by the fish-eye lense.

The thing, which turned out to be a man rather than a fish, sat down on the mattress and offered him a block of Swiss chocolate.

'You must be young Niall,' he smiled.

Girl with Ice-Cream

23

It was a boat, but its cargo was not fish. The colourful blue and green *bateau* was packed from bow to stern with a cargo of bulging suitcases and children, pale hunched children who did not look as if they were leaving on a pleasure trip.

'What's all that about?' Dominick asked Dalio, vaguely.

'You haven't noticed the big ship in our waters? It is to take the children to Africa – the Jewish children.'

Of course he had noticed. He had seen the three-funnelled monster steam over the skyline yesterday afternoon and thought he recognised the silhouette of *La Fontaine*, once the toast of the Atlantic liners, but long since superseded by the *Normandie*. But that was yesterday. This morning, he felt shakier and less intelligent than if he had been drinking brandy all night.

'Have you noticed another thing? We are losing this war.'

Craufurd turned gloomily back towards the quays where a group of men and women were waving at the boatload of children. The men were somewhat incongruously dressed, for these climes, in black suits and black and grey trilbies; most of the women were wearing furs and were holding handkerchiefs to their eyes.

'Things looked pretty grim in 1914, but it turned out all right in the end,' he repeated the conventional placebo with which everyone was trying to fool everybody else this summer.

Dalio spat into the harbour.

'The other was a clean war, a soldier's war. This war is filth. In the other war they did not try to destroy a man's livelihood.'

'Who is trying to destroy a man's livelihood?'

'The Italians, who else? They should never have let the Italians into this war.' Dalio's bitterness was making him illogical, 'They do not fight clean.'

Dominick motioned towards the mountains behind the Fort Carré, still wearing their spring coat of sparkling snow – the alleged battleground of the new war against Italy. 'We haven't heard too much from the Wops, have we?'

'They don't fight in the mountains, they work in the night, like smugglers – dirty,' Dalio assured him. 'You say your apartment was raided last night?'

Dominick nodded.

'Italians. They are attacking our boats too, they are killing my friends, ordinary fishermen. Come, I will show you something.'

They walked along the quay in the direction of the boat yard – 'Chantiers Navals d'Antibes' – past the plaque that commemorated the crash of the Tunis seaplane in May 1937, to the cluttered section of the harbour where Dalio kept his boat.

He pointed down to a small boat that was tied up beside his own.

'I found her capsized outside the port this morning. It is my friend Simon's boat. I could not find Simon or his son. *Disparus*!'

The craft was typical of the little glow-worm vessels that nightly plied their trade under the battlements of Grimaldi Castle. The feature of the conventional night-fishing boat was the gallows-like structure in the stern from which the acetylene lamp unit was hung, the brilliant cyclops eye which dazzled big and little fish into death by spearing. The gallows structure was still there, although it might. well have snapped off when the boat capsized. What was missing was the big lampshade and metal cage which housed the acetylene lamp. This had not been snapped off. There was a clean incision in the lamp's feed pipe, such as a pair of metal cutters would have made.

'That new lamp was his pride and joy,' muttered Dalio.

And the only thing that had interested Dominick's night raiders had been a lamp fixture.

The boatload of children was put ... put ... putting out of sight behind the Mole Extérieur, but the parents were still waving on the quays, and there was still clean, sparkling snow on the mountains behind them.

A picture postcard scene, in many ways, though it had touches of surrealism.

24

It took her a few seconds, blinking through dazed eyes, to realise that the sun was real and burning, and that the glass was smashed. Down there on the quays, among other less familiar sounds, her ears caught Niall Craufurd's high-pitched pitter-patter and the deeper, more musical tones of his sister. Poking her head out through the biggest hole in the glass she saw her employer two storeys beneath her talking to a fisherman with a faded blue beret. Captain Craufurd looked overdressed in that double-breasted Oxford blue suit of his with the slightly flash pin-stripe and stiffish collar. Mechanically, he pushed one hand down towards his waistcoat and glanced at a fine half-hunter. The old fisherman was gesticulating straight up towards where she leant, pointing excitedly. Following his direction, Craufurd swivelled negligently round and cocked an eye towards the offending window. He gave her an owlish wink and a curt wave of the hand.

'I think I was wrong ever to engage you,' he told her later over a café-cognac and a hot brioche. 'What would a presentable lady of nineteen, isn't it, possibly have to do with a couple of loud-voiced Craufurd nippers. What's the cliché? On the Riviera in spring a young lady's fancies turn to thoughts of love?'

'I can assure you . . . ' she started to reply.

'No, seriously, I owe you an apology – I mean forever lumbering you with the infernal brats. I solemnly promise, if our so-called civilization ever gets out of this mess, only to engage bad-tempered, ill-visaged, middle-aged nannies with squints. Pretty young ladies have other and more pleasurable functions to fulfil, I'm sure.'

She tried to mumble something but realised that she was facing straight into the sun and it was hurting her eyes.

'Here,' he said taking out a red spotted silk handkerchief. 'You've got cream all over your lips. Do you know,' he reminisced, lighting a cigarette, 'the first time I ever came here I must have been about your age – a young idiot of about nineteen. Some dim and distant relation had a place round by Juan-les-Pins. I was sent to her to perform that upper-middle-class sacrificial rite called "sowing your wild oats". I seem to remember I did, with a French lady of uncertain age who used to wander around in floaty diaphanous gowns. She also called me Nicky.'

Audrey Hopkirk was about to ask him who else called him 'Nicky' but decided the question would be impertinent.

'Look,' he suddenly said, 'forget the war. Forget our night visitors. Just enjoy yourself. Get around. Have a hell of a good time. In my day that was the only reason young girls used to push their pretty little noses into this smelly old rock-pool. I'm afraid I can't offer you the family limousine with complaisant chauffeur to drive you in state down the Corniche, but there's an excellent little place quite close where one can still hire a bike for a few francs. Who knows? A little exercise might suit you. Bring a flush to those pale cheeks. Don't worry about the kids, after all they have to be my responsibility whichever way you roll the dice.'

It was nice to escape from them all, feel the wind in her hair, though cycling was hard work in this mountainous place.

Audrey Hopkirk saw herself as much archaeologist as sightseer. One balmy afternoon she worked her way up a cliff that seemed to go on forever. Puffed out, she rested at the summit whilst minuscule waves rolled hundreds of feet below; in the distance sparkled Monte Carlo. This must be it, she decided, the place where the widower Max had driven that other gauche young impoverished 'paid companion'.

Evening had broken surprisingly early that day, and she had run the risk of getting stranded in the dark without a lamp (which she would not anyway have been allowed to use). She gave the bike its head and flashed down the mountain road at an impossible speed, the wind blowing her hair out in a stream behind. Elated by the ride she entered Antibes to pause by the harbour and watch the fishermen go out with their dim lamps bobbing above the waves. Standing there, leaning against her bike, her eyes had been drawn straight down by some compulsive force she would have found it impossible to explain.

There was a boat down there straight beneath her below the jetty, and the fisherman in it had presumably been just about to cast off. He still had the rope in his hand, whilst his blond-headed companion was pulling the protective old car tyres abroad. What concerned Audrey was that she had obviously caused the young fisherman awkwardly to freeze in his tracks, as she stood there towering above him, leaning on her bicycle. She noticed he was quite young. And that there was something compulsive yet strange about his eyes.

25

'Well, tell me,' Commissioner Lazzaron coughed. 'What *is* going on in Antibes?'

Inspector Clément took a deep breath and began again, slowly, methodically, in language he hoped a child could understand.

'Yes, yes, acts of sabotage. You've said that before. You have yet to explain what exactly are these acts of sabotage, who is responsible for them, what precisely are the preventative measures you intend to take?' Lazzaron clawed at a fresh packet of Gitanes cigarettes.

'Fishing boats have been attacked, men have been drowned, but that is not all....'

'What a disaster!' the Commissioner threw up his hands in mock agony. 'We've lost more than a few fishermen in this war, Clément, and there's nothing our department can do about it. If the French army can't win this war, we can't win it!'

'I am seeking your permission only to increase our patrol activity in Antibes, the local force is insufficient,' Clément repeated sullenly.

'You've heard the news, I suppose. Reynaud's government is finished. He got nothing out of his friend Churchill at Tours yesterday. They'll have to send for Pétain.'

'I want enough men to undertake house searches in the Antibes district,' Clément ignored this irrelevance.

'A few fishing boats,' Lazzaron laughed, less than heartily.

'An Italian agent is operating in the Cap, and there is other evidence,' the Inspector insisted.

'We'll need every gendarme we've got to keep public order. And that won't be enough.' Lazzaron breathed in Gitanes smoke. 'The moment the Communists get wind of an Armistice, believe me, it's got to come, there'll be trouble. They know that Mussolini has no love of reds – I can't say I blame him. They'll fight like wildcats to save themselves from the prison cages of Sardinia, and a good dose of castor oil. We'll need every man we've got to keep order.'

'I need twenty men in Antibes now,' Clément said.

'What is this obsession with Antibes? Have you got a woman there?' Lazzaron grimaced.

How did you explain what there was at Antibes to a stupid mule like Lazzaron? Inspector Clément asked himself in the butter coloured corridors of the Nice Préfecture.

There was a woman, yes. She was called Hélène Colmar. She was hostile to the police, but more afraid of some other force she was unwilling to describe. There was an Italian with a police file called di Cavazza who seemed unusually eager to avoid an internment which most of his compatriots, at least those whom Clément had arrested, had cheerfully accepted on the basis that it could only last a few days. There was an American who claimed to deal in fine art but who employed known thugs. There were strange losses at sea and weird rumours running along the Antibes waterfront. And there was an ocean liner filling up with children lying off the harbour. There was enough that was wrong with the Antibes area to worry any conscientious police inspector.

He had seen a picture in the woman Colmar's puzzling apartment. It had seemed, on close study, to portray the harbour of Antibes under moonlight; but the scale was unnatural, the perspective was false, and the figures were too large and grotesque for their setting. The situation at Antibes was worrying, as this picture had been worrying. But how did you make an unimaginative mule like Commissioner Lazzaron understand?

26

'Who is that, please?'

'This is Mr Craufurd's residence.'

'Who are you please?' The Frenchwoman's voice sounded distraught. 'Are you a friend of Nicky?'

'I'm sorry, Captain Craufurd is not at home,' Audrey Hopkirk said. She had been taught it was not the business of a servant, even an upper servant belonging to the upper middle-classes, to get into personal conversation with callers on the telephone or on the doorstep.

'If you are a friend of Nicky's, you must find him,' the foreign voice implored.

'I am the governess of Captain Craufurd's children,' Audrey decided it was permitted to explain. 'We are here for the summer,' she added, a strictly uncalled-for explanation.

'You must tell Nicky I must have my picture back now. I need *les pécheurs de la nuit,*' Hélène Colmar half-sobbed.

'Ah, the night fishermen,' Audrey Hopkirk remarked brightly. A star pupil at French, she was still looking for top marks. But now she bit her tongue.

'I never said he could have it. I never gave my agreement. If he is fond of me he will return it here to the cabin today.'

'I will tell Captain Craufurd as soon as he comes in.'

'No, you must find him now and tell him!' the Frenchwoman's voice suddenly became violent, or suicidal.

'I'll give him that message,' Audrey calmly replied.

When Craufurd returned she said that a woman friend had called, and perhaps a man. She thought she had heard a man's voice whispering to the woman at the other end of the line.

27

'All aboard the *Skylark*,' shouted Dominick Craufurd, sporting a faded but still outrageously stripey I Zingari blazer. 'Trips round the harbour and bay, courtesy of my good friend Dalio. No worries about upset tummies. Water looks calm as a mill-pond.' It was difficult to resist. God was in his heaven and the warm sun was extracting iridescent ripples of pure light from a Seurat sea. Dalio's two-stroke was chugging like an elderly asthmatic and the owner was attempting a grimacing semblance of a smile, whilst ugly swear words seemed to come noiselessly from under his breath through gaps driven in his teeth.

'Joining us, Miss Hopkirk?' queried Captain Craufurd, starting to haul up the anchor. 'Or maybe you prefer to landlubb. Bit anti-social, isn't it?' He looked across to her and saw a stereotype, a reproduction of something else – a young girl leaning on the quay against the handlebars of her bike. Pretty as a picture!

'All right,' he conceded good-humouredly. 'Shove off, if you must.'

'Take care of yourselves,' she called out apologetically to the children as the boat started to chug away.

'Niall says they could have one-man submarines out there,' shrieked back Oriana Craufurd.

'I'm more worried about magnetic mines, silly,' cut in her brother. Audrey Hopkirk turned, swivelling on her bike to throw them a final wave. There was a road which led straight through the town, then out, in the general direction of Grasse. The road led ever upwards, inexorably, sometimes steeply. In the dim distance were mountains, blanketed in heat-haze. Soon she had dismounted, pushing her bike at walking pace. It was a silly thing to do on a day like this. She noticed the old women sitting outside their cottages – gnarled faces, black dresses. They looked at her with hostility more than amusement.

It took her a bit of time to admit she was puffed. First, it had been grim determination to keep going, somehow to 'show 'em', though who 'em might be – her sardonic employer or the local inhabitants – she had not quite made up her mind. Then other considerations started to weigh. She realised that the old women were looking at her now with a sharper curiosity, a more vindictive malice. Being puffed made her look puffy. What a sight she must be! Her face must be as red as a beetroot, and she felt her hair flat and clammy, flopping down her forehead in one sticky mass.

She had decided to keep going. Somewhere there must be some hotel, or at least a reasonably clean restaurant or café where a girl could go to sort herself out. Instead she struck a length of newly gravelled road with tar sticking to her shoes. The only place for miles was an *ouvriers'* place, where a few trucks and cars had stopped. The 'ladies' was unmentionable (clearly frequented exclusively by men despite the sign on the door). Hastily combing her hair and throwing some powder over her face she fled.

Next door was a tawdry open shop where *ouvriers* hung about hammering at very old push-button machines, that clattered away and sent out staccato tracer bursts of coloured lights.

One man was doing well. His table was roaring along. Every few seconds a huge lady with diamonds on her breasts lit up at the end of the table and seemed to wink. But it seemed all lost on the man, who quietly went about the business of pushing in the slot to claim his extra balls, which he then sent crazily careering up the board with a deft touch on the flipper knobs. Although he had his back to her, he must have had eyes in the back of his head.

She could tell he knew she was there. When he finally turned round with that throw back of the fingers, a Gallic way of saying 'who gives a hang anyway?', he obviously knew everything about her.

'It passes the time,' he said half-apologetically. 'The thing's been fixed. But maybe that's all to the good. Otherwise I would be here forever.'

At first sight he struck her as a pretty ordinary young man, with his short, black hair, the kind who wore a dark suit and quiet tie and hung around the fringes at dances. A bank clerk or something.

'But then it's amusing to retaliate a little. To rock the thing forward and to the side – *comme ça*. But you've got to be careful. If you over-tilt – pffft! – kaput!'

As he twisted round to face her squarely she realised her first impressions had been hasty. This was no suburban rabbit. For one thing he was older than she had thought at first, nearer thirty than twenty, and his dark moustache was sproutier, more cavalier than the short-cut norm. His eyes were deep and brown and gave the impression of enormous kindness and depth, but each had in the centre a salmon-pink iris, as if someone had plugged them with a tiny gem.

Another thing – this man had seen life, had known pain. He had skewered round towards her leaning heavily on his stick. He was a bit of a cripple and the romantic thought crossed Audrey's mind that he might even be a *mutilé de guerre*.

'I come up here often,' he told her over a cup of coffee back in the *ouvriers'* café. 'Antibes is so derivative. It's good to get your nose back into something French. For instance this coffee. Taste how harsh it is. And often if you come here at four or five in the afternoon you'll get *crevettes* wrapped in a page of *Figaro*, smack out of the bay. Covered in butter and crusted in coarse salt.'

'I don't think I can get out at that time,' said Audrey Hopkirk. 'Come on,' urged the stranger, peering deep into her eyes the way she had seen hypnotists do on the stage. 'A girl like you. With a body like yours. Do you know what your body signals to me, Mademoiselle? It signals peace. Blessed restful peace. But then I am French. Didn't your father or your employer warn you about Frenchmen like me? How swift they are at seduction? eh? How they undress a girl with their eyes, eh? And then perform the same beautiful task with their hands? How they kiss like no Englishman knows? How their lips can unlock something in a young girl's body? How easily he can make an impressionable girl just out of finishing school – how can I put it – how can I put it – become maybe his slave?'

It had happened to Audrey Hopkirk once before (in the films they called it 'getting fresh'). Some young students at a local hospital had invited her and a friend round for a 'bit of a razzle-dazzle'. They had drunk gins and its and eaten curry at a spot called the Taj Mahal. Later they had gone back to their digs and somebody had opened a bottle of a liquid called Segavin. Her friend in the next-door room had been more in control and had ended up slapping the young man's face. Audrey, out of pity really for the pimply youth who panted over her, had been forthcoming. She had returned home with a splitting headache and great soreness between the legs.

This time it was different. The man aroused not a jot of fear or repulsion. He had leant forward, as one might do in a dimly-lit *ouvriers'* café, and given her just a flick of a kiss, his moustache barely brushing and tickling her lips. It was like an opening gambit at chess. A statement of intent. But, as he had hinted, young Frenchmen do not beat about the bush. Like many English girls of her age Audrey Hopkirk had never quite been able to reconcile the needs of the body and the demands of the heart. The word had never quite been made flesh. But this Frenchman knew a thing or two about love and life. Knew how to lean forward to light his Gauloise and, as he did so, slide his hand deftly beneath the table. Knew how to place it there, rubbing against her stockings high up on her thighs beneath the flaps of her skirt. Knew, too, how to give her plump thighs a playful squeeze before withdrawing.

'You must come here more often,' he said.

As she wandered back to the Craufurd family she remembered that she had not even asked his name.

28

'Nicky, darling, thank heaven I've found you at last. I spoke to this idiot little girl, this little English girl you have in your apartment – oh, Nicky, I'm so worried about my picture.'

'No need to worry, everything's under control. I'm going to find you a disgustingly rich buyer.'

'It's all I have, Nicky. All I have in the world.'

'That's why it's safely under lock and key. Until we've got the price we want. It's my headache now.'

'Nicky, I don't want to sell the picture now. It's too valuable to me, you understand – sentimentally.'

'You're not going to be able to survive this war on sentiment, sweetest. Believe me, I've looked at the balance sheet.'

'I must have that picture *now*, Nicky!' the telephone ear-piece let out a bakelite scream.

Dominick Craufurd fished a packet of French cigarettes out of his pocket and grimaced as the black tobacco crackled between his lips.

He loved France but hated its cigarettes. It was going to be hard to get through this war without Players Navy Cut.

'Why the sudden change of mood?' he asked the telephone mouthpiece.

'That American dealer of yours – I've found he's a thief.' Hélène was always gloriously illogical.

'But he wants the picture and wants it badly. That's why we mustn't put temptation his way. But we do want a good price for the *Night Fishers*. Trust me to guide you through this wicked world of art dealing.'

'Other people love the picture, Nicky.'

'Ah, so we have another buyer?'

'I want my picture back, now.'

'Supposing we have a talk this evening about it. Unless....'

'This evening will be too late, Nick.'

'Unless I was going to say, you have another visitor.'

'Tonight will be too late.'

With an expression of faint distaste Dominick blew out a cloud of Gauloise smoke. 'It's not possible, is it, that our friend Cavazza has returned to claim his, er . . . privileges?'

'There's no one here, Nicky.'

'It was just a thought.'

'There's no one here.'

'I'll bring a bottle of champagne. I'm sure there must be something to celebrate, though looking at the news I can't think exactly what. Perhaps someone has had triplets in China, or struck oil in the Arizona desert. Or two Eskimos have suddenly discovered the joys of nudity. Never mind, we'll find a reason.'

'I'm not joking, Nicky. I must have that picture or . . . I don't know what I'll do.'

'We'll talk it over this evening, my love,' Craufurd said soothingly as he hung up. Why did beautiful women always lie? was the first question he asked himself. He decided they flattered themselves that lying somehow enhanced their sex appeal. And of course they always lied badly. Did she think he couldn't hear there was a man in La Cabine?

29

They had once called him Il Gatto, and indeed there was something irresistibly feline about Jerome di Cavazza.

It was not just that you sensed that any moment he might start purring, there was a cat's agility built right into the marrow of the man. That was why, when he finally came back to search Les Ombres, the job was over in under half an hour. Admittedly this time he did not have the assistance of Marvin Huntingdon and 'Inspector Bazaine'.

He had drawn a blank, so that was the business end of his assignment with Les Ombres. That left him honourably free to pursue the pleasure side, and catch up on the twenty-eight nights he had so fairly won.

As he crossed the lawn to the wigwam pavilion surrounded by its bougainvillaea, he had a *frisson* of presentiment, the kind of warning that comes only to cats, and other favoured descendants of Egyptian gods.

He dipped his head beneath the canvas flap and got that warm animal lived-in feeling about the place.

Hélène Colmar was at home. In fact she had been playing cards, there was her Black Russian cigarette still smouldering in the ash-tray on the camp table, and her cards laid out opposite her opponent's. She must have left the table in disgust (so had her opponent, but maybe for different reasons). And, carelessly flicking over her final hand, Jerome di Cavazza could understand why.

In fact her hand was so bad that even Jerome could not at first make out what game she had been playing. It was a handful of rubbish. The hand opposite her was an entirely different matter, and it had been laid out in that slowly 'stepped' manner that winners sometimes choose to humiliate their beaten rivals.

There were seven cards in it and three (the first three shown) were nothing at all, just lowly number cards. The last four were a different kind of card game. A King of Diamonds. A Knave of Hearts and a Knave of Spades. The final card was the Queen of Spades. It was a game they had conjured up last summer, one of the sickest jokes in the history of cards. The winner was the first to pair the Lady (usually of Spades) with three other male picture cards. It was a game that had got nastily close to life. But there was a difference this time.

Up to now, the game of 'Liaisons' had only been played among the three of them. The beautiful whore, the queen, in question had never been directly challenged by any of her attendant drones. But now she had had her divine nostrils rubbed in it. All day he had felt disaster, and now it was staring up at him with both azure-tinted eyes almost out of their sockets.

She was lying on her rug of lust and her skirt had been taken all the way up past her waist and her undergarments ripped away, though her black pointed shoes with the red bows still dangled on her feet and black satin suspenders were revealed above her diaphanous silk stockings. And all those lower limbs suggested to Jerome was that they had, just a minute or two before, been engaged in a glorious orgy of love-making.

The neck had been neatly broken in one delicate twist, and the black gloves which the murderer had clearly worn for the purpose had been left equally neatly folded over the breasts.

Jerome di Cavazza, unlike his friend Dominick Craufurd, was allowed a decent human reaction for the woman he had adored above and beyond anything living, with the possible exception of his mother. Being an Italian he slumped down on the bed and howled into the night.

And, if he had looked up through tear-stained eyes, he might have thought it was just the breeze that was gently moving the folds of the tent; a breeze that almost seemed to bring a flush to the dead woman's face.

30

It was not just the death of Hélène that caused pangs in Jerome's heart. It was the remembrance of an old friend, Michel André, creator of a new card game as catchy as blackjack and somehow truer to life – to their life. And Michel André, for the past twelve months, had been no more.

They had set themselves a typically crazy and suicidal challenge – to climb the hard north-east rockface of the Zugspitz. The National Climbing Team of the Hitler Jugend had made the headlines by shinning their way up it last year. Now they challenged all comers to emulate their feat.

It was not an act of pure bravado that persuaded the three friends to commit themselves to that treacherous rockface. They were gamblers, it is true, but they were also, individually and as a group, extremely experienced mountaineers. And that particular summer they seemed to share one thing else, an adult contempt for young jackbooters.

There was also a further inducement.

Halfway up the Zugspitz and twisted away from the mountain resort of Grainau so that no probing telescopes could disturb its isolation, was a tiny hut, a halfway cabin, where the friends could light a fire, have a meal and a drink and a sleep before the dawn sun woke them and they clambered out to attack that ferocious rockface. Or at least that was the theory of the place. But, for the three gamblers, it was destined to prove something else, a testing ground for the new games.

'It'd better be worth the walk,' Dominick had quipped, cleaning the glass of his hurricane lamp down there in the *Gasthof*.

They had breakfasted in their rooms, and then a fat serving girl had turned up with three foaming glasses of Bavarian *hellbrau*. Jerome was over by the window surveying through his binoculars the ever-changing face of the summit as racing clouds scurried across it. Outside, a brass band was tuning up and the Swastika banners were dancing madly in the sharp May breeze. The local brass band of the Hitler Jugend together with an élite procession of young party members was to escort the three of them out of town and as far as the huge arrow hewn from stone which pointed the way up to the Zugspitz.

There was only one slight difficulty.

The third member of the climbing party was unaccountably late; not for the first time in his confusing life, Michel André had so far failed to turn up.

Of course, he had never failed to honour a bet, and Jerome happened to know he had had a bet on the side with one of the richer American expatriates in Antibes that they would beat the Hitler Jugend's time.

'Pity they can't play the Eton Boating Song,' drawled Dominick as the brass backing for the Horst Wessel grunted up to them. Jerome remembered admiring his friend's sang-froid and his cold capacity to take these crises in his stride. It was just like Michel André to set the whole thing up and then shrug his shoulders and saunter off. It was hard to criticise a friend but it sometimes appeared that Michel André had no sense of honour.

'We'll do it alone,' decided Jerome, emptying his stein in a flourish of bravado.

'No problem at all, old chap,' concurred Dominick Craufurd, tying up some ropes.

Jerome should have been proud, marching there through the Swastika-bestrewn street behind the band, with the simple Bavarians thronging the pavements. This was his hour. He and Dominick – alone. But inwardly he was weeping, as a young man might who feels these matters of friendship and honour very keenly.

Of course, he knew that people one loved, one revered, were not always perfect, but it was shameful to have Michel André's absence noted by the world at large, by grunting Bavarian pygmies in lederhosen and weasel-faced party officials, by people from the press and cameramen dodging out in front. Of course it was nice that one friend *had* turned up. Dominick, quietly striding out with a look of vague distaste on his pale face.

The Gauleiter's car overtook them just before the official starting point.

'Good climb. Good luck – grosse Deutschland wishes you well,' shouted the Party chief.

'That was a near squeak, old boy,' murmured Dominick as Michel André clambered out and, thrusting a haversack over his feathered hat, joined them without comment, and just one wave to the party dignitary in the Mercedes.

Michel André, there was that something about him. He arrived with that funny look on his face, a wry droop to that walrus moustache of his and a wink dropped at you out of the corner of the eye, and you had to start inwardly singing.

The three of them had piled on the pace, trying to put space and height and carpets of spring flowers between them and that Nazi send-off committee.

He could not feel the same way about Dominick. Dominick was very clever and worldly and cynical, and dressed about as well as the Duke of Windsor. He had a dash of hard Englishness about him that attacked the palate like angostura. You could love Dominick for what he had but he was not a little boy like Michel André, a little boy who broke all his toys, and teased all his friends and then came back and asked for more. 'Here have one of these,' Michel André had told him, putting a huge *Bratwurst* roll into his hand. 'You eat it, then you belch, and then you fart. That is called showing respect for the *Bratwurst*.'

'You haven't got a spare slice of game pie, by any chance?' Dominick had pointlessly asked. 'Nanny never taught me how to eat things krautish.'

And so Jerome had followed his friends up the lower slopes of the Zugspitz, a *Bratwurst* sandwich in one hand and an alpenstock in the other. The clouds drifted away and the peak was revealed distant but shimmering before them, and Michel André did his French imitation of a German mountaineer's song with Jerome filling in the yodels.

It was a thing to remember – the three of them gaily filing towards that distant and lofty inferno.

'Does no one around here play backgammon?' groaned Dominick that night by the light of the hurricane lamps.

'No, this is more à la mode,' said Michel André, stripping open a new pack. 'This is like climbing into bed with a lovely lady.'

'Which lady, damn you?' complained Dominick, deep into cognac. 'Just any old tart from the Place Clichy would do for some I know.'

'The idea of the game is to help the lady,' Michel André was saying, his walrus moustache twitching in the lamp-light. 'Because, confidentially, she needs help. Not me, not Dominick Craufurd, not even the ever-handsome dashing young di Cavazza, indeed it takes all three together to give her what she so delicately craves. But this lady is no lady. This lady, my friends, is a whore, but one the mere thought of whom brings the saliva dribbling down the lips.'

'No prizes for her name, damn you,' remarked Dominick filling up his gold flask again from the brandy bottle.

'This lady is Babylon. She is all whore. She is all . . . pussy.'

'I know we're by ourselves, but should we be speaking of her like this?' Jerome was asking.

'Which leads me back to these fellows,' continued Michel André, ignoring the interruption. 'My friends, real life is in these painted counterfeits, these knaves, these kings. There are eight of them in the pack and they are, to a man, what's the delicate expression, oh yes, I know . . . screwers. But the law of "Liaisons" states that four is company. The winning hand must contain one blushing Eve and three roosters.'

Up to then, arrangements had evolved as they might among friends. Hélène had stayed over at Les Ombres with Michel André because he had the biggest place. But her affection for Dominick and Jerome meant that either of them also had the right to saunter in of an afternoon, accept a glass of champagne and listen to Sidney Bechet's band on the wireless or Hitler's voice relayed over the mountains from Berchtesgaden.

Now, tonight, they discovered that these vague arrangements displeased Michel André's precise Gallic mind.

'My friends, I would like to announce a new rule. Before any of us gets his moustache into the lady's more honeyed areas, we've got to prove our ability at "Liaisons"!'

The night was young up there in the mountain hut, in fact it was only about eight o'clock, and none of them was exactly sleepy. The first game went to Jerome. He won the first kiss from Hélène upon their return from the mountains, and none of them could touch the lady until Jerome di Cavazza had exacted his kiss.

'But what happens if he buggers off to Palermo?' Dominick had enquired.

'Then we wait,' answered Michel André with his characteristic shrug 'Maybe she is an old lady before Jerome returns, but still we do not touch her.'

Half an hour later Hélène Colmar's future had been more clearly mapped out. Jerome might be the first to butterfly-kiss her lips, but it was Dominick who was granted the first entrée to her breasts, and, by a further win, was to be the first allowed to slide his fingers up the side of her skirt.

'What if she isn't wearing a skirt?' Dominick had needlessly asked.

It was suddenly past midnight. The three were aware of physical change; of one another's breath, blowing like a wind machine up there in the silence; aware of the clink of bottle against glass, the sulphur of the matches extinguished by the richness of Gauloises.

They became aware of something else. Heartbeats. Their own and one another's. Michel André had invented 'Liaisons', he had introduced them to 'Liaisons'. But it had not turned out his way. He had lost the first kiss, the first clinch, the first night. Now after twelve games he had surrendered his rights to his friends for the next six months. He had to sit there and entertain her, whilst they took their fill. So said the *règle du jeu*. And 'Liaisons' was a serious game. Michel André had not joked when he had stated that you break its rules at your peril.

Then Jerome had got up and walked outside, stood for a while looking at that peak against burning moonlight.

'Look,' he told Michel André who had come out to join him. 'Forget this game. That is our target, that is our objective. Tomorrow we'll talk further about the beautiful lady.'

'We are not schoolboys,' Michel André had remarked. 'But do not forget, Jerome, there are ways round every little difficulty. Honourable ways, I mean.'

'Sorry, it didn't work out too well,' came from Dominick, offering Michel André his flask as he started back towards the hut. 'Well, I'd better be turning in now.'

At first Jerome had thought it was reveille time, even though it was darker than when he had gone to sleep. He was being shaken.

'Sleep is for boys,' came his French friend's fierce whisper. 'We are men, we play all night.'

It had proved more difficult to wake Dominick. At first he had just sworn and curled up again. But he listened when Michel André explained. 'I lay awake and then I came to think of Hélène and that little silky property of hers, you know what I mean. And for a moment I felt very sad that I would not be dropping in to make its acquaintance for a few more months. That's a long time – and I have big balls. And then I thought ... I have friends. And friends aren't like ordinary people. They help. They give a man a chance.'

He began to talk about art, or rather about a picture.

The master had done it before his eyes, he had put the entire thing together whilst Michel André had sipped his champagne. It had all happened the evening before yesterday, one reason why he had been delayed. It was a picture to change the world.

'Picasso?' Dominick had yawned. 'He paints too much to be a really valuable artist.'

'This one is different,' Michel André had assured him.

They were friends, but they were tired. They were friends, but they had the Zugspitz to scale in a few hours. They were friends but ... there was something in Michel André's eyes and the way his lips clamped together that forced them to view friendship in a new light. To give him that new chance.

And, of course, had they been soberer they might have remembered that Michel André was in a classic d'Alembert situation: having lost the whole evening, he was in a good bet position to double up and win.

That was what he proceeded to do. At half past three it was all settled. Jerome had lost the early favours promised upon immediate return to Antibes. Dominick had forfeited his six month option on the lady's body. That had now reverted to Michel André, and he had kept his Picasso. It was a good time for him to 'leave the tables'.

The next day was public, not private. It was recorded by pictures, by eye-witness accounts and by radio interviews from Grainau and Garmisch-Partenkirchen.

And, like most well-covered, profusely described public events, it remains totally obscure.

But, of all the many accounts, the most reliable and also the most restrained must be that of Dominick Craufurd, the man exactly at the spot, who happened to be one of the mountaineering correspondents of *The Times*. According to Craufurd they had left the hut early and beaten all records on the final ascent of the mountain face in full sunlight.

Their haste was not just dictated by the wish to beat the record of the Hitler Jugend group. They had noticed the change of wind and a vast shelf of cumulus which was beginning to drift towards the rising sun. The summit 'victory' picture still survives. It was taken by a camera placed on a rock.

The three of them are grinning through their goggles, each man holding out in his gloved hand full handfuls of playing cards. On the way down, Dominick Craufurd had occasion to dwell on the superficiality of the d'Alembert principle.

This time, the Supreme Being had dealt the cards himself. For some reason, Michel André had lost patience with their slow descent. He had opened out a big distance between him and them, and would then wait for them to catch up when there was a question of roping.

On one such foray forward he must have mistaken the way and gone straight over the edge. It had been a gambler's choice. Visibility had been almost nil.

Michel André had just dropped out of life into the fog.

31

Think of a number, dial it. And see what Fate turns up. The first number he thought of was Dominick Craufurd's.

He heard Craufurd's voice at the other end of the line, the single word 'Craufurd' and behind it, he sensed, an extra glacier of English reserve. He was suddenly infected by the suspicion behind the Englishman's voice.

He said, 'This is Jerome, perhaps you know why I am calling.'

'Where are you ringing from. Rome?' No crack in the glacier of sang-froid. It was almost too good to be true – the unflappability of a stage Englishman.

'When you last saw Hélène, did you leave her well?'

'Haven't seen her too much lately. I honour my bets you know.'

'You saw her long enough to discuss the value of a certain modern painting, I understand.'

'Are you back in France and did you bring Hélène's boat with you?' Craufurd answered coolly. 'You sound very close, and I can't hear any jackboots in the background.'

Jerome wanted to shout, 'Hélène is dead, you cold-blooded, murdering Englishman!' But he told himself this was not time to be the passionate foreigner.

So he said, with his best imitation of an ice-cold Englishman, 'I would like to meet you now. We could have a spot of lunch, and perhaps play a game of cards.'

'Is it safe for you to be outside in daylight? I'm thinking of the political situation,' the cool answer came back.

'Suppose we meet at the Eden Roc restaurant. You always admired the view there. If you're worried about the expense I will pay the bill.'

'Do you suppose it's still open? This war has been rather costly on waiters.'

'I will meet you at the Eden Roc restaurant in half an hour, open or closed. It's up to you if you want to bring a gendarme.' The next number Jerome dialled was the police to report the death of a certain Hélène Colmar.

'I regret I cannot give my name,' he said, 'but I would be grateful if you could treat the lady's body with respect.'

In peacetime the entrance to the Eden Roc restaurant would have been shimmering with parked Bentleys, Mercedes, Hispano Suizas and Bugattis. This lunchtime there was only one car outside the restaurant, Dominick Craufurd's old Lagonda. Jerome parked his 'borrowed' Renault and walked into a restaurant that already had become a museum to pre-war culture: a mausoleum of chandeliers, plaster ionic columns and linen-covered tables.

Dominick was seated at one of these tables by a window that looked straight down on to the Golfe de Juan.

'Well, at least it's open,' he greeted his friend. 'They're rather dubious about lunch, but I've managed to winkle a bottle of scotch out of them while they're making enquiries. Oh, and I've found they've got Players Navy Cut. I thought I was going to have to smoke Gauloises for the rest of the war.'

Jerome helped himself to a whisky, and raised his glass. 'To absent friends, as you say in English,' he toasted, with bitterness in his voice.

Dominick watched him closely. It was unlike Jerome to gulp his drinks. Jerome usually toyed with them in the same way that he toyed at affairs with women. There was also a change in his friends's eyes. They were harder, darker, and more intense than he remembered, except perhaps when he was climbing mountains. They were eyes that might have been crying.

'Well, it's very nice to see you, dear boy, though, if I understood your telephone call correctly, this reunion isn't strictly social. Tell me, how is darling Hélène? You have seen Hélène, haven't you? As a matter of fact she rang me up this morning. She seemed a little . . . .'

'Hélène is dead,' Jerome said, 'I found her murdered in the Cabine this morning. Who could have done such a thing, Dominick?'

'Oh, Christ!' Craufurd murmured.

Jerome watched him push back his chair and walk over to the big window behind him. It looked down on the salt-water swimming pool where anybody who was anybody, from Jean Cocteau to Cyril Connolly, had splashed before the war, the coveted rock-pool where Hélène's golden limbs had stirred desire in the hearts of the weediest and most goose-fleshed bathers.

Jerome could not see how Dominick was taking the news. He slapped a pack of cards on the linen table-cloth and started to deal them.

'What about a game of "Liaisons" to take our minds off it?' he suggested. 'You know how to play "Liaisons", don't you, Dominick?'

Craufurd turned round from the window. Jerome watched him watching the cards. They were the cards Hélène had been playing with before she was strangled.

'Take a card, Dominick.' Jerome gestured at the stack he had placed between the two four-card hands he had dealt. 'You know the rules.

We are looking for accomplices for the Lady. Three men *au lit* with her, to be precise.'

'What are we playing for? It was usually Hélène if you remember,' Craufurd sighed.

'Let's decide as we go along.' Jerome suggested grimly.

Craufurd examined his hand. He said, 'Refresh my mind. We keep the Joker in the pack and if we draw him he's worth two male court cards, alternatively he can substitute for the Lady.'

'Correct,' Jerome nodded, 'but it's surprising you've forgotten.'

'My flat was entered last night by an unusually dressed gentleman from the sea,' Craufurd said, picking a knave of hearts and rejecting a seven of diamonds. 'Broke a lot of glass but didn't take anything much. My friend Dalio is of the opinion he was an Italian, but of course it wasn't you. You don't go around dressed in a rubber swimming suit, do you, Jerome?'

'I'm sorry, I am glad nothing was taken,' Jerome answered, looking sceptically at a two of hearts and beyond it at the inscrutable face of the Englishman. 'Incidentally, I met an old friend of yours last night – a Mr Marvin Huntingdon of New York,' he said continuing this dialogue of non-sequiturs. 'He was interested in a picture in which I understand you also have become interested – Michel's *Night Fishing*.'

'Huntingdon, there's a knave for you,' Craufurd chuckled mirthlessly as he discarded a six of clubs. 'There, if you like, is a suitor for the hand of the Lady – or do I mean the Law? Let me try and be a little more precise. I know of two people who have had access to Les Ombres recently, one of them is Huntingdon, the other is yourself.'

'The third possibility is that you killed Hélène,' Jerome said.

'Yes, that I suppose is a possibility from your point of view, assuming, of course, you are innocent.'

'We shall see,' Jerome said, laying his hand on the table. 'A two of clubs, a king of diamonds, a Joker and queen – Liaison!'

Dominick threw his hand on to the table – knaves and a queen only wanting for a third male court card.

'We didn't agree what we were playing for,' Dominick said, pouring himself another slug of scotch.

'The truth,' Jerome told him.

'The whole truth and nothing but the truth? That's an awful lot to ask for one winning hand at "Liaison".'

'One question. One answer for every winning hand. Since it's my privilege, I am claiming the truthful answer to the question: Did you kill Hélène?'

'The truthful answer is you must be mad if you think I could hurt a hair of that marvellous woman.'

'The truthful answer please. We always honour our bets.'

'Of course I didn't bloody well kill her,' Dominick spat out. He picked up the cards, shuffled them furiously and dealt two new hands.

'It's possible there is a Joker,' Jerome suggested.

Dominick looked up into his friend's eyes.

They were dark, intelligent eyes, women might have called them beautiful eyes, but it would be hard to say they were entirely honest, or ever had been.

'Assuming there is a Joker,' he drawled, 'what do you suppose he looks like? What do you suppose he does, apart from wearing cap and bells?'

'Perhaps he comes from the sea. Perhaps he wears a rubber swimming suit, and speaks with an Italian accent. That would be some Joker,' Jerome answered cynically, examining a hand that contained nothing over a seven of clubs.

'You don't believe in my night visitor, do you?'

Jerome shrugged. 'You've changed in the short time I've been away, Dominick old chap, you've become harder, perhaps more ruthless, possibly a little less.'

'Honest?' Craufurd suggested, discarding a three of clubs and collecting a king. 'If we're going to be perfectly candid, I could say the same about you, Cavazza. Incidentally, you haven't told me what you did with the boat.'

'There is one thing we know about this Joker, assuming he is not you or me,' Jerome avoided the question, 'he plays "Liaisons" – that's not a very common game, is it?' There was a wall of suspicion between them, but behind it was a friend whose intelligence Jerome needed to consult.

'Why should the Joker know anything about "Liaisons"?'

'Whoever it was who killed Hélène had been playing "Liaisons". We are playing with his pack.'

'Talking of "Liaisons", I think it's your turn to play the young George Washington,' Dominick said, laying out two knaves, a king and Joker, substituting for a queen. 'Liaison.'

'I didn't murder Hélène, if that's what you want to know.'

Craufurd raised a laconic eyebrow. 'As a matter of fact, I was going to ask another question which may or may not be related. What did they send you back here for?'

'Perhaps I haven't been away. How do you know I've been away?' Jerome gesticulated.

'Play the game, Cavazza!' Craufurd snapped.

'The question has to be phrased to elicit the answer "yes" or "no",' Jerome stalled.

'I don't remember that rule,' Craufurd said, looking at his old friend with an expression of near disgust.

'Oh, yes. Otherwise you could ask me to describe Einstein's Theory of Relativity, or the influence of Cavour on Italian nationalism or what my exact feelings for Hélène were, and precisely to what extent I was jealous of you and Michel – unfathomable questions like this....'

'Very well, I'll try and phrase the question another way ...' He cut himself short. An old waiter in carpet slippers had padded up to their table.

'Monsieur, I am sorry. The chef is not here and we have taken no delivery from the markets this morning. *C'est la guerre*. If you wish my wife can prepare you a plate of *crevettes*. I regret it is all we have. If a plate of *crevettes* with perhaps a Chablis of 1937 will be acceptable....'

'Perfectly acceptable, I'm sure,' Dominick waved the old walrus away and then returned an interrogatory stare at Jerome's face. 'Is it small fish or big fish I wonder, little prawns or something more substantial?'

'Small fish, small beer,' Jerome answered. 'My mission is so trivial it is almost laughable. Now you've asked your question, let's try another hand.'

'You still haven't told me what you're here for.'

'You've asked three questions already,' Jerome said, dealing the cards.

'Next time I'll expect a more helpful answer,' Craufurd scowled, picking up his hand.

Jerome had a queen and three numbered cards.

Dominick had a queen and two knaves.

Jerome discarded and drew a three of clubs.

Dominick drew an ace, no use in 'Liaisons'.

Jerome was luckier this time.

Dominick looked poker-faced over a ten of clubs.

Such conversation as they had been exchanging stopped. The two men were totally intent on the play.

And then finally Dominick said, 'I think that does it,' and laid a queen and three jacks on the table.

'I think I have a more satisfactory Liaison,' Jerome said. He turned up a queen, one jack and two kings, a winning hand.

'My question is not of too much importance,' Jerome tried to imitate his friend's casual drawl. 'All the same it could be a clue to the identity of ... the Joker. There was a painting in La Cabine. You know it of course. Picasso's sketch for *Night Fishing at Antibes*. It was missing when I found Hélène this morning. So I feel I should ask you, just as a matter of formality, have you got this painting? Yes or no?'

'It's pretty rum, isn't it?' Craufurd pondered, holding his whisky glass up to the sun which was just beginning to slide into the frame of the window.

'I mean it's not as if it's the finest thing the old boy has ever done, a pretty hurried draft if you ask my opinion. Nothing really to warrant all this interest.'

'Yes or no?'

The fierceness of the question surprised Dominick, and the expression in his friend's eyes pushed an odd crazy suspicion into his mind.

'Could there be another reason why you want an answer to this question?'

'I am asking the questions,' Jerome said.

'Is it conceivable that *they* want this picture too?' Dominick thought aloud. 'No, it's really too absurd to make any sort of sense. Unless your people have decided it's the only scrap of France they're ever likely to get their grubby hands on. But what the hell does your friend Musso know or care about modern art? It's true Michel, that last night on the mountain, spoke very highly of his damned sketch. He had the look in his eyes, you remember, don't you, like a cat that has swallowed the cream or perhaps one should say the champagne. He insisted there was more to it than met the eye, a great deal more. It could have been another of Michel's jokes. But his jokes tended to be immensely practical, immensely well-planned....'

'You have the picture? Yes or no?'

'What exactly is the answer worth to you?' Dominick countered, lighting a Players and sending a smoke ring reeling away across the deserted restaurant.

'We honour our bets, don't we, Dominick?'

'Very well, if you insist, I've got the damned thing.' Craufurd sighed. 'If you like I'll tell you exactly why, but perhaps we can defer that until you are safely locked up.' It seemed that Craufurd's elegantly tailored blazer had concealed a lightweight army revolver. It was now pointing, somewhat dejectedly, at Jerome's abdomen. 'I honour my bets. I play the game,' Craufurd apologised, 'but bearing in mind what you've admitted you are acting for an enemy power. I really can't let you run around scot-free!'

Keeping Jerome covered, he snapped his fingers for the waiter and picked up a telephone.

'I'm awfully afraid I must ask the waiter to report your presence to the French police. I imagine it's extremely unlikely they will shoot you as a spy considering how badly the war is going for them. Damn, where is the old buffer?'

The flak over Toulon was no joke. Lieutenant Toni Maggia had never seen anything like it. Certainly not in Ethiopia and not even over Madrid. It seemed these French bastards had saved the whole ordnance of France for Toulon and their precious fleet. The length of the Milhaud Piers and the Noël Docks was a sheet of angry flame, and from the Mourillon Navy Yard across the Bay they were throwing everything they'd got at you, from wing-shattering high explosive to stomach-curdling tracer. And this wasn't to mention the contribution of smoke and fire Admiral Darlan's beloved warships were making, or the swarms of Morane, Saulnier and Vought fighters that were buzzing around like killer bees.

'Hey, Tenente, this is crazy. Let's go home,' Giuseppe, the starboard gunner shouted over the intercom. Maggia's rear-gunner did not need to shout over the intercom. He was supposed to be manning his exposed Breda machine-gun a few paces behind him on the flight deck. Instead, big Alfonso was thumping him on the back, shouting, 'Who ordered this crazy mission? They've got to be crazy!'

They were right. It was suicide to stick around anywhere in the lethal airspace over Toulon. Take evasive action! Get down on the deck fast where you're no longer a crawling duck in a shooting gallery!

Lieutenant Maggia put the three-engined Savoia into a dive and levelled out at wingspan's altitude over the sea.

'Okay, boys, take it easy,' he reassured them over the intercom. 'We're going home to bed – in one piece so the girls will still want you.'

They roared over the Iles d'Hyères and on towards Saint-Tropez, shimmering in the late afternoon sun, suddenly so close you could almost reach out and touch it. The next thing they knew they had a speedboat's view of the promenade at Cannes. It was then that Maggia remembered his bomb load.

'Hey, Giuseppe!' he shouted to the starboard gunner who was also the bombardier, 'get rid of those eggs, will you?'

Giuseppe stumbled towards his bomb-sight and jerked open the bomb-bay. Splash! Splash! Splash! The consignment started to hit the water and sink harmlessly.

But Maggia had reckoned without the Cape of Antibes, which was now approaching with the speed of an express.

'Hey, Giuseppe! No more bombs!' Maggia yelled, pulling back belatedly on the stick.

But it was too late. One of his last bombs was even now bounding along the surf towards the base of Eden Roc. Now another was rapidly losing height over the restaurant.

It was the first and last clutch of bombs to be dropped on the Cap in the campaign of 1940. But it was effective up to a point. For instance, Giuseppe's final throw shattered the windows with the azure view and brought the roof down on the bar counter. It sent Jerome sprawling among the deserted tables, and buried Dominick Craufurd under a pile of decorative plaster.

It left Cavazza for several minutes in some doubt as to whether he was alive, and it was some further minutes before a curse and the sound of debris being thrust aside reassured him that his friend Craufurd had survived. Once he was certain on this point, he dusted off his suit and made his exit. The game of 'Liaisons' had gone too far.

32

The heavy police Citroën snarling to a halt created more vibrations, more suffocating clouds of dust, a new dose of dinning in his eardrums. Only this was a different menace from the Savoia bombers; the reek of burning oil was more objectionable to Jerome di Cavazza's nostrils than the stink of high explosive.

Another thing, the black monster had almost knocked him off his feet. Even so, the car that erupted through the bomb debris had been driven both brutally and lethally. It seemed to have one object, to finish off the job the bombers had attempted, at least so far as Jerome's life was concerned. And it had failed by a matter of centimetres. Jerome's evasive dive took him down to road level and strung him around a fragment of his borrowed Renault.

Next moment he was inside the car, his arms pinioned by two gentlemen in black leather jackets. 'Signor di Cavazza, I think,' said a partly bald-headed man, twisting round at him from the passenger's seat next to the driver. And then Jerome saw him against a dazzling blue slant of sea.

'You do not know me, but I know you,' said the portly man, offering him a Gitane. 'I am the Commissioner of Police round here. Commissioner Lazzarone.'

'Lazzarone. That's great! Lazzaron. Lazzaroni. A most convenient name.' The driver was enjoying his own private joke, rocking backwards and forwards in his seat, and every time he lurched forward his foot hit the accelerator and the car spurted dangerously along the twisting backroads of the Cap.

'It was unwise . . . really very unwise for a man of your intelligence to put his neck straight into our noose,' the Police Commissioner was saying, giving him a smell of last night's escargots. 'You're not exactly a grey figure, Cavazza. In fact you might be flattered to know your name has featured high among wanted and potentially dangerous enemy aliens in our police files. And now we seem to have scooped you up.'

'Come on, stop the teasing. These jokes are good, but some of us haven't got the time or the stomach to laugh,' growled the driver as the Citroën took off down the almost deserted coastal road towards Cagnes-Sur-Mer and Nice.

'I could have you shot,' persisted Commissioner Lazzaron. 'Put up against a wall and . . . flick!'

'Balls,' guffawed the driver.

'Relax, Cavazza, you sloppy degenerate. You are amongst friends. *Amici*. We are here to kick the stinking entrails out of people like our excellent Commissioner of Police here. Lazzaron. What a joke. Well, we'll make a good Italian of him yet. It's simple – just add an 'e'. Lazzaron-e. At heart he's a spaghetti chewer like you and me.'

'Who are you, I don't understand . . . ' choked Jerome, appalled by the sheer aggregated sweat of his five companions and, it would seem, compatriots.

'Lazzaron-e,' laughed the Commissioner. 'Well, that may be going a bit far. But it remains true that my grandfather was a customs collector at the time when Nice was still good Italian soil, and Garibaldi was a name to conjure with.

'Like thousands round here I'm a multi-national. That is why, when the armies break through and come surging into Nice and beyond, you'll witness a miracle, Cavazza. A sudden huge increase in the number of Italian flags seen waving in our streets. A sudden glut of Chianti flasks.'

'Very little will change,' guffawed the driver. 'Lazzaron, sorry, Lazzaron-e, will keep his job. That is he'll still be working his arse off for us. But time is short, Cavazza,' — swerving the Citroën off the road, into a cypress grove. 'And some of us here are interested to see if real coarse Italian blood is still pumped round your decadent playboy's veins. In fact some of my lads would like to see it spurting right now.'

'I think I must introduce a fellow countryman, Centurione Pugno,' the Commissioner was saying. 'The Centurione represents the New Italy, that is, when it comes to directness and speed, he doesn't like to be outdone by his German allies.'

'The Commissioner is too polite,' said the Italian, sliding out a long fish-skinning knife, 'I'll put it more bluntly. If I fail to get co-operation I am liable to return to my trade and slit his throat like a tuna fish.'

Jerome now had a good view of the man, standing up there amongst the olives and cypresses, framed by the sparkling sea and yet giving it one glance. He was a short wiry specimen, black as an African, and one of the more noticeable things about him was the veins pulsing away in his thick neck. His dagger was gently tickling the main artery in Jerome's temple.

'Look, Cavazza,' he threatened, almost pushing his carious teeth and venomous breath straight down Cavazza's throat. 'What's your filthy game?'

'Calm yourselves,' remonstrated Lazzaron, putting a podgy arm round each of them, 'and, Centurione Pugno, put away that knife, I beg you. We are all Romans at heart.'

'That's why I left Italy,' said Jerome twisting himself out of Lazzaron's grip. 'Some of my fellow countrymen have the power to make me vomit.'

'Look,' said Lazzaron, his tiny piggy eyes swivelling round in excitement. 'We all seek ... we are all good Fascists. Even so, it is vital to understand the whole picture. I think maybe I can help. Now our friend, Centurione Pugno, he is very straight. If he wants an enemy's secret weapon he goes over and seizes the thing – not a replica, mind you, but the real schemozzle in perfect working order. And, having got it, lays it at the feet of his Duce. But there's something even better. A common-or-garden scrap of paper. I mean the plan. Now if the Duce had that, he could cut corners. In a matter of weeks, if I understand the thing correctly, he could have his models coming off the assembly line and into the hands of men who would put it to good use. Men like Centurione Pugno here. Now isn't that better than blotting out a few fishing boats?'

'What have you been doing, Pugno?' sneered Cavazza.

'Our friend has been fixated on lamps,' explained Lazzaron, 'and quite right too. And, if you swiped every bloody lamp in every stinking little fishing boat from Cannes to Menton, you might discover a weapon that could win the war. But you would have to kill an awful lot of fishermen to get there. Now Cavazza's purpose is the same. It's just that his orders are more subtle.'

'It could also be that you can't let a stinking pig into an art gallery,' interjected Cavazza.

'Ah, art, now that's interesting,' sighed Lazzaron. 'I referred to that scrap of paper that could alter the world. Of course it needn't be vulgar wood pulp. It might be hardboard or even canvas. It could be in disguise – a little enigma, a tiny problem in Chinese chess.'

'I think Commissioner Lazzaron had better explain,' suggested Jerome.

'You both have different orders and different ways of going about it,' Lazzaron began. 'But you're after the same thing....'

He mentioned a certain art collector who also dabbled in profitable espionage. He recounted a conversation in Ventimiglia between that art dabbler and one of the pushiest officers in Italian Naval Intelligence. The only clue they had to go on was a work of art – a decadent non-representational piece of work from a Neo-Marxist dauber called Picasso that might make the Duce spew; but all the same he'd give his back teeth to get his paws on it. He put together a jigsaw of the recent ownership of the said piece.

'My men have been smart,' he said. 'My information is that it is now out of the hands of a slut called Hélène Colmar. And anyway the lady is no longer with us. To cut a long story short, it's in the possession of a friend of Cavazza's. Though for how long . . .' and he gave a Franco-Italian shrug of the shoulders. 'It shouldn't be too difficult to get it away.'

'A man, a governess and a couple of kids . . . a pisshole apartment with rusty locks and decrepit doors.'

While Lazzaron had been talking, Pugno was engaged in slicing pieces of bark off a pine tree with his fish knife. Now he sank the thing deep into the trunk, a little trickle of sap flowed out.

'Cavazza,' he said quietly, 'this is your balls-up. So I am giving you exactly half an hour. Then I bring you good Italian reinforcements. I gather there are children and a very young woman. That's good. We Fascists have a way of putting a little pressure on a young windpipe. As for the girl – my men are in excellent training. For the last week, since we left Genoa, we've been living like hermits . . . eh? But we'll deal this one out Sicilian style. In Trapani when you see a nice slither of tripe hanging up in a shop window, you share with your friends, eh? Each man carves himself a nice fat slither, eh? As for the man, your English friend, well, there's another Sicilian custom – from Agrigento this time. When they got an old bull and they want to make the meat tender for the table they slit an artery in its throat and string it up. Then they gently flay it till the flesh comes off in their hands.'

'I will get the picture for you,' said Jerome di Cavazza.

33

No, this was not work for an officer and a gentleman. This was work for a common thief. Jerome di Cavazza was disgusted at the cheap ruse he had invented to get Dominick out of his flat, and how easily it worked.

'Dominick, my dear old fellow,' he had purred down the telephone, 'our conversation was rather rudely interrupted yesterday, was it not? There was so much more I wanted to discuss with you, preferably not with a revolver pointed at my stomach. Could we meet under a flag of truce – say at the Café d'Ancre in a quarter of an hour?'

So all Jerome had to do was to wait in a quiet corner of the café under Craufurd's flat until he saw his friend come briskly down the stairs and walk purposefully away into the golden Antibes evening.

He knocked at the door of Dominick's flat as a formality. His plan was to blow open the lock with his Beretta automatic, get the damned picture and go home, looking in on the way, of course, to tell

Commissioner Lazzaron and his seamy gang of patriots, or traitors, to call off their thugs from the sea.

The door opened just as he had brought out his Beretta. A girl with dark cropped hair, young enough to have come straight out of school, an English school, was looking at him with large and direct greenish-blue eyes. Jerome had not been thinking much about England recently, but now he suddenly found he was recalling the fields of Kent and the lanes of Hertfordshire and the whispering weir where you could see the Thames pass over from the lawn of the Compleat Angler at Marlow. This was the England that Audrey Hopkirk's eyes suddenly reminded him of.

'Who are you?' said a voice like a bird singing in a clump of leafy elms.

'I am a friend of Dominick's.'

She said, 'You don't look awfully like a friend of Captain Craufurd's — with that pistol in your hand.'

It was a funny thing. Looking at her he had forgotten all about his Beretta. Now he noticed another thing. There was a door chain between himself and the eyes of the English girl.

'I'm still a friend of Dominick's,' he claimed truthfully, or falsely (it was so difficult to be sure). 'I'm here out of concern for his safety and yours.' This, at least, was more or less true.

'And that gun is to protect us?' she asked sceptically.

'Please let me in and I will explain. There is not so much time.' Now he remembered to pocket his Beretta.

He was surprised when she removed the chain and opened the door wide enough to let him in. She nodded towards the living room. The hallway was narrow so he had to brush against her body to pass her, brush against her young firm breasts. She was wearing no perfume; he supposed English girls of this age never did, but he could smell the freshness of her, like apples in an Evesham orchard.

Dominick's children were sprawled out on the carpet of the living room. They were playing a game of 'L'Attaque'.

'Bad luck, I'm a Sapper so I take your mine, and this, if I'm not mistaken is your Flag.' Niall Craufurd was saying, like a chip off the old block.

Then he beamed his bird-bright eyes upwards to examine the visitor.

'Not the man from the sea, are you?' he asked.

'No, I'm not a man from the sea.'

'You look like a foreigner, though,' Oriana decided, 'you look even more foreign than a Frenchman.'

'What charming children!' He turned back to the young governess. 'I've heard so much about Dominick's children. They're so like him, aren't they? Now let me see if I can remember your names,' he grinned, making the mistake of turning back towards the children;

because it was at this point that Audrey Hopkirk brought the Martini jug down on his head and he pitched forward onto the 'L'Attaque' board crumpling an army of Commanders-in-Chief, Espions, Scouts, Sappers and Mines.

He could not tell how long it took him to get on to all fours, because he had passed out. But he knew that vital time had been lost and now the governess was pointing his Beretta at his head and saying, 'You'd better explain yourself. And let me remind you you're not the first funny visitor we've had to deal with.'

And young Niall Craufurd was suggesting, 'Ask him if he's an Italian spy. He looks like a Wop to me.'

Still half stunned, Jerome's hazy mind could only appreciate the girl's ankles. She was wearing thick brown knitted socks such as would be considered appropriate for a junior governess, but they did not disguise the svelte contours of her legs and ankles. Often Nature got it wrong with English girls. Faces as sensual as rose blooms got stuck on hunched bosom-less torsos. Or a buxom body and tapering waist was meshed with a bottom and a pair of legs that might have been cast in suet pudding. But when Nature got it right with English girls, it got it perfect, Jerome thought, letting his mouth brush against the girl's thickly stockinged ankles.

'And don't think I can't shoot if I have to,' Audrey Hopkirk said, mistaking this tribute for a hostile move.

'She can drive a car if she has to,' Oriana Craufurd chipped in. 'She can handle all the gears except reverse.'

'It's really so simple,' Jerome tried to soothe as he got painfully to his feet. 'I am looking only for a picture, an insignificant picture – I want nothing else. I know, I know, you think I am a thief; but let me tell you the most important reason why I must have this picture. There are other people who want this Picasso. They are not old friends of Dominick, like I am. They are not as polite as I am. Their heads are too thick to be stopped by a glass jug.' He rubbed his head and found a streak of blood on his hand. 'They will carry sub-machine-guns – or worse – not just a fairly inaccurate pistol. And I am distressed to think what would happen to you, particularly you,' he gestured romantically towards this embodiment of England's green and pleasant land, 'if you do not let me have the picture now.'

'So it's the Picasso you're after.' Audrey eyed him scornfully.

'You can promise Dominick I will return it as soon as the war is over.'

'Why are you all so keen on boring old Picasso?' she asked him over the muzzle of his Beretta. 'He can't even draw properly. A child like Niall here can draw better than Picasso.'

'Believe me, Signorina, it is a matter of life and death for you and me and the children here that you tell now where the picture is.'

'If it was a Constable I could understand what all the fuss was about,' the dewy voice of England told him, 'or a Landseer or even a Munnings. I know it's not very smart to like Munnings, but he really can make you feel you're there on Epsom Downs on a June morning. You don't know where you are with a painter like Picasso.'

'I respect your opinion,' Jerome nodded. 'I can see from your eyes that you are a girl of supreme intelligence. All the same you must believe me that the world does not share your views. And here perhaps you will allow me to say that I know the world better than you do.'

'I bet you haven't seen a Stuka really machine-gunning real people, like Miss Hopkirk has,' Niall Craufurd riposted.

'Please,' Jerome begged, 'there's so little time.'

'Oriana,' the governess commanded, 'I want you to telephone your father at the Café d'Ancre – he's left the number on the desk pad – and tell him we have an Italian visitor who says he's a friend.'

She turned her head to check her instructions were being obeyed just long enough for Jerome to be able to make a dive for the Beretta. He timed his leap well. The pistol fell out of her hand without a struggle. And she made no effort to stop him pinning it to the carpet with his foot. In fact, all he needed to do now was to reach down with his right hand and pick it up. But he postponed this obvious movement in order to keep his hold on her wrists a little while longer – slim, lithe wrists like her ankles.

'I mean no offence,' he said, 'but I think you have the most beautiful eyes of any girl I have ever seen.'

He drew her right up to his face, and kissed her hand with a shy enquiring smile.

She did not try to pull her wrist free. She just stood there watching him kissing her hand, like a student at a botany lesson.

He closed his eyes. He was thinking of the Evesham Valley, the half mysterious, half inviting Malvern Hills; he was thinking of the mist-shrouded fields that ran down to a reviving plunge in the Cherwell; he was thinking of punts at Henley, and then suddenly there were sounds that made him think of walls running with blood.

If there was a saving grace about Centurione Pugno, it was that he was always thorough. For example, dashing now through the downstairs Artiste Assoiffé bar with his second in command, Capo Manipolo Battaglia, he could not resist giving the bottles behind the bar a burrp with his Beretta sub-machine-gun. Well-stocked shelves were turned into a seeming soda fountain as Ricardi bottles exploded, Marc and Martell bottles became gushing pieces of jagged glass, bottles of Martini, St Raphael, Byrh and Calvados vomited from the violence that was being done to them.

The noise of the destruction echoed to every corner of the building.

Jerome had expected that it would take weeks of careful courtship;

but suddenly, weeks ahead of time, he was lying close to her on the carpet with one arm wrapped like a snake around this English rose. Of course, it was not quite the scenario he had been dreaming about for the last five minutes, he had to keep his other arm free to scoop the children onto the floor. And there was the fact that Italian sub-machine-gun bullets were now making tinder wood of the apartment door, and some of them were ripping through the living room to shatter the windows and desecrate the walls. Besides, Miss Audrey Hopkirk was struggling as ferociously as a Cheshire cat.

'I warned you, I warned you, dear Miss Hopkirk,' he whispered in her exquisitely proportioned ear and could not resist kissing it. When Nature decided to get it right with English girls, it got everything right.

'You're as big a crook as the rest,' she snorted as she broke free. Now she swooped up the Beretta and aimed two shots at the apartment door. One did not make it. It shattered a miniature of the Duke of Wellington in the hall. But the other produced a cry from behind the door. Capo Manipolo Battaglia had been hit in the leg.

'Quick,' Jerome urged, 'there must be an escape onto the roof.'

Miss Hopkirk's answer was another shot from his Beretta. It was a good shot but it missed Centurione Pugno who was crouching in the door frame ministering to his wounded comrade. In another sense it was Miss Hopkirk's least successful shot because it stung him into a mood of total destructiveness. With one thrust of his boot, Centurione Pugno burst into the apartment with his Beretta blazing.

How did he succeed in herding Miss Hopkirk and the children into the shower room? He thought, then and afterwards, it was one of the miracles that hover around love at first sight. Like the hero of a Boccaccio romance, he had the sense that there were other forces at work to pull the strings. But it was not a complete fairy story. The delicious English girl still had his Beretta and she was showing every intention of putting another shot through the shower door in the direction of the intruder.

And this could have been fatal. Pugno was hell-bent on destruction, but so far he had found no particular target for his hate. He had ripped the 'L'Attaque' board into ribbons of cardboard, and made a miniature Warsaw of Dominick's drink cabinet. He had made mincemeat of an early Graham Sutherland. Now he was making a surrealist nightmare of the fake Jacques Emile Blanche. A shot from Audrey Hopkirk would have switched his smoking sub-machine-gun on to the shower room door as instantly as a fireman's hose on to a fresh outbreak of fire.

'I love Constable, I love Landseer,' Jerome murmured taking Audrey and the pistol into his arms, 'I love Keats and Shelley and Byron and all the genius that England has given Italy. For the love of

Constable and Keats will you be so gracious as to come with the children onto the roof.'

It was Niall Craufurd who got the window open, but then he hesitated. 'Daddy said we had to promise not to climb on this roof.'

A stray shot from Pugno's swivelling sub-machine-gun decided them all. Or perhaps it was those benign romantic faces that pulled the strings.

Dominick Craufurd had been wrong to the extent that it was not a difficult roof to climb. And it was not all that difficult to make the crossing onto the neighbouring roof and clamber over its red tiled apex to the safer side.

Jerome was almost grateful for the hand grenade that Pugno lobbed into the vacated shower room. It gave him another excuse to grab Miss Hopkirk in his arms and press his mouth against her cheek, nestle his nose under her chestnut hair, plant a protective hand on an orchard-ripe young breast....'

'If you love Constable, I adore Constable,' he whispered, 'because I am crazy with love for you.'

34

'Jesus,' the little man whistled, 'what hit this place?'

'A masked man with a sub-machine, and the silly thing was he was looking for a Picasso,' Audrey laughed, 'Can you imagine doing all this for a painter who can't even draw?' she giggled shrilly. She was on the point of indulging in a fit of well-earned hysterics.

'They did this for the *Night Fishers*!' the little man cried. 'Jesus, you'd better have a drink!' He turned to the blitzkrieged cocktail cabinet and found that Craufurd's bottle of scotch had been miraculously preserved. He poured himself a hefty slug and slipped a tablet on his tongue.

'By the way, you haven't told me who you are,' Audrey enquired, half-sobbing, half-laughing.

'I'm a friend of Captain Craufurd's,' the little man told her.

'Do you know, they all say that. Every one of them says that. Isn't it odd!' Audrey burst into peals of laughter.

'Did they get it? Did they get it!' the little man shouted at her, perhaps to stop the hysterics or perhaps because he badly wanted to know.

'Do you know,' said Audrey Hopkirk, 'I'm afraid you will have to excuse me. I think I'm going to be sick.'

'Did they get the *Night Fishers*?' the little man bawled after her.

He had not noticed before but there were two pairs of eyes on him, two pairs of eyes taking in every vital inch of him from the adjoining bedroom door.

He felt his heart take a leap at his ribcage. Then he realised that the eyes were positioned at an even lower level than his own. Hell, they were just a couple of kids, he reassured himself. This whole place, this whole eerie coast was beginning to make him jumpy. Bad for his heart.

'Psst. Are you looking for the Picasso, too?' one of the kids whispered.

'We know where it is,' a little girl's voice added.

'You know where the *Night Fishers* is?' the man's voice raced up the scales.

'Hush,' cautioned Oriana Craufurd, 'you'll bring Miss Hopkirk back.'

'Tell me, where the godamn hell is it?' the little man screamed under his breath.

'Here,' a rectangular brown paper parcel slid through the doorway, 'you can have it if you promise never to bring it back,' Niall Craufurd whispered.

'It's a beastly, horrible picture and it's brought us nothing but bad luck,' Oriana explained.

'Where in hell did you find it?' the little man demanded, grasping the package with both hands.

'Where Daddy hid the horrid thing, under the floor under Niall's bed. Niall can draw much better than Picasso can,' Oriana whispered.

'You're a great couple of kids,' Marvin Huntingdon wheezed. 'Here, you'd better have some chewing gum.' He thrust a hand into his jacket and found he had only one stick of Wrigleys left. Maybe he'd treat them to a Hershey bar some other time.

Huntingdon had come prepared to negotiate with Craufurd. He was prepared to double his offer, if there was no other way to get his hands on it even treble it. But here were Captain Craufurd's heirs handing it over for free. You didn't stay to argue with a deal like that, Marvin Huntingdon decided, as he tucked the parcel under his arm and made a dash for the street.

Later, Dominick said to Miss Hopkirk, 'If you were going to shoot at someone, I wish you had shot that little skunk Huntingdon.'

35

'I don't quite understand you,' the Vice-Consul at the British Consulate at Nice complained peevishly. 'You say you are an American citizen, I really cannot quite understand the problem.'

Philip Hickson-Smith was admittedly flustered. It was a torrid afternoon, a dash too torrid for early June.

'Look, I'll phone Wilbur Vanbrugh at your Consulate. I'm sure he'll be delighted to take this, eh, brown paper package under his official protection.'

'This is not just a parcel,' yelped the sweaty little man, mopping his bald dome yet again with that nasty spotted handkerchief. 'This is something of the highest historical, artistic and financial importance!'

'Really,' sighed Philip Hickson-Smith, warily fingering the roughly packed object with its coarse brown string. 'I must explain, Mr, eh, eh, Huntingdon. You see that filing cabinet over there? It is my personal responsibility to reduce the contents to ashes by late afternoon. Then I have over a thousand British subjects who seem to have left it much too late to want to return home. I mean they had all winter to make their arrangements. To add to my problems, the Consul has asked me to arrange for a certain Person and his Wife to be convoyed safely out of his villa in Antibes through Arles, Toulouse and over the Spanish frontier. To add to my problems the gentleman has somehow managed to mislay his passport.'

Whatever the muddled reasoning that had guided his footsteps some twenty-odd years ago, Philip Hickson-Smith knew that it was not for this he had joined His Majesty's Consular Service. The whole world and his dog, the unattractive poodle variety, had seemed hell-bent on gate-crashing their way into the hallowed cloisters of the Consulate. Official passes had gone by the board. Everyone was ranging about the halls and vestibules, gate-crashing in and out of his office, gabbling every language from Bronx to Montenegran.

'Look, Mr, eh, eh, Huntingdon, I really think it would be best if you could deposit this valuable parcel with Wilbur Vanburgh of your Consulate. I'm sure he'll know exactly how to handle it. Incidentally, are you all right? You do look rather ill.'

'Look, can't you get it into that aristocratic cranium of yours, I haven't got time....'

Hickson was no doctor, but this man was well on his way to a cardiac. He had leant right over the desk and was shaking him, podgy fingers ruining the line of his lapels. 'Don't you understand, this package is worth a life – any life. That's why they'll be waiting for me outside the US Consulate. It's the one place they'll think I'm sure to head for. All I'm asking you is to put this painting into your goddam diplomatic bag and get it to London. I'll see it's collected from there.'

'You're not seriously suggesting, Mr Huntingdon, that other people are interested in this picture of yours?'

'Look, you pernickety-nosed fool, if you don't take delivery of this, Christ knows what's going to happen....'

This was impossible. The man had let go of Hickson-Smith's lapels, but only to fall on the carpet under the table and come up the other side gripping his trousers, shrieking and imploring.

'I'll see if I can find the Consul,' said Hickson-Smith, standing up and somehow managing to disconnect his trousers from the American's clutch. 'I'll be back in a mo . . . Relax, Mr, eh, Huntingdon. Just sit back.'

Now this was more easily said than done. There were all these sweaty foreigners clogging up the passages; he had to push through. And there was no help. When fifteen minutes later he returned to his office with the nasty suspicion that the Consul had personally been evacuated from his own consulate, maybe never to return, he had other things to worry about than why all this *profanum vulgus* had been left to roam at will without passes.

Because one of them would never roam again.

Mr Marvin Huntingdon, citizen of the USA, art historian of the world, had quietened down a bit, that is he sat hunched in a posture of hopelessness across the Commercial Attaché's desk. His bleating accent would never again assault British eardrums. That oncoming cardiac had taken its course.

It took Hickson-Smith a bit of time more to discover his blessed brown paper parcel had disappeared. This was perhaps the only saving grace about the whole proceedings.

At least one thing was clear.

This inconvenient American had expired from a heart attack.

36

The Hôtel Negresco has not changed that much in forty-odd years. It still broods gothically over the Promenade des Anglais. It still mixes the snazziest cocktails and boasts the most expensive pick-ups. It still mounts exhibitions of the most avant-garde painters and has some of the most old-fashioned plumbing to be found anywhere on the Riviera. It is still crammed full of chic and surprises, like the *trompe l'oeil* effect of hiding three hundred bedrooms behind a deceptively tortuous façade.

Dominick Craufurd was a habitué of the Negresco and its endless game of mirrors, its constantly perplexing labyrinth of corridors. He had diced, loved, gambled, talked and slept in maybe at least a quarter of those three hundred bedchambers. Yet even he had been known to wander for fifteen minutes or so in search of a particular room, and a highly specific assignation.

The serpentine-shouldered man at the reception who, although nearly eighty, had returned to duty the moment his son had been sprung into arms, gave him a weary impassive nod that did not tremble on familiarity and yet just hinted at some prior acquaintance.

'*Numéro* 478, Monsieur le Comte?' he flatteringly croaked. 'Ah yes, you must be seeking Monsieur Huntingdon.'

It needed a man whose sensitivity had been turned as tautly as was Dominick's at this moment to detect a certain wryness behind these bare instructions. 'The gentleman left in a hurry earlier today. I don't know if he has yet returned.'

The lift, one of the Proustian museum pieces of the Negresco, wobbled him up to the third floor, and cranked to a halt.

Ah yes, that's correct, thought Dominick. There are rules to this game too. The management or the architect has placed a limit on the permutations offered by this maze. The third was the ceiling. You could wander for hours down these perplexing corridors but at least you knew there was nothing up above. Or was there?

Having gone quietly round the place and returned to his point of starting and then repeated the performance, Dominick had still been unable to crack this Chinese puzzle of a possible fourth floor. Number 478 was an impossibility and yet he knew for a certainty the management never lied.

A buxom chambermaid gave him a Gallic shrug but no enlightenment, a shuffling guest turned a deaf ear to his enquiries. But Craufurd was a bridge as well as a roulette player. He knew the twilight world of feints and deceptions. He could tell a false door from a real one without having to open it. And today he was in top psychic form. What seemed like a deserted broom cupboard was in fact an uncarpeted staircase leading to a new and hitherto unexplored floor. There, second on his right, was a door with a number on it: 478. But it was locked, and the lock was of the grandiose old-fashioned kind. It was a door painted white, which led nowhere, therefore it must lead somewhere.

After a quick glance down the corridor, he drew his automatic and shot the lock. He entered an immense disused bathroom, such as might have been constructed for a visiting Bonaparte or a king of Egypt. Giving the huge marble bath a playful tap and dropping his head to avoid the glistening crab's claws of its shower fittings, which must have taken pride of place in the Paris Exhibition of 1880, he opened a connecting door into a huge and deserted room that must have been at one time the bedroom of honour.

Hastily, he crossed the carpetless floor-boards. There was only one way to progress, and that was straight into a magnificent *garde-robe* that stood in one corner. Before he drew the double doors open Dominick caught an unsatisfying image of himself reflected straight back from two fake Empire mirrors. His suit was crushed and unpressed. His tie was crooked, uncovering a gleaming brass collar stud, his face was flushed. Worst of all, there were deep circles beneath his eyes, circles which had never before encroached on the Craufurd visage. Could this be age? He paused a second to follow tiny ghosts of future wrinkles burrowing out from below his eyes. No, not ghosts, more solidly demonstrable phenomena. God, I look old, he thought. Worst of all, he was unshaven, and that was unforgivable. Dominick was ashamed that even the old buffer at the reception had seen him in this condition.

He also paused for one further reason, to try to pick up any sound of following footsteps. And then he reflected that the Hôtel Negresco was probably the last place remaining on earth where one could fire a revolver and no one turn a hair. He then swung open the double doors of the *garde-robe*, expecting to find it stuffed with fancy dress. Instead it led through to another door. This was where the more faunish guests must play sardines. Flicking his lighter on, Dominick stopped and read 478, and under it a card stuck straight on to the door. 'Marvin Woodrow Huntingdon,' the inscription read. 'Dealer and Negotiator in antiques and fine art. Hôtel Negresco, Nice.' He pushed at the door handle and surprisingly it opened. But then there was no need to lock such a camera obscura. The bed was unmade and some remains of breakfast were laid out on a little table in the middle of the room. For the rest there were two small chairs, a sofa collapsing into one corner and a few daubs propped up against another. The carpet was resplendent but worn to shreds, and an old-fashioned washing basin stood upon a rickety stand. The small window was open and air was puffing through grimy grey blinds. The window looked out into a black courtyard, four storeys below, which must have been all of four metres square.

But there was something that drew Craufurd's eyes, more even than the canvases stashed in the corner, because it tickled a more personal funny bone: a pair of heavy ivory dice lying on the table beside a scrap of broken croissant. They were aristocrats of dice, two or three times the size of the vulgar modern versions and with the dot numbers rendered as stars in an antiquely faded red. They felt good to the palm, too. A man could hold them and weigh the odds; hold his fortune between his fingers and roll it forwards. Dominick idly flicked them on to the table. He had thrown a six and a two. The second throw gave him a one and a two. The third a double two. These fascinating dice were just beginning to unlock a chamber in Dominick's memory, when his hands, still cradling the dice, were grasped and twisted sharply behind his back.

'You are under arrest for the murder of Monsieur Marvin Huntingdon,' an asthmatic voice rasped at him.

Commissioner Lazzaron let out a shrill whistle from the side of his mouth. One pair of hands delivered a softening thump on the back of the neck, another pair deftly frisked him, feeling and finding the lump of the gun in his coat pocket.

'Of course I could have you shot here and now,' the Commissioner told him. 'But your neck looks made for the guillotine.'

'This is a funny kind of questioning,' Dominick was able to observe quite drily. 'I have always been a good friend to France, although I admit these are difficult times. But think for a moment of the money I have put into the coffers of the various casino municipalities around the coast by way of the roulette wheel. You owe me some kind of hearing. As an honorary Frenchman, I invoke the Code Napoléon.'

The Commissioner spat out a thick wad of black tobacco. He then put his mouth within inches of Craufurd's, whilst his men handcuffed the latter's arms behind his back. 'Consider the evidence,' he growled, poking a podgy finger into Craufurd's stomach. 'Huntingdon is your friend, your business colleague. (Poke.) You sell him a certain picture, eh? (Poke.) You follow him, eh? (Poke.) You murder him in the British Consulate, eh? (Poke.) You come here to collect – for your crime.'

'I wish you wouldn't keep on hitting me in the stomach,' said Craufurd quietly.

'However, we are just, we give you one more chance. Where is it? I said, where is it?' — shouting the question straight into Craufurd's mouth.

'You know one thing,' said Dominick Craufurd, 'you really should consider using a mouth wash.'

'Take him away and get to work on him,' was Lazzaron's instruction.

Dominick Craufurd felt humiliated. He had never been forced to wear handcuffs before.

37

One man had made the mistake of wandering down to the quayside at Antibes that warm June evening. His name was Stephanak, and he was a middle-aged Czechoslovak refugee who had gauged all too correctly that Hitler's Third Reich was about to catch up with him. They had told him there was a seaplane that left Antibes harbour every Monday and every other day for Tunis. A tip to the right person, plus a hundred percent *pourboire* on the air ticket could, they said, get a harassed Central European safely out of reach of the Gestapo's tentacles. The seaplane seemed to have migrated for the summer.

Its accommodation was too scanty to handle a massive exodus. But it had a more capacious substitute – 'it's the biggest boat for miles', they had said.

Apart from the fishing boats, and their lobster-faced, foreigner-hating skippers, there was only this large yacht that seemed to measure up. This was the mistake Stephanak made in the failing light of this June evening. He should never have approached the *Belle Bête* with or without a fistful of francs. It was only because he was there that Pugno's knife slid into the back of his neck as easily as a spoon into jelly. Stephanak plunged forward into the water, unaware of the fact that he had been blocking the retreat of one of the war's first commando raids.

Normally a bit of fighting served to unwind, to mellow, the violent disposition of Centurione Pugno. But the mood of Pugno, as he swung aboard that playboy's toy called *La Belle Bête*, can only be described as excessively mean.

'Get the surgeon,' he bawled into the heavily sweat-aromaed galley decks below. 'The pigs tried to kill Capo Battaglia.' But it was not Battaglia his thoughts were on. They had a different focalising point: the sneering visage of one Tenente Cavazza. It could fairly be said that Pugno had only one desire left at this particular moment: to sink his Sicilian knife deep into the traitor's bones through the thin covering of fair, hairless skin; and then churn it up a bit so that his hand could feel the shape of each one of the Tenente's innards in turn at the end of his sensitive blade.

'Take her out,' he roared at the helmsman. 'We still fight like women. We must learn to be men.'

At first he thought it was a heap of crumpled rope. And it almost tripped him up as *La Belle Bête* swung wide away from her anchorage and made for the open bay. But it was rope that moved, and moaned. Pugno sank his boot in harder, and the moan crescendoed to a scream. He looked down on a ridiculous goatee beard, red wine slobbering over cracked lips, red eyes. He saw the face of Prince Baccarat.

'Your ticket ends here, my friend,' he stated, and himself smiled at the joke. 'We must say *arrivederci*.'

The dotard sickened him with his drunkenness and his fawning. He might have been good cover at one point. Now he was disposable garbage. How he hated the sight and the smell of him.

'Throw him away,' he ordered as the *Belle Bête* started to cut smoothly through the water. A splash accompanied by a low moan told him his commands had been obeyed.

The old luxury liner, *La Fontaine*, was fully lit as the *Belle Bête* streaked past. It was a tempting sight, a sitting duck. And its sinking would finally blood the pussy-foots under his command, strengthen their will to iron. To send one man, just one man with a limpet mine, so that they could all watch it shatter into a thousand pieces of twisted metal, the sea surface littered with corpses, now that was tempting. But it was also a trifle public, and his instructions were specific on this point. That was why, as they finally reached the open Mediterranean, Pugno decided to go for weaker game.

38

The walls were not all that thick down in the cells of the Nice Préfecture. Dominick could clearly hear what his neighbour in the next cell was shouting. The man's complaint was that he was a Spanish officer who had fought on the wrong side in the Civil War. Worse, he had picked precisely the wrong enemy. He had brushed with an Italian regiment on the Ebro and, as far as could be understood from his frantic mixture of Spanish, Catalan and bad French, he had not been too particular in his treatment of his Italian POWs. He was trying to tell anyone within hailing distance that the Italians would crucify him if they found him here in the cells of the Nice Préfecture. He was begging anyone who had an ounce of compassion to let him out for the love of God.

Craufurd had been there only twenty-four hours, but he doubted if there was an ounce of compassion to be had in these precincts. Certainly there had been nothing compassionate about the evening meal he had just been served. War was war, police stations were police stations, but the liquid slime that had been handed in to him had been truly diabolical.

It was soup fit for a dead man.

So, when he heard the footsteps approaching, he thought of the vagaries of French justice and its archaic punishments, like Devil's Island and Madame Guillotine. He thought of its bumbling magistrates and often arbitrary rulings and hazy notions of habeas corpus, which were certain to be aggravated at a time of national disaster. He thought of a creaking mechanism and a sloping, none too hygienic blade coming down, just as he heard the heavy footsteps approaching.

A key turned. He was out of his cage, but there was no gain in light. It was as dark as the tomb down in the cellars of the Nice police Préfecture.

'We are going to let you go, but first there are a number of questions I need to ask,' said the voice of Inspector Clément.

'That's all right, Inspector,' reassured an English voice which Dominick began to recognise as that of Philip Hickson-Smith, 'I can personally vouch for Captain Craufurd. He's entirely bona fide. I can assure you he would never dream of committing murder on Consular promises.'

'Nevertheless, there are a number of questions I insist on asking the Captain.'

'I am sure Captain Craufurd will be anxious to help you as far as it is in his power,' Hickson-Smith's diplomatic voice soothed, 'but, as I explained to the Prefect, Captain Craufurd has been recalled for military service – against the common enemy, of course.'

The Vice Consul put a hand on Craufurd's shoulder, an unusual gesture considering the genteel disapproval Hickson-Smith felt for this particular expatriate, and guided him towards the concrete stairs and daylight.

Inspector Clément followed, still insistent that there were questions he must ask.

'They've got my name. They've got me on their black list. Those fascist bastards will crucify me if they find me here!' the ex-Spanish loyalist shouted; but no one was listening to him.

At the entrance of the Préfecture, Inspector Clément grabbed Craufurd by his blazer lapel and said, 'Admit it, this Italian di Cavazza is your friend'

'I think he is my friend.' The evening sunlight had hit Dominick like a searchlight aimed straight at the eyes, he was dazzled, groggy and more than a little confused.

'You were both friends of the woman Hélène Colmar, you both had dealings with the murdered American Huntingdon. Why is it that wherever you go there is death?'

'I think Cavazza is my friend.'

'But you think he could be guilty of these murders?'

'That's all right, Inspector.' Hickson-Smith tugged Dominick towards his parked Riley.

'If you suspect your friend di Cavazza you should be more co-operative. He is, as you must be aware, an agent of a hostile power.'

Clément held on. 'I am far from convinced you have told me all you know about di Cavazza, about these murders, about what is happening out at Antibes.'

'Inspector, why not leave Captain Craufurd to me. I promise to examine him thoroughly on all these questions. I will have the advantage of being able to talk to him absolutely frankly – without the obstacles of the language barrier.'

He steered Dominick into the front seat of his Riley and drove off with a rapid series of gear changes. Inspector Clément watched them go with an expression of marked dissatisfaction. He had to admit Lazzaron had a point. Why had Craufurd been caught in the murdered Huntingdon's hotel room?

'I assume I should say thank you,' Dominick acknowledged, as they drove through the empty streets of Nice. Most people were at home or in their hotels listening to the news of the fall of the Reynaud government. 'By the way, have I really been called up?'

Hickson-Smith ignored the question.

'It frankly hasn't made things any easier. On top of everything else one could have done without this entanglement with the French authorities,' Hickson-Smith complained at his windscreen. 'But then I suppose it's asking too much of Providence that anything should be simple.'

'So you wanted me out of prison. I must say I'm surprised,' Dominick told a seaside street deserted of everything except palm trees.

'As you know, one has been quite frantically busy,' Hickson-Smith complained to the palm trees. 'The problem of evacuating a certain ex-monarch and his morganatic bride should be enough to put any consulate at full stretch. Quite apart from the other demands one has to cope with at a time like this. I confess it should have come to my attention earlier. But since Mr Churchill assumed the reins of power one has been bombarded with a quite impossible mountain of memoranda. So I really cannot plead guilty for having overlooked it.'

'Overlooked what?' Dominick wondered.

'A demand, it seems totally bizarre to me — but then who is one to question our new masters? — an urgent demand to acquire a certain painting, by a certain Monsieur Pablo Picasso. As I say, the request is highly confidential and apparently extremely urgent; but I'm really not in a position to go chasing after stray Picasso paintings. That is why I had to talk to you and, as it turned out, pull every string available to the Consulate to get you out of the hands of the French Police.'

'Would this painting have anything to do with the subject of Night Fishing at Antibes?'

'So you *do* know something about it,' Hickson-Smith exclaimed wanly. 'Perhaps all one's efforts have been not entirely in vain. The maddening thing is — and I trust you will treat this in strictest confidence — the infuriating thing is I believe the picture in question was delivered to the Consulate by this American Huntingdon. And it's even rumoured you sold it to him. Anyway, it was lost in the confusion resulting from his ... quite unanticipated death. Exactly why this painting should be of interest to Whitehall totally escapes me. However, if I can tell London that you, as our local art expert, are vigorously looking into the matter, it may appease them.'

'London wants the picture, and you bloody well let it go!' Dominick shouted at the silent pleasure domes of Nice.

'It's your pigeon now,' Hickson-Smith said as they drew up at the British Consulate. 'We've scratched your back, I trust you'll do us the favour of scratching ours.'

This was an unnecessary remark, by an unnecessarily pompous civil servant, in Dominick Craufurd's view. He needed no old school exhortations or menacing to go out in search for the sketch of the *Night Fishers*. What Hickson-Smith had told him only multiplied his curiosity.

'Dominick, my darling, what a stroke of simply divine fortune to find you here!'

The reddest of red lips were pecking at his mouth and a blanket of expensively scented powder and rouge was pressing against his cheek. From a crowd of anonymous refugees, an old familiar face had suddenly loomed up out of the past.

Dolly, Lady Orient had been an acknowledged beauty even before ragtime accelerated into the Charleston. In fact some unkind tongues had suggested that Dolly had been the original inspiration of the famous Boer War Song.

Modern cosmeticry and surgery had preserved something of Dolly's legendary good looks; but science had been unable to cope with all the blows that time, life and her lovers had dealt. Layers of make-up were failing to disguise the fact that she was nursing one hell of a black eye.

'Darling Dominick, I wish you'd tell them I don't wish to be evacuated, I don't want to be evacuated, I refuse to become a dreary little refugee. They're quite mad, darling, if they imagine one can live anywhere except Villefranche.'

'Dolly sweetest, let's be honest – you just can't wait to be raped by a sweaty Italian blackshirt. You know Dolly's life-long tragedy is that she wasn't a Sabine woman in the days of ancient Rome. She was only *just* too young!'

The young man who spat out this barb was also a familiar face to Dominick, a pale, acne-marked face belonging to the vitriolic Riviera society reporter Quintin Thorne. It was no secret that Thorne was Dolly's constant companion – 'lover' would have been too romantic a word to describe his role in Lady Orient's disorganised life.

'They're trying every conceivable threat and bribe to get me to desert my beloved Villefranche.' Dolly's visible vocal chords moved with agitation. 'Can you imagine, they thought I would be thrilled to bits with the idea of travelling in the same convoy as the Prince of Wales, or whatever he calls himself now, and that dreary Wallis. I wouldn't travel in the same ocean liner as that boring, vulgar little couple!'

'Rumour has it you went a long way with his grandfather, but then he was more your period, wasn't he, Dolly darling?'

'For Quintin, it's different,' Lady Orient explained indulgently, 'he's too artistic, he's too sensitive to be locked up in a concentration camp, he needs civilised people around him.'

'Whereas you'd have the time of your life with all those sadistic guards, wouldn't you, Dolly darling – it would be a busman's holiday for you!'

'You must excuse me, I have to get back to Antibes,' Dominick said.

'Is there a party? I've been absolutely starved of parties this summer. Oh, Quintin, my pet, do let's forget this evacuation nonsense and drive out to Antibes with darling Dominick.'

'There's no party,' he told her, trying to detach a jewelled claw from his sleeve.

Dolly ignored, or was too deaf to hear, his objection. 'Lots of bubbly and lots of fun just like in the old days,' she gurgled, 'I'm dying to see darling soulful Jerome again and dear wicked Michel André. How is that sweet, unspeakably wicked man?'

'Michel André is dead,' Dominick reminded her.

'Dead? I refuse to believe it!' Dolly cried at Dominick's retreating back.

The Lamp

39

Luckily it was June. His clothes had dried out faster than he had expected, and the miserable creature which had lurched out of the sea in the darkness somewhere on the long curving strip of beach that linked Cagnes-sur-Mer to Antibes was now almost recognisable as a bearded human being. In fact, there was almost a hint of a swagger about the Prince's gait as he moved through the narrow streets of Antibes. The smells of the shops and the cafés had worked wonders on his spirits. 'I'm still lucky,' decided the man who had broken the bank at Nice, as he settled in a bar in the Place des Nations. Antibes was quite one of his favourite places.

There was just one problem, Prince Baccarat discovered, as his hands probed his still-moist pockets. That Italian peasant had pitched him into the water without a sou.

'Waiter,' he called with something of his old élan, 'I will take a glass of Ricard if you will be so good,'

'Can you pay for it?' the bar-owner queried, eyeing a bedraggled old man who looked as if he had been fished out of the sea.

'My name is Prince Bakaloff. I would fancy you can observe that my credit must be good.'

The barman told him to clear out or he would charge him for leaving moisture on his furniture.

And yet he was still lucky. Behind the sour barman's head was a flip-over calendar which clearly stated that it was 11 June. Ones, elevens and one hundred and elevens were the Prince's winning numbers – the numbers that had broken the bank on an April evening, so long ago.

In point of fact it was the 18th of June, not the 11th. The sour *patron*, stunned perhaps by the final catastrophe of Italy's declaration of war, had allowed time to stand still behind his bar. But this was immaterial to Prince Baccarat. 'I have an instinct that Dame Fortune has relented,' he muttered to himself as he stepped almost nonchalantly out of the bar. Besides, he had just had a minor inspiration.

'Forgive me, Madermoiselle.' He raised a non-existent panama hat to a voluptuous passer-by, 'I would be grateful if you could direct me to the coast road. I have a friend with a villa on the Cap. A certain Monsieur Michel André, you may perhaps have heard of him. He is a quite remarkable young man.'

She gestured vaguely but prettily westwards, and he was strongly tempted to invite her to join him over a bottle of Dom Pérignon in the nearest café; but then he remembered his temporary financial embarrassment. There will be time later for the appropriate divertissements, particularly if young Michel is at home, he thought, as he headed for villa land.

High up in the blue June sky, another squadron of Italian bombers was making white trails for Toulon. Who would bother about a damp old man limping along the coast road in search of a young millionaire he had not heard was dead?

40

She sat there in the café, sipping the harsh coffee until it went tepid on her. This is the time, she kept on telling herself, the gentlemen stands you up. She had never felt dowdier in her life. That bloody brown suit, the over-ironed frilly shirt, the much-laddered stockings. She had constructed a makeshift line up there at the top of the house by the skylight, and her clothes hung out there in the soft June breeze every night, breathing in the Mediterranean ambiance but not apparently looking any the better for it.

She had read in the papers that up north the Panzers had broken through again, she had heard rumours that '*Les Anglais*' were on their last legs. But, apart from the occasional hostile plane circling high up there in the blue, this was still the eternal Riviera. Her limbs had begun to stretch languorously to a new rhythm. She had experienced the daydream that she would like to be caressed by somebody very sophisticated and very rich . . . and very French.

Her employer, Captain Craufurd, certainly had been rich and might conceivably still be. But his charm was variable. Now that he had had his telephone connected, though not bothering to do anything about the rest of the devastation in his apartment, he was talking into it most of the day, or so it seemed, in that cold-as-an-icicle voice of his. As she left, he had given her a friendly wink. Now she must return. With colour rising fast in her face, Audrey Hopkirk had the nasty realisation that not only had she been stood up, but the rest of the stubbled brigade in the café seemed to know it.

Finally the *patron* momentarily left his cash-till.

'You do not ask where your boy friend is?'

'Boyfriend?'

'Frenchman are not like English,' the proprietor observed. 'They do not . . . their ladies.' Audrey Hopkirk was relieved she did not understand the crucial word. 'He has been delayed. That car will take you to him.'

She glanced outside and saw a dirty black Renault which had obviously once been a cab, with the meter box wrenched off. Beside it, a swarthy man in overalls was waiting against the wall.

'Where are we going?' she asked, as the Renault coughed into life and began to lurch off.

The driver spat at the dashboard and stamped his boot hard down on the accelerator. Peering forwards, Audrey Hopkirk noted that none of the dials was moving. They rattled straight through Antibes, and out the other side. The car was climbing, heading towards the cypress-crowded peninsula. As it tried to hold the switchback road, she caught tantalising vistas of translucent blue water framed in hibiscus and oleander.

And then the car just stopped. At first she thought it had run out of petrol because there was no house or restaurant visible, just a crazily twisting pathway. The driver jerked a thumb at her, motioning to her to get out. Clutching her handbag, she complied.

'Psst,' said the driver, ejecting a thick glob of saliva towards a burgeoning orange bush. 'Psst', he repeated, as Audrey stared at him blankly. The man was trying to make his meaning plainer. To do so, he wound down the window and showed her his thumb again, blistered and red. Slowly he lifted it and held it, pointing upwards between his bloodshot eyes. Then he put it into his mouth and sucked on it. Finally he took it out and jerked with it.

She now saw what she had missed, a gap in the hedge which led to a circuitous drive. As the noise of the departing car gradually evaporated, she trudged on. A resplendent villa suddenly erupted before her eyes.

Audrey had only one yardstick to compare it by; in all her limited experience there was only one possible comparison: Grampington Place, Lord Pennard's country seat in Oxfordshire. But Sandy Pennard's place was romantic in a different kind of way. It had old barns and shooting boxes, it seemed to be woven into some fantastic threadbare tapestry.

This place had no charm, on the contrary it was exceedingly overdone and vulgar. And it possessed an ominous foreignness. As Audrey's feet took her firmly up the drive she saw that the front door was swinging open, though all the windows were shuttered and closed.

41

Who was this discourteous cable writer who signed himself Alexander? Whoever he was, thought Philip Hickson-Smith, he could have no conception of the realities of the situation here in Nice.

'And what, I would like to know, is supposed to happen to Carlo?' Lady Orient was screeching at him like a demented cockatoo. 'Am I supposed to leave him behind with everything else I treasure in this world?'

'Dolly darling, I know your brain is addled, but can I remind you that Carlo is an Italian national.' Quintin Thorne grimaced under a hand-coloured photo portrait of King George VI. 'The Iteys will welcome him with open arms.'

'Of course they'll welcome him, silly boy! He's the most inspired cook in Europe. I refuse to be separated from him!'

Philip Hickson-Smith took a deep breath and tried again. 'As I have pointed out to his Royal Highness and ... er, the Duchess, the expedients we are taking may only be temporary. Between ourselves I am confident there will shortly be an initiative by America or some other neutral power, and everyone will be able to get round a table again to hammer out a realistic peace formula,' said the young diplomat of the Munich school, fingering the cable from the mysterious, peremptory Alexander. 'You may be reunited with your chef sooner than you realise.'

'I'll die in England. It's become so impossibly middle class nowadays,' Dolly Orient sulked.

'I am afraid it is essential you join our convoy.' Hickson-Smith applied his bedside manner. 'There is just the possibility, if you were to fall into Italian hands....'

'Dolly falling into Italian hands! Can't you just see it!' Quintin Thorne grinned. 'They wouldn't have a fly-button left between them.'

'... there is just the possibility,' Hickson-Smith ignored this lewd interruption, 'considering your connections and ... er, your station in life that you could become a hostage, a bargaining counter which might prejudice future peace negotiations.'

'My terms are quite simple,' Dolly Orient cawed. 'I'm going nowhere without Carlo, and certainly nowhere *with* those vulgar little Windsors. And how about my butler Tootsie, he thinks England's so grey and grisly?'

The door slammed on Hickson-Smith's fraying nerves. He wondered if the world had gone mad this summer. Would no one listen to reason? Once again he had been forced to divert vital energies from the Windsor case into patient negotiations which seemed to have led nowhere. And now there was this cable from a mysterious nonentity in Whitehall with a Greek name.

Code name: SKYLARK

Imperative you acquire picture in question as matter of supreme urgency. On PM's authority all efforts to be directed to this end. Expect immediate cable reporting success.

ALEXANDER

Events had been moving so fast, it had entirely escaped Hickson-Smith's notice that a Mr A. V. Alexander of the Labour Party had joined the Government as First Lord of the Admiralty.

42

'This is all so ... well, unexpected,' she told him as he came down the oak staircase with its fancifully Gothic carvings and corbels. 'I had imagined....'

He was wearing a yachting blazer with crested brass buttons and a striped tie that looked vaguely familiar. An anonymous-looking pair of grey flannels and plain black shoes reinforced her hopes that this young man was nothing if not orthodox, even though he lived in a villa that vaguely worried her with its perversities of taste. All that fake baronial oak illuminated by glaring chandeliers with thousand-watt bulbs could have been made for an Odeon cinema foyer. Then there was the confusion of paintings, some stacked and some hung, some abstract and some again embarrassingly full frontal. And the quiet tread of his feet over deep purple staircase carpeting also worried her. Most men needing a stick to help them walk would have come down those stairs with an off-beat thump. He made no noise at all.

'I'm sorry I could not meet you in town,' he apologised. 'You must understand. It was affairs of business.'

'You live here all alone?' she asked him, at the same time cursing herself for the straight naiveté of the remark.

'That is my misfortune,' he said. 'At one time, I was happy here.

My father built this place for me. He worked in Lille – we were opposites. He went to bed with his office ledgers. I liked fast cars, champagne and girls. He hated me for it, then he finally saw his way to sink me. He took me up into this rubbish dump and gave me all the garbage I could see. He settled my hash.'

'But this is beautiful,' she protested. 'In its way, that is.'

'It is sick, like France,' he told her, steering her out onto the drive and over a velvet lawn freshened by whirling sprinklers. 'It tastes foul in my mouth, so much putrid fruit. But my father was right. I do not know how to spit it out. No, the villa is just bad taste. That's boring and normal. You may prefer my little wigwam commonly called Le Bijou. Now that really is quite something. It's a joke, like vomit.'

Audrey had not quite worked out whether the villa was romantic, ugly or really rather horrid, but she knew exactly what she thought of the huge leather marquee, with its plain pine furniture, a huge couch and enough pelts, skins and furs to fill a trapper's yard. It was so perverse, you almost had to giggle.

'This is my chamber of melancholy,' he informed her softly. He motioned her towards a huge tiger skin, and from nowhere produced a bottle of champagne, in a bucket of ice.

'What beautiful glasses,' she exclaimed fatuously.

'They are eighteenth-century, I think,' he told her, as he ran his soft white hands round the well-turned stem. 'Many beautiful women have drunk from them. But I'm afraid you are the first virgin to touch them!'

Her hand trembled as she reached for the glass. As if to steady her, or maybe protect such a precious heirloom, his hand closed over hers. Then she was looking into brown eyes, which would have seemed quite tender but for the tiny pinkish jewels that flashed coldly from their centres.

'We will kiss, I think,' he told her. 'I will teach you the French kiss. It is really a matter of national honour – to show a pretty young English girl how a Frenchman makes love!

Audrey Hopkirk's champagne glass slipped from her fingers and landed harmlessly on the thick fur. She had dreaded that first kiss, and wondered if he too found it embarrassing. It was usually done in the upright position, standing, or at worst sitting up. But she now found herself stretched full-length on the pelt with the jettisoned glass tickling her ear. His tongue had slipped straight into her mouth and she tasted the champagne. He withdrew for an instant and she came up for air, not forgetting at the same time to pull down her skirt. But the Frenchman calmly pushed it up again. His lips were engaged in an area which up to now had carried barbed-wire entanglements – and then she could feel the ends of his moustache and his teeth puncturing the flesh.

'This is impossible,' she thought, and also said.

'You are right,' his voice buzzed beneath the layer of skirt. 'Your employer Captain Craufurd would not behave like this, eh?'

'My employer,' she stated pompously, 'has always behaved. . . .'

'Like the cold fish he is,' he added. 'But then we all know his complaint. His great English school did him a great disservice. It turned him into a pederast. He is like our André Gide.'

'That is untrue,' she told him, brushing aside the proffered champagne and leaping from the rug, her face flushed, her words coming in rapid bursts. 'That is vile. And besides, you do not even know Captain Craufurd.'

'Oh, but there you are very wrong. I know the type. I admire it. The icy nerve. The total lack of concern for other people, even beautiful women. He is an ossified pig – the very type that has made Britain great – with one redeeming feature. He is a gambler. He could have an even cooler head than mine.'

Of course, all this talk about Captain Craufurd was sheer funk, sheer postponement. She realised she was more than slightly fuddled, and it was for this reason that the sequence of events leading to another and potentially more caressing penetration would seem, on recollection, distinctly foggy. The only thing she would recall was emitting the monosyllable 'ouch' at a *moment critique*, and fearing that this word might be a shade disparaging to the myth of the French technique.

At any rate it had the effect of making him stop and indeed leave – though whether this was a blessed relief or an unmitigated calamity she could not quite decide.

She must have nodded off, for suddenly it was pitch-black and a venomously chilly breeze was making the stiff flaps of the canvas dance. She felt terrible, like the prim, dull, legendary girl men knocked over with a few glasses of party cup. Such girls, they said, ended up with a pain in the head and a pain between the legs.

'You know I never thought I would be so head in the air . . . ' she told the slim form that was now advancing towards her, holding a candelabra.

'Now, that's funny. . . .'

There was something translucent in his hands. He was giving her hair, blonde hair, a complete wavy set. But this was no wig in the charade sense. It was a professional hairpiece, cut short and permed in the fashionable style.

'You will wear this,' a voice told her. 'I cannot explain. It is just necessary. . . .'

He bent down to work it over her hair – it tickled her ear-lobes, and she giggled. She was wondering, inconsequentially, what her uncle in Leamington would think if he could see her now.

The only trouble was that the giggle was being strangled in her throat as his hands moved to embrace it tightly.

43

The thought was crossing her mind, something for which there was no background experience whatever: was he going to put his hands round her neck and snap it? Or was there something more to it – the neck play an extension, in his case, of the love play?

'Excuse me,' he muttered in that deeply resonant voice, but this is wrong....'

His hand was on her throat. Then it moved up. Secretly, she had feared (or hoped) it might drop down, curl its way again under her blouse.

'This is not too good, eh,' he whispered.

It was the wig, it must have gone askew, the way it sometimes happened to a pantomime dame.

She felt the thick blonde curls flicking against her cheeks.

'That is more *à la mode*', he muttered.

There was something about his face – such a straightforward face, almost ordinary, as if it might belong to some junior bank clerk. But someone had said the face is the mirror of the soul, and she knew this man's soul was not as ordinary as his face. This might have been thought to be very perceptive in an innocent English middle-class girl of nineteen, but in fact a great mesmerist, a supreme conjurer, had helped her along the path.

The thing had caught her eye, illuminated as it was by the quirkily Gothic candelabra. It had been propped up there against an old stagecoach trunk: just a crude, to her eyes even garish, daub about the size of a piece of foolscap; a couple of misshapen, badly drawn figures bending over what looked like a boat with a light, just as she had seen in fishing boats off Antibes, swinging above them, illuminating a squirmy congregation of fish.

Of course she recognised the thing, and wondered why it was here. But what struck her most was a man's head and face. She could tell that from the mouth sneering downwards, whilst his deadly tripod hovered murderously above the water. The face was the face of her lover, and Audrey recognised for the first time the implicit and terrible evil hidden within it. But there, beyond argument, in the face of the quiet young Frenchman ... Oh Lord, could this really be him?

'And now ... ' he was breathing hard as his hands slid down her dress. 'And now ... ' as his fingers began to probe for the holes high up in her embarrassing pair of stockings.

It was instinct, any woman's instinct, not a young girl's. Her legs rapidly unbent and scissored to curl right round him and hold him in a crab's clutch.

As her eyes opened, glowing with simulated passion, her legs locked tight round his as if to crush him.

A shudder of pain went through his body as she rammed her knee into his lame leg. A tear or two squeezed their way out of the hard pink agate. And, as she gazed in wonder, his hand was out from under her skirt and was whipping across her face as he spat directly into her mouth. 'Bitch . . . ' he salivated at her. But she had the advantage. Pushing up with all her force, she rolled him over, screaming with pain, onto a huge bearskin. He was hurling words at her, words she had never heard and could hardly decipher for the drumming in her ears.

She cracked her knee-cap hard against his leg. Then she was through the flaps of the tent; into deep night, the moon shining, the stars twinkling, whilst up there searchlights cut swathes across the warm Riviera sky.

She smelt jasmine, honeysuckle, hyssop and coriander. Her nostrils tingled deliciously to the distant aroma of juniper. Then, as she gave a final twist round towards the wigwam, she saw a humped form, a four-legged beast, burst through the canvas with the howl of a wolf at bay.

Audrey Hopkirk kicked off her stupid high-heeled shoes and ran.

44

The Italian Commander was standing at the window of his soot-flecked hotel bedroom overlooking the tracks of Ventimiglia station. He had poured himself a glass of chilled Tuscan white wine. It seemed the best answer to the hot confusion that was going on under his nose. An ancient steam engine had just wheezed into the station towing a string of olive-green freight wagons. Now a lack-lustre team of soldiers was beginning to remove the tarpaulins to unload this fresh cargo of war.

Not that the Commander was interested. For days he had watched tanks, howitzers, half-tracks and heavy artillery and all the fruits of Italy's northern factories being ponderously unloaded at this station, and, as far as he could see, it had advanced Italy's cause by exactly 500 millimetres. Besides, the Commander's thoughts were elsewhere. He was thinking about a young, rich, amusing but essentially decadent young Frenchman who had claimed a deep sympathy with Fascist Italy's ideals.

He had talked in riddles, but that had pleased the Commander. His conversation tended towards ambiguities, too. In fact, he had believed they had understood each other perfectly. He still believed they had understood each other, but now there was just a shadow of doubt, like the haze of black smoke the ancient steam engine was intruding on the razor-sharp clarity of this stifling afternoon.

'I have a marine painting which could be of interest to the dedicated collector,' the Frenchman had said at their first meeting in a back-street café in Bordighera a few months before the war. 'The fact that it is painted by a certain well-known Spaniard of dangerous left-wing leanings needn't trouble you. Even radical art can conceal striking truths. By the way, do you mind if I drink whisky?' he added, pushing away a glass and looking around for the waiter.

'I've come a long way to meet you, Monsieur André,' the Commander had said, not too indulgently, 'I hope it is not merely to discuss left-wing art, which as you know is prohibited in Italy.'

'You have fishermen. They work by night, in darkness underneath the waves, and they stalk bigger fish than tuna. This painting could illuminate the work of these men. It could be surprisingly illuminating.'

'Tell me more about your marine painting,' the Commander had replied with an unamused smile.

'Ah, the sketch for *Night Fishing*. It's a remarkable study in its way and certain to be of profound interest to all students of modern art. But first, let's return to the matter of your fishermen of the deep. It should be a field in which your mighty Empire excels. You have your own sea, your own *mare nostrum*, a great fishing tradition. But you have a potential enemy whose power is based on successful boat-building, and you have a potential ally who has a proven capacity for fishing in dark waters. In fact you have potential enemies and allies who can, at present, surpass you in an area where you need to be pre-eminent, bearing in mind,' the young riddler had added, 'the recognised shortcomings of your land forces.'

'I am a reasonably civilised man, 'the Commander had said, 'but I do not react sympathetically to cheap jokes at the expense of Italian arms.'

'We are talking about adding new lustre to Italian arms – incredible lustre,' the man André had replied cooly.

'This lustre you talk about – could it win a war for us?' the Commander had enquired, flicking specks of the Frenchman's cigar from the tablecloth.

'In an afternoon, – or perhaps I should say in a night,' the Frenchman had said, draining his whisky glass and signalling the waiter.

'Your are making extraordinary claims for a picture by a Spanish socialist.'

'Yes,' the Frenchman had smiled pleasantly, 'and of course it's small for a Picasso and, since I was there, I can tell you it was hastily executed. But I don't think the Italian Government will regret their investment or the advance they are going to make me. As with all great art, one must look below the surface.'

They had played a sophisticated game together in that seedy café in Bordighera, a game of riddles and meaningful nuances. But now there were a number of straight questions the Commander would like to have asked this witty traitor. Unfortunately the man André was dead. He would clearly have to wait for the delivery of the painting.

The tarpaulins were off. Any spy or authorised observer had a clear view of the supplies they were now unloading from the freight train. The Commander watched two soldiers grappling with a sign that read 'Via Vittorio Emanuele'. Two others were lugging a similarly styled sign with the words 'Strada Mussolini'; and now being handed down from one of the freight wagons were the nameplates of a so-far non-existent station called 'Grimaldi'.

They had advanced precisely 500 millimetres, and were unloading the street signs for the new Italian-occupied Menton. 'What kinds of fools do they have at the Commissariat General?' the Commander asked himself with an exasperated smile.

45

Audrey Hopkirk ran smack into a net, a web that closed around her. She almost laughed when she realised the trap was nothing more sinister than a lowered tennis net. Sprinting across the clearly delineated tramlines, she made for the cover of a thick hedge that seemed to stretch endlessly into the night. The shock did not knock her out, it was a warning not a death trap. In spasmodic but lessening throbs the electric charge admonished her for her temerity, gave her a second warning, then a third – each time with decreased force. Finally, the throbbing passed out of her body, leaving her numbed and trembling.

Of course, she could not stop here. Somehow she had to escape from this evil garden of shocks and perfumes, down there to the comforting quays, and the little cafés; the fishermen bobbing out to sea, Captain Craufurd up there in his room, squirting the soda into his scotch with that coldly quizzical look. She knew the general direction and yet had the shrewd idea that the shortest distance was not a straight line between two points; that, to get out, she had to climb further back into the recesses of this hell.

Which is why she started up the hill, running parallel to the aromatic hedge which puffed night scents like poison gas. There had to be an easier way through. Stopping for a second to pull a thorn out of her toe, she heard a crackling above the rustle of the breeze in the trees, the mocking of the cicadas, something like the interference on a wireless set. The crackling seemed to come from a tree to her left, and she was able to make out a box attached to a branch like a dovecote.

Then a crack of pure sheet lightning flashed for a hundredth of a second across the sky. It almost blinded her. Red, purple and ultramarine spots danced across her eyes, forming conglomerate bubbles of colours that kept on joining and then bursting apart like frogspawn under a microscope.

The voice when it came, there from the dovecote high up on the tree, was full of coughs and crackles and yet unmistakeable.

'Do not move,' it croaked at her like a gramophone record with a blunt needle. 'Stay still. There are traps everywhere.'

For a second she was convinced. Yes, there was some diabolical conjuror up there, controlling every effect, including her own destiny. But the conjuror had a physical impediment. He stuttered, in fact he had to pronounce every word and syllable twice. Only this was no ordinary stammer, it was a multiple impediment. And she knew her tormentor suffered from no such affliction. The speakers up in the trees could not be properly synchronised. His words were not just being relayed to her through a storm of crackles, they were being echoed.

In other words, the conjuror was as blind as she was. His fingers on the switchboard might be lethal, but he was bluffing. He had not yet tracked his victim.

There is a gap in every hedge, and she did finally discover this one narrow wooden door with a rounded top. She pushed through into utter darkness. The space was gigantic, maybe as great as a hundred feet square. She said goodbye to the hibiscus, the coriander and the brutally sweet aroma of that ghastly hedge. She remembered the airlessness of huge marquees in summer, and knew more by instinct than anything that she was in a huge tent; no moon, no stars, no clouds fleeting fast across her eyes. Tiptoeing forward with arms outstretched like a sleepwalker, she was aware of a slimy coily thing there beneath the arches of her feet. Stooping to touch it, her finger traced a length of rubbery hosepipe. It was obviously an electrical lead, a heavy mains coil. Suddenly she realised that she was not alone in the tent.

'*Bonsoir*,' a voice said, a mechanical nondescript voice that needed no reply.

The black was not quite black anymore, more the deepest maroon she had ever seen. And from this whirligig of maroon objects a shape began to emerge: the billowing canvas drapes of the marquee; the huge masts that sustained it, and over the floors a mass of thick purple wires – like human intestines.

From the end of the tent an explosion of cauldron-hot red took a flying leap straight into her brain, singeing her pupils as it travelled: but an explosion without sound or substance.

She heard a suppressed whistle, like air escaping from thickly tarred bronchial tubes.

Her spectrum was once more a dark tapestry of richly fabricated maroons, calm opacities of colour, but her eyes were smarting excruciatingly as if she had peered at the sun through a magnifying glass.

'*Alors*,' wheezed the nondescript voice, as to itself. The tent was transforming itself into a greenhouse. From startlingly bright sea green it opted for the greater peace and subtlety of apple. And, coming towards her, was a green man with a huge head and padded shoulders sticking up bold and square, reflected on the screen in front.

'What do you want? I am English. I am here with my employer, Captain Craufurd. He will be missing me. He will be sending out a search party to find me. He has important connections....'

'*Hein* ... !' the green shadow stated.

She felt she had no physicality, no body, just a reflective surface. That was also how Georges Bizet happened to view her. She had the beauty, the strictly transient appeal of an ant in dissolution under his burning glass. But the pleasure was onanistic, a *bon-bon* for him alone.

There had been a time when he had tried to please others – he, Georges Bizet; tried to feed their trivial minds with words. But his scripts, all written between two and four in the morning by the light of a guttering candle, had ended in the rubbish bin. Too soaring, too poetic, even 'pompous', one film director had claimed. He had his idols – Renoir, Carné, Cocteau, Clair, but one of this select group had yawned at Bizet's sombre monosyllabic prose, another had made a gesture to wipe his arse with a story line. All this had led him straight here; to the wretched little schoolgirl blinking up at him, or rather her flickering tangerine-coloured shadow (for she would be what he made her); the ant curling before the glass.

'*Ma petite*,' he crooned, almost to himself, '*ma petite*....'

Sparks, carpenter, props boy, studio hand, second clapper, focus puller – he had been all these things, taking literally René Clair's advice to 'learn our game the hard way'; except the game he was learning was his. His time as clapper boy had him round the camera where all crimes must be perpetrated. Focus pulling was like magic, got him into lenses, reflections, and glass and ... *La Lumière Blanche*.

In a flash, in a blinding flash.

He blinked at the figure in the middle, groping for him, casting a giant shadow. He had given her as yet just a tantalising touch. You wait till we go full throttle.

Should he warn her? To keep her eyes open, to go for instant kill? That would be less cruel. His bouncing light could penetrate eyes tightly clenched, scythe through shielding hands. But it would be cruel, take time, like torture. If only he could speak to her....

He wanted to say: lift up your head, curve your arms behind your body like an angel of God and I will dazzle you with beauty. You will go out in a blaze of glory.

But he could not.

Audrey bent down in a world of delicate periwinkle – blue, hands and arms doubled over her eyes. Georges Bizet adjusted his triple-filtered goggles. Audrey Hopkirk's hands were searching for the oily black snake she had almost tripped over. Georges Bizet was fine-tuning his apparatus. This was the moment that sent him trembling – when time stood still. It had first happened by accident, well, almost, in a back studio just outside Cannes. It had been a tragic mistake. Fiddling with the camera, he had brought in his bulbs and things the previous night – and those screens of zinc, mere dinosaurs: a minor matter compared with what he was now capable of.

He had been bending down, as now, with his filter goggles on, waiting to trigger off the thing. That prop shifter – the dirty, smelly one, slacking again, taking things up, then putting them down again, fiddling away, always farting. A flash as as if a fuse had blown – the man cartwheeling away holding his eyes, howling, bashing his way blinded out into the open street. As the hues were darkening to sombre purple – the prelude to his little trick – Audrey Hopkirk took the black snake in her hand and pulled it. She heard the click-away of a connection, and fell back with the force.

Night descended on Georges Bizet, a night with no sun god. With a snarl of rage he burst towards the centre of his studio where the stupid girl was hiding.

There was a restraining hand on his shoulder, a glint of a cigarette lighter.

'Michel....'

'Thank you, my dear Georges. It is kind of you, to entertain my guest. Of course blind girls are like blind mice. But in the case of this young lady I am glad you left her her eyes.'

46

As chance would have it, he had found the door to La Cabine open. He had tip-toed in, discreet as ever, calling 'André'. Nobody had answered, but still his luck was in. Here on a table was a chilled bottle of 1929 Krug which had been consumed only as far as the neck label. There were two glasses beside the bottle. One had been used. One had not.

There was also a plate of scarcely tasted caviare. He sampled it. Genuine Beluga. Lucky too if you were cultured enough to be able to read the auspices! He poured himself a glass of champagne and stuck a self-indulgent finger deep into the caviare. Then he settled back into a Western-style rocking-chair and examined his surroundings. His eyes were biased. A peasant's hut would have seemed like a palace after *La Belle Bête* and the indignities his captors had inflicted on him. This was no peasant's hut; it was like an ante-chamber of paradise compared to the stink-hole *La Belle Bête* had been. All the same he wondered why a rich young man like Michel André would choose to erect this curious leather tent over his love bed.

'A toast to love and chance – my winning combination,' Prince Baccarat finally decided, raising his third glass of champagne to the wigwammed double bed.

Lazily, his eyes toured La Cabine (or was it Le Bijou?) now made rosy by the effects of the champagne and the muted lighting. He took in the picture of Sitting Bull, the Confederate flag, the saloon room graffiti of the old West. And then his eyes bulged slightly. He had noticed the picture of the fishermen with lamps, propped against the old stage-coach trunk. Perhaps it was the effect of the drink, but the picture was stirring curious depths in his memory: a certain evening (was it spring 1938 or summer 1939?), sitting on a floor nursing a bottle of Mercier (was it on this floor?), Michel André shouting about Pablo Picasso, two types of genius combined in one frame, a painting so valuable it would change the world. And he remembered certain things his captors had muttered aboard the desecrated *Belle Bête* about a picture of fishermen probing the sea, and how they would be lucky if they could lay their hands on it. Well, it was the Prince's day for luck. Prince Bakaloff was not a particular admirer of Pablo Picasso. He preferred, in so far as he had preferences, the lighter touch of Matisse and Braque. But beggars, even temporary beggars, couldn't be choosers. Prince Baccy drained his glass of champagne and gingerly removed the painting from the wall.

47

It was a dismal little *boîte*, the kind of place he would never return to – unless he were led there by those blind goddesses, Luck and Instinct. But after his eight-hour siesta session in a ditch his thirst was acute.

The champagne was not Krug, Cliquot or even Mercier. To be precise it was *vin ordinaire blanc* livened up with a squirt of soda water.

So that was not so lucky. Nor was the undoubted fact that the rascally *patron's* wife behind the bar would certainly attempt to charge full Epernay rates for this dyspepsically farting potion. (Even so he spent even longer sampling it than might a gourmet in the Caves d'Epernay.) Don't ride your luck, *mon brave,* blind instinct jogged him, settle up now with the good lady, whilst you have a few remaining sous tinkling away in your pocket.

Clutching in his other hand a hastily wrapped brown paper parcel, Prince Baccarat stumbled his way up towards the bar.

And that lucky combination of numbers in the date 11 June credited him with a few more chips from the bank. The grim-faced *patronne* had after all a heart of gold. Dismissing with a shrug his proffered wallet, she poured him out another glass of her home-made 'champagne' *sur la maison.*

It was Pavlov's dogs all over again, he sagely reflected: feed them enough of this execrable piss-water and they'd begin to enjoy it, they might even toast the late Baron Mumm (a companion from Prince Baccarat's misspent youth) with it.

'*Merci,* Madame,' he said, giving her a bow that dated back to the St Petersburg days, when the angelic infant he had once been had learnt harmlessly to roll a dice or two.

'*Merci,* Monsieur,' she riposted, sliding towards him an illegibly scribbled multiplication table. Not that he himself had to add up the digits, the *maison* had performed that perfunctory task for him, and put a circle round the brilliant answer, further underscoring it heavily with a blunt crayon. 'Eighty-five francs,' muttered the Prince mechanically, going through the ritual and nervously frisking every pocket he had. Eighty-five francs, now that was a nice round number, but it was not his kind of number – in fact multiples of five and ten, not to mention low figure doubles, were to him like a prison sentence.

Eighty-five francs, that was impossible for this vilely gaseous gut-rot. Eighty-five francs.

Of course he did dimly remember, just an hour or so back ordering drinks for the house, even if most of his fellow imbibers had now fled the place to pee away in some alley the effects of his hospitality. How long *had* he spent in this pissoir? As the Prince's sinuous fingers fluttered like a misdirected moth through his pockets, the *patron's* wife emitted a whistle from the side of her mouth.

Prince Baccarat's luck was trembling in the balance. He was to be flattered by the appearance of *Le Patron* himself, who now stepped wearily from the room behind the bar, brushing the sleep from his eyes. This man frankly lacked the charm of his wife. Coming round the bar, he took the Prince straight by the throat and spat into his teeth the sum required.

Prince Baccarat's problem was that he had nothing to leave as a token of good faith. He thought of paying the fair price for the *vin ordinaire* they had all been consuming but a second look at the *patron* persuaded him that even on 11 June no man was lucky enough to get away with that. His fob watch, his rings, all had gone – rifled from him while he had snored in the ditch.

There was one thing left. He went through the formality of untying the clumsily wrapped brown paper bundle he carried.

He tried to give this piggy-eyed adding machine a primary lesson in surrealism. He mentioned Braque and Derain, Léger and Kandinsky. Then whipping the painting out, he religiously mouthed the words, 'An authentic Pablo.' But the miserable *patron* was no Marvin Huntingdon. In fact he seemed more ready to break the canvas over the owner's head. 'Wait a moment,' commanded a voice from the end of the almost deserted bar as the Prince stood there trembling with eyes tightly shut, awaiting the impact of art on his head.

'Let me see that.'

He was not the kind of man you would expect to see in the seediest *boîte* in Antibes. He was well dressed, well almost, if you made allowances for these hard times. His suit, a shade of light lemon, had seen better days but in its prime it must have been quite something. And he was certainly familiar, even though he was clearly suffering from the crisis of nerves that seemed to affect people living through these days in acutely differing ways. Here, it took the form of a hectic flush in the face.

'That is not bad, eh,' the man said appraisingly, taking the painting out of the hands of the *patron*. 'Not bad at all....'

'That's Picasso,' gasped Prince Baccarat. 'You understand. It must be worth a fortune, many times the price of this hovel. It's not signed but you can tell it's genuine. A genuine Pablo Picasso.'

‘Picasso,’ laughed the young man hollowly, ‘now that’s going it a bit. But it’s quite a good daub, I’ll give you that. In fact I have no hesitation in certifying it a genuine fake. Look, it’s even dated, as all fakes are.’ This joke pleased the *patron* and his wife so much that, forgetting the bill for a moment, they poured the peacemaker a bumper of ‘house champagne’. Which was how Prince Baccarat found himself playing a quiet little hand of vingt-et-un with his saviour at a table in the corner.

Of course the young man was very kind, but really he was stupid to put up those crinkly batches of crisp ten-franc notes. Did not he know that, today of all days, Prince Baccarat could not lose on ones and sevens. The Prince was still thinking this when his saviour turned tormentor, got up from the table to seize his winnings, wrapped once again in brown paper, and giving the Prince a flashing smile prepared to depart. When the Prince protested about the date, the men replied, ‘But, my dear Prince, I thought you knew. Today’s the eighteenth of June.’

The Prince remembered the man’s name. It was Cavazza and his nickname was Signor Otto.

48

‘Daddy, where’s Miss Hopkirk?’

Dammed if Dominick Craufurd knew where Audrey was. He told his son, ‘Dammed if I know!’

Oriana Craufurd, sitting up in her camp bed, looked knowing. ‘Do you know what I think? I think she’s with a man.’

‘Have you any proof of that?’ her father snapped. Then he wondered why the thought of Miss Hopkirk being with a man should annoy him. ‘No doubt she is,’ he added more placidly. ‘She’s a young girl. Young girls tend to like young men!’

‘Do you know what I think? I think he’s the Frenchman. The one who telephones.’

‘Who telephones?’ He was not snapping, he was shouting this time. ‘I asked you who telephones? Why the deuce didn’t you tell me before about this?’

‘He’s a friend of yours, Daddy,’ Oriana Craufurd coolly out-stared her father. ‘Besides, he made us promise not to tell. It’s all about a surprise for you.’

Dominick finally lit the cigar that had been dangling from his mouth. Once, his wife had told him not to smoke in the children’s room. The children no longer had a children's room in the strict sense of the word, and he no longer had a wife, but the instruction had stuck in his mind. He lit the cigar, but was careful not to blow the smoke in the children's direction.

'Surely you are mistaking the Frenchman for my friend Jerome Cavazza.' He was trying to speak calmly, if possible soothingly, again. 'Italians speak quite like Frenchmen. Well, you ought to know, you've met him – curly-haired fellow who wanted to steal the silly old picture.'

'No, it's not the Italian, we know the Italian. He kisses Miss Hopkirk too, but it's not him.'

'He *kisses* her!'

'It's the Frenchman who buys her ice-creams,' Niall Craufurd piped in from his camp bed. 'He bought Miss Hopkirk two ice-creams!'

'That's a secret, Niall, you weren't supposed to tell,' his sister scolded.

'Shut up!' Dominick rapped out.

He thought, yes, his nerves were beginning to fray. Half-irritably, half-apologetically, he stubbed out his cigar. 'Perhaps you will be kind enough to describe this gentleman to me,' he said as casually as he could pretend. 'Describe the French gentleman who buys Miss Hopkirk ice-cream.'

'He's dark and not as old as you are,' Niall volunteered.

'Most Frenchmen are dark, and a good many of them are not as old as I am. What else?'

'He buys me ice-cream too, if I promise to go home like a good boy.'

'So he can speak English?'

'That's not fair to Miss Hopkirk,' Oriana cut in. 'You promised not to tell you'd followed them. That's why he gave you an ice-cream.'

'Will you shut up and let me get to the bottom of this!' Dominick flared at his daughter. Again he was angered with himself. In his thirty-five years of make-shift living, he had had to deal with a good many nervier problems than the temporary disappearance of a fairly average-looking governess – if you did not count the way she looked in a bathing suit, running like a young animal towards the sea. Why were his nerves going now?

'I asked could he speak English?' he repeated, trying to keep the edge out of his voice. 'Perhaps almost as well as an Englishman?'

'He can speak English; but he can't walk very well,' Niall Craufurd decided. 'He walks with a limp.'

The ice-cream parlour was closed like everything else in Antibes that night; yellow shutters reflecting the yellow moonlight. He pressed a bell. He could hear it sounding through the old building like a whimpering dog. Dominick Craufurd asked himself, had he taken leave of his senses to be ringing on ice-cream parlour doors at ten minutes to midnight? The voice that shouted down at him from an upstairs window was no reassurance.

It said it was late. It was nearly midnight and besides there was a war.

'Monsieur, il faut que je parle avec vous,' Dominick shouted up at the window in his public-school French. *'C'est absolument nécessaire que je vous pose quelques questions à l'égard d'un homme boiteux qui se promène avec une canne. Une jeune fille est disparue. Vous pouvez peut-être sauver!'*

The voice said it was late, and there was a war. It said that, if Dominick did not go away, it would send for the police. It added that it had had enough trouble from footsore refugees over the past fortnight. It would not put up with any more.

So Dominick withdrew into the hot, misty Antibes night, gently cursing the ice-cream parlour proprietor under his breath, but more harshly himself. He was by nature a gambler, and a gambler was by nature cool. Yet for the past hour or so he had been behaving like a panicky novice, scattering his chips across the board in a brainless effort to recoup.

There was a smell of vegetables and flowers at near compost stage. He found he was walking through the old market place in the direction of the outer harbour – in fact he was taking the long way home. Under the moonlit statue of General Championnet he realised why. He wanted to see if that damned *Belle Bête* had returned to port.

There were quite a few things wrong with the Antibes seascape that summer: the Italian bombers, for instance, which had replaced the traditional brightly coloured pleasure planes. There was also something wrong about the absence of sails on the water, and the dominant outline of the luxury liner *La Fontaine,* and the sad boatloads of children who were daily being ferried out to its overcrowded decks. Aesthetically, there was something wrong about the machine-gun nest they had set up in the tower of Grimaldi Castle – to say nothing of the useless noise it made. But, if there was a single thing wrong about the scenery of Antibes that summer, it was *La Belle Bête*. Perhaps he was being unfair to it, but it seemed to Dominick that everything that had gone wrong, badly wrong, with his life that summer dated from the arrival of this grey old two-master in the harbour.

To put it at the very least, *La Belle Bête* was an omen, a decidedly unlucky omen. There was another thing that was wrong about *La Belle Bête*. It brought people back to life who were supposed to have vanished for good. It had ferried Prince Baccarat back from oblivion. Who else had it brought? Was it possible it had brought a dark Frenchman who spoke English perfectly and claimed to know him intimately, and walked with a limp? It also seemed to play a part in settling other people's hash.

He had climbed down on to the outer promontory of the harbour. A furtive crew of night fishermen were loading their tackle into their floating lamp-stand. War and the black-out were supposed to have put a stop to the night fishing industry; but the fishermen would have explained with a salty curse, 'We have to eat.'

Further along the promontory, Dominick could make out another furtive figure. It was alone and walking rapidly in the direction of *La Belle Bête's* twin masts.

Dominick Craufurd never ran anywhere if he could help it, it was not in keeping with his image of impeccable *sang-froid*. But now he broke into a run.

The man he was pursuing was not a night fisherman. He was too elegant and slim for that particular breed. Also, he carried a large parcel under his arm.

'You'd better stay exactly where you are,' Dominick panted.

Jerome di Cavazza turned round with a sad smile, his features clearly identified by the moonlight.

'Have you got a gun?' he sighed. 'It would make a difference, I mean as to whether I do what you say, or tell you to take a jump in the harbour.'

'You know I have a gun,' Dominick reminded him gruffly.

49

Now the children were asleep. The Picasso painting was propped up on the mantlepiece. Dominick Craufurd and Jerome Cavazza were sitting in armchairs, gradually disposing, in a gentlemanly way, of a bottle of Stock. The only hostile thing there was Craufurd's service revolver which was lying on the table beside his brandy glass.

'Have you ever looked at this painting, really looked at it?' Craufurd wanted to know.

'Oh yes, I've looked at it,' Jerome shrugged. 'As you know Pablo is not one of my favourite painters though of course he's a charming man. If you ask my opinion, I think Giotto was a more effective primitive, and a better draughtsman incidentally.'

'If you will forgive me saying so, those are remarkably superficial thoughts for a man who has been prepared to kill for this picture.' Dominick pushed the Stock bottle towards his old friend. 'Did it never occur to you to ask yourself *why* you were ordered to take this picture?'

Jerome thought about it for a few seconds. 'An Italian officer doesn't really question his orders,' he said, winking.

'Then Italian officers are bloody fools!' Crauford snapped. 'Have you looked at the night fisherman?'

'Excuse me, which night fisherman?'

'The one with his head closest to the water. For your information, I may say, this is the fundamental difference between the preliminary painting we have here and the eleven-foot masterpiece which is now in the Guggenheim Collection in New York. This figure is beaming a powerful torch on the water, whereas the figure in New York painting is dangling a fishing line. Another difference: the face here is brilliantly illuminated. It's a young, handsome but strangely malevolent face. Does it remind you of anyone?'

Jerome looked at the painting. 'There is a certain similarity,' he smirked.

'To the life,' Dominick nodded.

'All right, it's Michel André,' Jerome acknowledged after a little more thought. 'But is that really so strange? We know Picasso painted the picture for him a month or so before he died.'

'So young, wasn't it a tragedy,' Dominick snarled.

'Have I said something wrong?'

'Now look at the reflection in the water,' Craufurd ignored the question. 'This is another difference between the preliminary painting here and the finished article in the Guggenheim. Here we have a reflection, but the funny thing is it doesn't reflect the face.'

'A lamp where the face should be.'

'A lamp with a monster bulb – much bigger than the normal night fisherman's acetylene lamp. What do you suppose Picasso was getting at?'

Jerome thought and then shrugged. 'Who can tell with Picasso? People write many ingenious explanations in the art magazines, but if you ask my opinion Pablo paints whatever comes into his head.'

'Some critics say every Picasso is a record of his last conversation. He had been talking to Michel André when he made this painting. What do you suppose Michel had been telling him?'

'It's difficult to tell now he's dead.'

'Put it another way. What was it that Michel André told Picasso that your Government, for one, finds so fascinating?'

Jerome helped himself to more Stock. At the same time he slipped a hand along the table towards the revolver, but Dominick covered it fast with his left hand while his right hand continued to gesture indulgently towards the bottle.

'You don't know what this bloody picture means, yet. You're happy to try and sneak it off to your tinpot, jack-booted criminally incompetent superiors. I call that dangerously irresponsible. On the other hand, you're often not as charmingly naïve as you'd have us think.'

Jerome acknowledged the double rebuff with a raised brandy glass.

'Honestly, Dominick, I find it difficult to get all worked up about a piece of canvas when the enchanting Miss Hopkirk's still alone out there somewhere in the black-out.'

'I appreciate your concern for Miss Hopkirk,' Dominick answered icily, 'but I'm not sure I agree with your promise. Have you noticed the girl with the ice-cream cone and the bicycle on the right hand of the picture? I think that could be significant.'

'Will it find Miss Hopkirk?' asked Jerome, raising both hands in the air in despair at his friend's dogged obstinacy. The picture was a picture when all was said and done. Yet Dominick Craufurd was staring at it as if it contained the answers to all the conundrums of life.

'Look at the second fisherman,' he said in a mystic faraway tone of voice which reminded Jerome of the first lesson he had learned about upper-class Englishmen, namely that they were all mad. 'Here the difference between our painting and the Guggenheim version is less marked. But in our version the hair is blond, brilliantly blond. Does that suggest anyone to you?

'It's Bizet, who the bloody hell else did you think it was?' Dominick growled.

'Ah, Bizet – and Michel . . . .' Jerome began, scanning the two lamp-lit figures.

'I told you you should have looked into the picture. I suspect incidentally you will find that our friend now walks with the support of a stick.'

'Captain Craufurd, this is Audrey,' the gentle yet slightly home counties voice came clearly down the line. 'I'm sorry I wasn't back in time to put the children to bed but, as I think you've gathered, there've been a few snags. Mummy was quite right, it really isn't wise to speak to dark strangers. I'm very sorry, but this is meant to be a rather melodramatic call, Captain Craufurd....'

'Where the hell are you,' Dominick shouted into the mouthpiece.

'Ask her if she's all right,' Jerome hissed.

'By the way, you all right?' the Englishman repeated.

'I'm supposed to appeal to your natural gallantry. I think I'm supposed to weep pitifully too. It's rather like a Dornford Yates novel, isn't it? Only I'm afraid this time it's real life. I'm to tell you that I'm in danger, real danger if you don't deliver the picture. Doesn't that sound like a film or something? I'm not allowed to tell you what my fate is to be but perhaps it will be glaringly obvious to you, if you've been to the films and seen the marvellous things they can do with special effects these days? I don't know if you ever saw the film about the *Titanic* but....'

'Miss Hopkirk, are you all right?' Dominick shouted down the line.

'You still call her "Miss Hopkirk" at a time like this,' Jerome gesticulated in amazement.

'Dominick, *mon cher ami,* how delightful to hear your voice again after all this time.' Another voice had come onto the telephone, an urbane, purring male voice straight out of a supposedly buried past. 'You really are a sly old son-of-a-gun trying to keep a treasure like Miss Hopkirk to yourself. Particularly since we used to share everything, *n'est-ce pas*?'

'How do you share anything with a murderer who's supposed to be dead,' Craufurd snarled.

'You speak of death,' Michel André purred back. 'Personally I think death is to be recommended, especially when it is followed by resurrection, Dominick, *mon cher,* I can perfectly understand how it quite intoxicated Jesus Christ. And of course I've only just begun to roll away the stone. I can promise you my resurrection is going to be even more spectacular than the original.'

'I'd forgotten you were a blasphemer too,' Dominick said.

'In the case of Miss Hopkirk, resurrection may be less predictable,' the feline voice continued, 'although she is admittedly an angelic-looking creature with eyes that are almost divine. And, please believe me, I do intend that those eyes should become sightless and this vital young body perhaps less vital if I do not get the picture, Dominick. I may be a blasphemer, but you, my friend, I regret to say, are a thief. In other times I might have said. "Keep the picture. What is a picture between friends?", but I have principles now. I want the Picasso back, not because I necessarily admire the vain old fart, but because it is a matter of principle.'

'Michel André, the man of principle, that's a new one, isn't it?'

'Let me confess, *mon vieux,* I experienced a revelation when I went up into the Bavarian Alps to commune with the God of History. I looked down on my past life, our past lives, and thought how petty and squalid it had all been. We had the intelligence and the imagination to conquer the world, but we played with chips and dice and pieces of card for contemptible sums of money and, let us be honest, the favours of a *whore.* We were like France and England playing with our little party politics, our putrid little ideas of toleration and liberalism while all the time the God of History was beating on the door. Up there like Moses in the mountain, the God of History bestowed on me a new creed – a creed to carve on tablets of granite. Shall I tell you the first commandment: a man is a fool if he does not use his intelligence like a bayonet, like a machine-gun, or if you like a flame-thrower.'

'He's stark staring mad,' Dominick murmured to Jerome.

'Of course Jerome Cavazza is with you,' The voice at the end of the telephone had resumed its conversational tone. 'Do please give him my affectionate regards. I always thought he was the most romantic of us, didn't you? I think it is possible that he was actually in love with Hélène. I cannot believe that a fake romantic like Jerome is going to permit you to sacrifice La Belle Hopkirk for the sake of a painting.'

'How do you know I have the picture?'

'Intuition, dear old friend,' Michel André said, 'Oh and of course I've talked to Prince Bavaloff.' But I must tell you there can be no more delays, even for friendship's sake. I want that picture within one hour.'

'Why don't you let Miss Hopkirk go and let's play for the damned picture, that's what we would have done in the old days, wouldn't we?' Dominick said, this time in an almost friendly tone.

'*Mon cher ami,* all our games are over.' The voice of Michel André sounded like ice.

'Very well,' Dominick sighed. 'You can have your bloody painting, but not until you've given us back Miss Hopkirk – unharmed.'

The arrangement was they would meet at the gates of Les Ombres in an hour and a half.

'Just one request,' he concluded. 'Please don't bring any friends who aren't old friends,'

50

'I suppose you realise you've come through on the night line,' the ultra-English voice said peevishly (it was part of its diplomatic training never to betray outright irritability). 'I appreciate your difficulties, Craufurd, but we *are* trying to keep it open for a very urgent call from a Very Important Person not all that far removed from where you're speaking.'

Dominick swore furiously down the British Consulate's night line.

'I'm afraid we have absolutely no mandate to investigate suspicious activities in French private houses,' the diplomatic voice of Philip Hickson-Smith persisted, wearily but unruffled. 'I'm sorry. Even if there is a lady in the case – I beg your pardon, an English passport holder – it is still in the first instance a matter for the French authorities. I'd much prefer it, Craufurd, if, instead of adding to all our difficulties, you'd bend your mind to the small matter of a certain painting in return for the little service I was able....'

'This matter is connected with the damned painting,' Craufurd barked.

'Are you saying you've got the wretched picture? I must say it would be an immense relief to get this particular chore off my plate.'

'You could have the painting if I can get action on the girl.'

Dominick had suddenly become cagey. He was not going to hand the picture over to be registered, filed and perhaps forgotten by this callow civil servant. It was obvious the painting was much too important to get wrapped around with red tape.

'Have you or have you not acquired the painting?' Hickson-Smith asked with a genuine hint of irritation.

'Are you going to help us to get Miss Hopkirk?'

'I've told you how I'm placed here,' Hickson-Smith complained. 'I don't want to sound pompous, but I have a major affair of State on my plate.'

'I'm getting damn-all help from my people,' Dominick said, slamming down the phone. 'Perhaps your people can do something.'

Jerome di Cavazza shrugged. 'Perhaps they can. Perhaps they can't. But that's not the answer, is it, Dominick? If you are fond of that governess of yours, you must hand the picture back to Michel André. That's my hardest hunch to date.'

'You're fond of her too, aren't you?' Craufurd answered gruffly. 'From what I understand you're a damned sight too fond. You kiss her, I hear.'

'Don't you kiss her? She's very sweet.'

'What the hell would you do in my position?' Dominick sighed.

'I'm not in your position,' Jerome smiled, reaching for Dominick's silver box of Players cigarettes and politely indicating the weapon that lay a little further along the coffee table. 'After all, you're the man with the gun.'

'If you had the gun, would you hand this picture over, knowing what we know about this picture?'

'You seem to see more in this picture than I do,' Jerome said, blowing a smoke ring. 'As far as I can see, it is still a matter of oil-based colours splashed, one must admit with some *élan*, on to a piece of canvas worth perhaps eight francs. I admit there is evidence that it has a value beyond its face value. But I cannot see how it could ever compare with a pair of eyes as innocent as an English April. You were smart to buy a little more time from that maniac. But now even that time is running out, my friend. You must let them have the picture, otherwise you will be guilty of a murder, perhaps even of someone you love.'

Dominick's face pinkened. Perhaps he was even blushing. He said, 'A lot of people seem to want this picture. My people. Your people obviously. The whole damned picture is a killer, I'm sure of that. It would be totally irresponsible to let it go without a fight. By the way,' he added, 'an English April isn't all that innocent.'

What the devil were they looking for, these two Antibes fishermen figures with such a remarkable resemblance to a certain Antibes resident called Michel André and his friend, the film lighting man, Georges Bizet? Put it another way, what were they actually doing, Dominick Craufurd asked himself perhaps for the final time. Plainly they were catching fish by torch-light. The blond figure had a whopper skewered by a fork. But what really seemed to be absorbing the two men was the reflection of this giant lamp in the water. It wasn't a standard lamp, which Picasso had made the memorable centre-piece of his *Guernica*. It didn't really resemble the acetylene lamp which the night fishermen used. Dominick had never seen a lamp quite like it. But then of course it was customary for that cunning old fox to paint objects as if you had never seen them before.

'Forget it – it's a picture', Jerome told him. 'And Miss Audrey is a young girl.'

'Is it in the picture or behind the picture?' Dominick asked himself, ignoring his friend.

'You've promised as an English gentleman, you will return the painting. Michel André is not an English gentleman. You mustn't risk disappointing mad André.'

'Picasso paints on practically anything that comes to hand – tablecloth, table, window, anything,' Dominick mused. 'He'd paint over a map of a diagram if anyone asked him. It would have been just like André to ask him. Always had a rum sense of humour. A fishing scene, masking perhaps . . . well, what do you think, Cavazza? You ought to know more about it than I do, you've got orders to steal it . . . shall we say a fishy scene disguising a naval secret?'

'It's painted on canvas.' Jerome pointed out. 'Don't think I haven't examined it. There's no backing, nowhere where a document could be hidden.'

'My hypothesis is that the painting has been *on* a document.'

Jerome lit another of Dominick's cigarettes. He said, 'You may be right. You may be wrong. I don't care. I am willing to risk my commission in the Royal Italian army. I am prepared to risk dismissal from the service for Miss Audrey's safety. Why are you being so obstinate, so insensitive? No one has given you orders to steal the picture.'

'I get the impression you're rather taken with our Miss Hopkirk.

Wouldn't mind adding her to your list of conquests. I'm not sure she's really your type.'

'Of course I want to go to bed with her, you English idiot!' Jerome shouted in desperation. '*Mamma mia,* that's better, isn't it, than not caring a sausage (or do you say a fig?) whether she is alive or dying.'

'I won't be a moment,' Dominick said, going to the door. 'Oh, by the way, you can take my automatic if you want it. But then you don't really, do you? You're thinking more in terms of unconditional surrender.'

He came back into the room with his grey side-burns slightly flecked with dust and wood-shavings. Dominick had been in his carpentry cupboard. He was carrying a paint-stripping spatula and a grimy blow-lamp. 'The gentleman *is* an artisan,' he quipped.

He set the blow-torch down on the coffee table, lit the primer methodically and worked the fuel pump. Then he looked up and saw Jerome eyeing him with amazement and horror. 'Don't worry,' he said, 'I'm going to give him his picture back – in some shape or form.'

The lamp was flaring now, a blue tongue of flame, licking away the little brown smoke puffs of paraffin.

'The first commandment of Michel André,' he explained, '—a man is a fool if he does not use his intelligence like a flame-thrower.'

Then, with his purring blue flame, he walked over to the picture on the mantlepiece.

'You mustn't do it!' Jerome yelled.

'Even for the sake of ultimate truth?'

'You cannot! You cannot! It is a work of art. It's not perhaps a Raphael or an Andrea del Sarto or a Mantegna; but it is still a work of art. It's worse than raping a nun, Dominick. You will scream in the Inferno!'

'Worried about your orders, old boy?'

The lamp flame tickled the elongated Picasso face of the woman who resembled Hélène Colmar with an ice-cream (a portrait, the critics said, of the painter's mistress Dona M'aar) and gave it the blistered appearance of a Guernica victim. The flame moved down and melted the woman's twin ice-cream cone into rivulets of paint. And then the walls of the harbour started to run with globules of molten greys, blues and acquamarines. The room began to reek of a burning masterpiece.

Now Dominick started to work furiously with his paint-scraper. As the blow-torch played on Picasso's illuminated harbour, he scooped out swathes of charred and clotted paint which a few seconds before might have been worth thousands of dollars in any New York auction room.

At points he had dug clean through to the canvas on which the picture had been painted. And this was the worrying thing. It was plain, if charred, canvas – nothing more, nothing less. Dominick released a nervous jet at the blond fisherman with the strange likeness to the cinema lighting man Bizet. For a second the fair hair burst into a small halo of flame. Then the whole figure dissolved, as Craufurd's frantic blade shovelled it out of all hope of immortality. It was still just bare canvas below the surface. The painted face of Michel André seemed to be more than just smiling at him, it seemed to be grinning from ear to ear. The image literally went up in smoke as Dominick punched it with his flame. That mocking malevolent face was surely hiding something! At least, that was Dominick's desperate prayer. His paint-clogged stripper showed that it was not hiding anything.

'There's nothing behind the picture, believe me,' Jerome whispered.

Dominick put the blow-lamp down on the mantlepiece. He did not notice he had forgotten to put it out. But he did see the great tracks he had carved across the face of the half-incinerated painting, and could not see a shred of a map or a chart or a diagram, just bare canvas.

'There could have been something. There could have been. It was a gamble; but, damn, there could have been!' He found he was having to grip the mantlepiece to steady himself.

'It would perhaps be tactless and obvious for me to say this was a costly experiment,' Jerome suggested. 'For both of us....'

'Yes, it would.'

'But perhaps I may be allowed to ask how we are to save Miss Audrey, let alone ourselves, without a picture?'

'It's a fair question,' Dominick acknowledged, staring into the terrible void he had created in Picasso's harbour.

'There's a possibility that, if we wrapped it neatly back in its parcel, Michel André will not inspect it for damage as we will inspect Miss Audrey for damage ...' Jerome shrugged uneasily. 'A one to a million possibility.'

Very slowly Dominick turned his back on what he had done. He said in something like his old tone of voice, 'You're quite right, we've really got nothing we can decently exchange for Miss Hopkirk. We'll have to get her out by force.'

'You and me?' Jerome enquired sceptically.

'You, me and anyone else we can scrape together,' Dominick decided. 'You've got some useful connections, haven't you, Cavazza?' he asked with a gleam of the old rivalry. 'Those flipper-wearing, fisherman-slaughtering thugs of yours are itching for a crack at somebody, well, aren't they?'

The Net

51

'It's a moot point who's the traitor,' Dominick had remarked. 'It's odd to think that technically speaking we should be stabbing each other in the back. Certainly, some of my denser superiors would find it hard to get used to the thought of a cashiered British army officer fighting alongside a gang of Italian blackshirts just a few days after war was made official.'

'Wait a moment, my friend,' Jerome di Cavazza had replied. 'Nobody has yet said *Rien ne va plus*. There's always a game after the game, but we're going to need a fair deal of luck to defeat a ghost.'

'Particularly a ghost who cheats,' said Dominick pensively. 'I wonder how many cards our dear corpse is keeping up his sleeve.'

It was curious waiting here by the road opposite the entrance to the villa grounds of Les Ombres, that grotesque side-product of the French cinema, now closed and shuttered. He remembered seeing it from this same point a year or less ago during the Sudetenland crisis. He had driven up, intending to leave his car in this very siding and saunter in through the grounds, gratefully sniffing the heavy mélange of oleander, coriander and hyssop that pervaded this part of the villa grounds. And, as now, the villa had stood out there in the moonlight, showing thirty or so blank holes, thirty darkened windows. And yet it had been party night. The guests included Jean Cocteau and his dazzling young protégé, Jean Marais.

As he had wandered up the drive, letting his cigar smoke weave its way through the villa herbs, he had to blink suddenly – or rather keep his eyes closed for a good half-minute. Somebody had thrown a mains switch and the full villa lighting system had surged into action. Maybe it was the quietness of the moments just before, the nocturnal peace of the garden and park, but Dominick had seen this as a vile invasion of his personal privacy.

He had wondered what bulbs could hold this kind of lighting power, but, as the effect softened into delicate roseate pink, he had given a chuckle and proceeded, amused at Michel's lavish bordello effect. It was that clever fellow, Georges Bizet, or whatever his name was, up to his tricks again.

The plan was foolproof. You could not fault it on logic, it was one of those increasingly rare things in life, a hand at bridge which had to win out, whatever the opponent did, like having all the big cards in one hand. It all stemmed from his Machiavellian friend Jerome holding the joker, in the portly well-fed shape of one Commissioner Lazzaron, who in turn was no gambling fool since he held trump cards in both French and Italian (and nothing as risky as an English king or jack). An urgent telephone call to police headquarters and it had been laid on, three large police trucks, containing an extraordinary force, considering how the war stood, of armed Frenchmen and their Italian enemies.

First, he had thought they must still be a mile away, then they had rounded the final hairpin, spinning round in front of him and pointing straight up the drive of Les Ombres.

You had to hand it to these frogs, they looked as if they meant business. Each truck had a searchlight mounted on the cabin and they were flicked full-on. Of course the place was dead, a repository of old and bitter memories, like rose petals turning to dust. The hammering of Commissioner Lazzaron on the over-opulent brass knocker caused echoes in the mind as well as in the house.

Dominick and Jerome watched them quietly from the end of the drive as they detrucked and spread themselves out around the villa.

'Stop wasting time,' muttered Dominick to Jerome. 'You won't find them there. Let's go and run 'em to earth ourselves.'

Holding a torch in one hand, and feeling with the other the comforting shape of his old service revolver in his jacket pocket, Dominick Craufurd made off up the drive at a rifle regiment's jogged canter. Stumbling through a mass of bougainvillaea, he seized hold of a camouflaged figure who had his machine-gun aimlessly pointed at those dead shuttered windows. 'He's a lucky man, his bird has flown,' thought Dominick, knowing that, if Michel André had really been lurking there, there would now be one French policeman the less.

'Look,' he whispered, 'get your men spread out over there. See those bushy-topped trees against the horizon – that's where our friend is skulking. Look, you tell him,' he finally beseeched Jerome. 'Tell him in his own lingo, unless we get moving over there we're all dead men – a collection of sitting ducks.'

It came at them through the whispering of wind against leaves, through the cicadas and the panting of the Italian. It was borne on the air: a voice, her voice.

It said, 'Help. Please God, somebody help me.'

'That's all right,' he caught himself muttering. 'That's all right. We're here. The main thing is, don't panic.'

'That's her voice, isn't it?' asked Jerome.

'Yes and no, our friend is up to his tricks again. Keep your head down, you fool,' Dominick yelled at Jerome, who was already sprinting over the lawn towards La Cabine. Then he was following him although he knew it was stupid, panicking just as Michel André had planned, the blood pounding, his breath coming in asthmatic jerks

– too much booze, he thought, too many John Player Navy Cut – oh, those palmy, balmy days of peace.

Of course, Jerome was nobody's fool. He had found cover – the best possible. Down there beneath the shimmering bougainvillaea, his startled face appearing wreathed in a mass of flowers. The man was a soldier, apart from being a cunning Italian – his Latin romanticism only skin-deep.

'This needs thought,' he whispered unnecessarily to his companion.

It was about fifty yards in the open from where they now hid, fifty yards before they made that billowing tent.

'Where the hell are your lot?' Dominick panted. 'What the blazes are they playing at?'

Jerome's answer was to take Dominick's head between his two hands and twist it ferociously to the far left.

Over there on the extreme left flank of this chaotic non-battlefield, willowy figures were detaching themselves from a fringe of silver birch saplings, twisting, bending forwards and breaking into a run. Five, seven, ten, twelve. Then the usual happened. Three bloody fools had got themselves right up in front, outstripping the main pack. 'Hold back, you damned fools,' swore Dominick.

'Please,' pleaded that voice. 'Please help me. Can't you do anything?'

The running figures were much closer now, you could pick up the thudding of their boots on the grass, the hoarse forcing out of breath, the smothered Neapolitan obscenities.

'Hold it, not so fast, you bloody cut-throats!' Dominick silently willed them.

There was something wrong. They had not got that far to go, the front three must have covered well over half the distance.

'Let's go,' decided Jerome, rising to his feet and giving Dominick's still recumbent body a sharp kick.

'Wait,' Dominick implored. There was something about this, something very odd. 'Christ,' he thought, as he realised that eyelids were as nothing, bits of gossamer wafer, that frizzled before the sun's great fireball.

A pain shot into his brain like the worst hangover headache he had ever had in his life. And then the whole thing quietened into a Paul Klee abstraction of deep maroon holding a myriad of pink and blue stars.

Dominick had reacted like a child, bending both arms and holding them as a double shield across his eyes. The spiky multi-coloured stars went out one by one, leaving him with an endless ocean of maroon.

When he opened his eyes, dropping the arms back to his sides, he saw nothing but the dense blackness of the sky.

'Good God, Jerome, I think I've gone blind,' he heard himself saying, whilst the sweetest voice in the world still purred into his ears. 'Please, can somebody come. I need help. Please. Please.'

And from the blackness a friendly arm was outstretched towards him and he felt the warm clasp of Jerome di Cavazza. They were holding on like two people who had not seen each other for years. Except that in their case they could not see each other.

'God, you Italians,' complained Dominick Craufurd. 'You and your bloody shaving lotions. You smell like a Parisian harlot.'

'And you, my dear friend, stink of honest true British grit and sweat,' riposted the Italian. And then they both laughed, because the dawn was breaking again; not that incandescent fireball dawn of a minute or so ago, but a gradual lightening of blackness, a sharpening of vaguenesses into soft and then more defined silhouettes, consummated for Dominick in one vision of the handsome, mud-stained face and brilliant teeth and flashing smile of the one Italian on earth who made any kind of sense. And then the dawn stopped lightening, and they knew it was still night. But they knew that they could see in Michel André's infernal moon-lit garden, knew too that tomorrow the dazzling blue of a Bonnard sea sandwiched between pine trees would be theirs once more.

It still stood there after all this, that damned flapping tent, great folds of stuff vaguely flopping to and fro in the breeze.

What had happened? Where were the attackers?

To find them, you had to swivel your new-found eyeballs backwards, across that perfect lawn; and, further still, towards the line of birch saplings from which the whole endeavour had originated.

When you saw them you could not fail to wonder why spotting them had been so hard. They were floodlit in a sombre landscape, joyously luminous characters, phosphorescent images against the night. And they were drunk. They staggered around, the three of them, like alcoholics, flailing for one another with their arms and falling over together. They were really quite droll, and Dominick with his resurrected sight felt inclined to chuckle at their antics.

Not so Jerome, who had left his cover in the foliage and was streaking towards them in the open.

And then came the most surprising thing of all. Jerome appeared among the Italians like a ghost. He had only a shadowy semblance to put beside their phosphorescence. One of the clowns was now on the ground and his arms were around Jerome's ankles and Jerome was stooping down to help him to his feet. And the man was crying, shrieking out something in the execrable Italian of the South.

They were acting like clowns; but the reality was, they were as blind as bats.

52

Flicking on his pocket torch, Dominick Craufurd broke into a fast trot, up the hill along that thick hedge and over the skyline. If it was anybody's war it was England's war.

Something started in the hedge high up and Dominick froze. He looked in vain for the obvious answer: a startled bird cawing away into the night. He was disconcerted to feel that his pulse-rate had shot up, he felt a rare sensation – the frantic knocking of his heart, which only happened when he was dicing for the very highest stakes.

From the other side of that bramble wall of a hedge, a twig snapped. What was it? The safety-catch released on a playboy's tiny revolver? Dominick stopped, and tried to sharpen his hearing. It was a high-pitched whistle, which he was at first unable to place, a shrill penny whistle of birdsong. As a boy brought up in the country, he knew them all, and this was the most vulgar of the lot, the common starling, that brillant aper of other birds. There was one problem: every starling would be comfortably ensconced in some barn or garage roof at this unearthly time of the night. At two in the morning, they didn't fly around and they certainly didn't trill.

'Michel,' he intoned softly. 'Michel. Michel André....'

The starling shut up.

'Michel,' continued Dominick. 'It seems a long time since....'

You couldn't see through the damned hedge, but shooting was another matter.

The first shot buzzed past Dominick's ear, and as he tumbled to the ground his thumb switched off the torch. Five more shots in rapid succession penetrated the hedge at the point where his body should have been.

'And now it's my turn,' he shouted, blazing into the hedge with his service revolver.

'Help me! Help me! Help me!' a voice repeated mechanically in the darkness. Something told him there was no longer anyone there.

53

Oriana Craufurd slipped out of her camp bed and called softly, 'Daddy.' There was no answer. She went over to her brother's bed and shook him awake.

'Where's Mummy?' Niall Craufurd asked.

'Mummy is in the north fighting the Germans with Uncle Sandy.'

'Where's Miss Hopkirk?' Niall demanded more pertinently.

'I don't know,' Oriana confessed, 'I know Daddy is worried about her.'

Finally, Niall mentioned the last parent figure on his list. 'Where's Daddy?'

'I'm afraid we're all alone here,' his sister told him.

It was dead of night, but the harbour was filled with children. Oriana and Niall Craufurd did not know the meaning of instinct. But, in default of a mother, a governess or a father, they felt they had come to the right place.

Perhaps the children's parents did not look so jolly. The moon revealed pale-faced women in black picture hats fussing around their offspring like distracted hens, grey-haired men in trilbies holding tiny tots in frantic embraces, and letting tears run down their adult cheeks when by rights it should have been the children who were weeping.

'We've still got two places left on *La Fontaine,*' a fisherman was shouting. It looked as if he already had a boatful. His fishing smack was crowded from bow to stern with chattering, giggling children, all of them, or so it seemed by moonlight, dark-haired and dark-eyed. As it happened, all of them were Jews.

The fisherman's teeth glinted in a merry smile. He seemed strong and reassuring with the tow-rope of his fishing smack twined round his muscular forearm.

'It's just a trip round the harbour, isn't it?' Oriana asked.

'It's free. Paid for.' The friendly fisherman smiled.

'Just round the harbour,' Oriana instructed him, putting her centimes back in her leather purse.

And then they were moving across the slick waters of the harbour towards the silhouettes of the twin lighthouses. And the children were laughing, and some of them were cheering. And only a few were crying.

'Do you think Daddy will be cross with us?' Niall Craufurd asked his sister.

‘He’ll be pleased,’ Oriana reassured her brother, ‘he was always sorry he couldn’t give us more boat trips.’

At first the big liner was just a splodge on the skyline. But then it began to get larger and larger. Before long it was a black edifice towering over the little fishing boat.

Now the children stopped laughing and smiling, and even the cheery fisherman looked glum under the gigantic shadow of that obsolete liner, *La Fontaine*.

And it was at this point that Oriana and Niall decided they wanted to go home, even though there was no mother or governess, or, at the moment, a father, to go home to.

54

At least they had some booty to show for their efforts – a film projector, a lot of cinematic gadgetry, and some spools of film worming out of their metallic cans. It was Jerome who managed to get the apparatus going whilst they all squatted on the ground to enjoy the peep show (those of them, at least, who still preserved the use of their eyes). England expects every man to do his duty, Dominick thought to himself, and I sit here with these thugs. The stuff went on forever, with big gaps in which the film ran blank. Much of it had been shot from a boat at night. The camera had been slung low over the side and sometimes the waves had splashed over it. Fairly arty stuff, for what it was worth; a cinema fanatic intrigued with the effects of light on water.

Then, in a new sequence of shots, the camera had been taken off the gunwale and lifted higher in the boat. A searchlight seemed to shoot out through dense blackness and discover an object bobbing in the water: a fishing smack. Then they were closer and it was obvious that the boat on which the camera was placed had a high-powered engine, possibly that of a playboy’s speedboat, although the upper trappings of the craft, as caught occasionally in the camera, seemed more those of the conventional sailing boat. There was a half-minute gap. Now they were back to the business of playing light on empty water; empty because the distant bobbing fishing boat, which they had been approaching with such speed, had clean disappeared.

As if bored with looking at the empty waves, the camera shifted its position, and at last one could see the crate on which it was mounted. One could see a mast, a pile of rope and a frequent object astern most local craft, the characteristic lobster-pot device of the fisherman's acetylene lamp.

Then the camera dipped down for a moment, and the first evidence of humanity appeared. It was an old face and it sported a white beard and a spotted handkerchief knotted round a gnarled neck. And the whole thing glowed like a saint in a sentimental religious painting. In fact the only part that was not positively phosphorescent was the eyes. They were black holes.

There was one other spool in which they were interested. But, unlike the rest which were in sixteen millimetre film, this one was much slenderer, the amateur photographer's eight millimetre to be exact. It showed Audrey Hopkirk caught in a very relaxed mood. She was sitting at a table in a café smiling shyly at the camera and licking a double-cone ice-cream, it was very candid stuff and the girl's unforced posing suggested that the camera was concealed from her.

'What does this all mean?' Jerome exclaimed.

'Draw your own damned conclusion, remember we're enemies, Cavazza!' Dominick shouted, as he lunged out into the night.

45

The puzzle was no longer the painting, but the harbour itself. Tonight, or rather this morning, it was a very different harbour from that depicted in the Picasso painting. The picture had assumed a warm summer night, warm enough for a woman with a bicycle to be wearing a summer frock and to be enjoying a double ice-cream. The picture had been suffused with moonlight or acetylene lamplight. Giant luminous-winged moths had reinforced the effect.

The reality was dark and chill, in spite of the grey suggestion of dawn in the sky behind Fort Carré. It was a feeling reinforced for Dominick Craufurd by a numbing sense of despair. Where were his children? Where was their governess? Was there any meaning in this shadowy harbour scene, except nothingness?

He had an instinct they would have come down to the harbour, perhaps to look for Dalio, but he would not have been prepared to lay too much money on his instinct. But what else did a man do, when he was stumbling from exhaustion and lack of sleep and frustrated misery, except to stare at the meaningless lapping of the water against the quays.

A blank canvas. A null waterfront. Was the meaning of the painting and the harbour nothing except death?

The glow of a cigarette approached in the demi-light. It was Jerome, rapidly smoking his way through another borrowed packet of Dominick's Players cigarettes.

'Why the hell don't you leave me alone?' Dominick snapped. 'I don't want anything more to do with you and your cut-throats.'

'I have made a tour of the harbour,' his old friend said in a kindly tone. 'There are no boats going out except just a party of Jewish children for the refugee ship.'

'Children? You said children?'

'They are not on the fishing boat. I made a very careful check.'

'Children. The *La Fontaine*.' Dominick twitched into life. 'For Christ's sake let's talk to the boatman.'

'There are so many children for the big ship,' the fisherman's glinting teeth grinned up at Dominick. 'All day. All night. How can I remember the children's faces? Besides, there are other boats.'

'They would have come down to the quayside here some time between twelve-thirty and two-thirty.'

'In the darkness all children look alike,' the fisherman gesticulated.

'My children are fair-haired,' Dominick shouted down into the fishing boat. He was conscious of the snobbery this assertion implied, but he was too tired and desperate to care.

'Dark-haired, fair-haired – in the darkness they are all the same.'

'So you saw two fair-haired children!'

'You will excuse me, Monsieur. The big boat is departing in an hour.' An engine vibrated into life. Dominick heard the plop of a rope landing on a deck. And suddenly a burst of disjointed phrases started to explode in his mind.

'Did you ever see the film of the sinking of the *Titanic* . . . ?'

. . . 'Amazing the effects they can achieve with lighting.'

'He must have the picture before morning.'

Stray phrases from Miss Hopkirk's Delphic telephone call which suddenly began to coalesce into a meaning.

And then a series of images began to swim into his mind's eye: shafts of filmed light playing on water; beams of luminosity glancing on waves, increasing to an intensity that defeated the camera, a white screen unable to convey anything more than a white screen; a fisherman staring into the camera, black shadows for eyes; a lot of meaningless footage, assuming those searching probes of light had no target but. . . .

'Did you ever see the film of the sinking of the *Titanic*? Audrey Hopkirk had asked, irrelevantly it had seemed to him at the time. But then he had been concentrating on the painting, and not on the reality. The reality of the situation at Antibes was that there was an obsolete luxury liner called the *La Fontaine* riding at anchor on the skyline, a mightily tempting target for anyone mad enough to want to bring the war to a few thousand helpless children. The Night Fisherman of Antibes had a mammoth fish to fry.

He hardly heard when the fisherman called from his slowly-moving craft. 'There were two children who spoke English. I don't remember if they were blond.' Dominick's instinct was racing to catch up with the weird twists of his old friend Michel André's mind.

Then the fisherman shouted again, 'Yes, a girl and a boy – English. Two trips ago.' And Dominick knew that his children were doomed.

On the far side of the harbour, under the sea wall, the final piece of the puzzle was ready to slot into place. But Dominick had not been looking at the far side of the harbour. The evasive ferryman had been occupying all his attention.

Even now as it moved out into the middle of the harbour, it did not invite special attention.

Another night fishing boat with lamps unlit, in deference to the black-out regulation, appeared to be making an unobtrusive exit from the harbour for a spot of illicit fishing on the more neutral sea. What was unusual, in Antibes harbour of all places, about a long boat with two small lamps mounted port and starboard, and a larger lamp mounted in front of the small cockpit on the bow? Or a crew of two men wearing berets, for that matter? Or the fact that they were carrying an outsize sack? There would have been nothing unusual if the boat had passed across Dominick's field of vision a quarter of an hour before. But just now the grey streak behind Fort Carré had broadened and lightened into a more passable impression of dawn. And Dominick saw that the fisherman who was standing near the main lamp had radiant blond hair.

A quarter of an hour ago it had been possible for the ferryman to say, 'Dark-haired, fair-haired, in the darkness it is all the same.' But now the blond hair of this fisherman gleamed like a strand of dawn under his beret.

'Bizet! Bizet! Bizet!' Dominick's exclamation ran round the gloomy harbour like a demented seabird's cry. And then he became unintelligible. 'The torch ... those bastards ... Oriana, Niall ... before she sails ... *La Fontaine* ... God help them!' Pieces of the puzzle falling back out of place.

But Jerome had eyes too. He had seen the fair-haired fisherman and he noted the unusual silhouette of his lamp – a monstrosity of a fishing lamp. And, if his friend was finding it difficult to express himself, he could not fail to notice that Dominick was struggling with the rope of a motor launch, the key to which the owners had almost certainly kept.

'No,' he said, laying a hand on his friend's shoulder. 'I know another boat, perhaps better equipped for us now. Besides, I am sure

Centurione Pugno will be pleased at the chance to settle accounts with our old friend.'

'No more alliances with the enemy!'

'Have you really any choice?'

And so, ponderously, slowly, *La Belle Bête* put to sea again. It cleared the twin lighthouses of the harbour mouth, just as the sound of the Italian army's dawn barrage started rumbling over the mountains. But no one on *La Belle Bête* was listening to the Italian army.

56

Sliding through the Straits of Gibraltar had been a calculated risk. But now *U436* had completed her voyage.

From his periscope, the U-boat commander surveyed the *mise-en-scène.* It was a peaceful enough night: just a few fishing smacks going about their predatory business – their acetylene lamps smouldering astern, like so many stars on the dark sea.

Far, far to the right loomed a larger shape.

It was the liner *La Fontaine,* crammed with at least double its normal complement of passengers – but then they were half the normal size.

57

The little blue fishing boat had, like all the others, a licence number from the municipality of Antibes (*numéro* 334976). It also, quite unnecessarily, carried a name, *Le Roi Oedipe,* scrawled in crazy orange Silly Symphony lettering on the side.

Two night fishermen were in the process of loading it up by the wharf, a process that drew wisecrack comments from other men in faded blue dungarees returning to port, their holds full of flailing loup de mer and red mullet. Over there past the double bastion wall of the inner harbour, the massive towers of Grimaldi Castle were just beginning to assert a heavy outline. The heavy starlit night was blushing at the edges, about to become suffused with just a hint of peach. It was a celestial moment, but it drew nothing but grunts from the two fishermen loading their equipment on to *Le Roi Oedipe.*

'*Merde,*' muttered one of them, turning to face the taunts of two hoary old fishermen, staggering across the quay with a huge sackful of lobsters. 'Don't you know the old proverb? The late fishers grab the juiciest flesh!'

If the two old men had a sackful of wriggling fish, the two late-night fishers had one too. But no one had time to stop and ask them why they were putting their catch on to the boat, rather than taking it off. Suddenly, with a staccato popping like an old machine-gun, the *Roi Oedipe* chugged out into the dark to be lost among the fading stars in the heavens and the bobbing stars in the deep.

Of course the wiseacre fishermen of Antibes were right.

The latecomers were in mortal danger of missing the catch.

Which in Michel André's book meant the difference of two and a half million deutsch marks in his numbered bank account in Zurich. He had been delayed so long, there was a strong possibility that the big metallic shark lurking down there somewhere in the waters off Antibes might have given up and decided to sink its teeth elsewhere.

For a perfect demonstration, Project Oedipus needed pitch black such as had existed for the past nine hours; although Georges Bizet did argue that, if his device could prove itself equally effective in half-light, it could be an even grander coup.

But what if the audience had grown tired of waiting? Michel needed *U436* because the whole test had been laid on for one passenger on it, and one man alone, a certain 'Hamburg Professor of Physics.' There was, however, an extreme contingency plan, to be exercised only in the direst need. Michel André decided to exercise it. He had decided to break radio silence and contact the U-boat direct.

'Oedipus awaits his golden pins ... ' was the message he was tapping out. 'Urgent ... Oedipus awaits his golden pins ... Oedipus awaits his....'

They were off-shore by over à mile and a half before Michel André got his confirmation.

It did not crackle over the radio. It manifested itself like a huge grey pipe arising from the deep. Beneath it dozed a killer shark, gently gliding towards its prey.

58

The two Craufurd children had inherited from their sometimes distant father a certain very British imperturbability. These genes had been reinforced by the unquestioned axiom of their early school days. The boy Niall and the tomboy Oriana both knew the hard fact – 'only sissies cry'. Which meant that the dark-haired diminutive passengers who crowded around the deck, tripping over ropes and soaking up handkerchiefs with their tears (not to mention wailing and chanting in a strange language which certainly was not Latin and least of all French), had simply not been to the 'right kind of place'. In fact, their lamentations were enough to make young Niall's lips curl with a kind of proto-cynicism.

He had been watching two very ugly seamen turning a wheel; and the anchors come scraping up, clanking against the ship's sides.

'What will he do, I wonder,' mused Oriana Craufurd, referring to the only meaningful 'he' in their young lives.

'Probably charter an MTB, I should think,' said her brother, turning over in his blazer pocket a gnarled conker with sixty-three victories to its credit.

'You mean an air-sea rescue ship?' asked his sister, no stranger to *Jane's Fighting Ships*.

'No, I mean an MTB. Bet they've got some docking in Toulon.'

'Well, he'd better hurry up,' said Oriana, who was made of less stern stuff than her brother. 'Liners are dangerous in wartime.'

'There aren't any U-boats in the Mediterranean, silly,' scoffed her brother. 'They'd never get past Gib.'

'Not so sure,' disagreed Oriana, an equally keen reader of *Wartime Weekly*. 'They said they'd never get into Scapa Flow.'

'Well, that was a fluke.'

It was a funny kind of voyage. Normally, when a liner got underway, it gave a triumphant departing blast on its hooter, and crowds at the jetty wished it godspeed as it gently slipped its moorings. But the *La Fontaine* was now moving fast out to sea without so much as a whisper, and to make matters more uncanny there was not a light to be seen aboard her.

Oriana was the first to spot it, but then her brother needed taking down a peg or two. She had been leaning against the rail watching the black oily waves part before the vessel's curving prow. Even when she spotted it, she said nothing, being determined to be sure of her facts. Finally, when there was no doubt, she turned cheekily to Niall.

'Well, clever face,' she mocked. 'If there aren't any U-boats in the Mediterranean, what's that periscope out there?'

59

It was like a valve in a radio, but not much bigger. It slotted in, an object like a bulb in a torch, but more elongated. It fitted neatly and easily into the acetylene lamp frame on the stern of the *Roi Oedipe*. And it could be said to serve the same purpose, to dazzle fish to their doom.

But there was something else to be done.

Michel André was busy pulling down the old triangular strip of brine-hardened canvas that did for a sail. In its place he roped up, with the ease of a man who understood yachts, something a shade newer and more shiny – a deep metallic silver. It certainly spruced up the *Roi Oedipe*.

'How about her?' asked Georges Bizet, gesturing to the writhing sack in the bottom of the boat.

'Oh, release her, but keep her gagged,' said André. 'She wanted a grandstand view. Let her watch if she can stand the glare.'

Audrey Hopkirk had had for over half an hour one fear, that she might choke to death. The codliver oil stinking sack in which she had been trussed became worse every moment. At the very bottom of it her fingers had encountered a huge reeking spider crab, which had somehow managed to get itself abandoned there, apparently for the last few weeks. When she had been tossed into the boat, every bone in her body had screamed out.

Now she was taking in deep gasps of air. The wind had changed to a sharpish north north-west and seemed to be made up of sparkling effervescent particles. She drew the ozone gratefully deep into her lungs.

At least she could now tiptoe gingerly about the fishing boat, although heavy snakelike coils of black wire made her progress difficult. The two men in their bleached-out blue overalls, black berets and spotty red scarves were too busy connecting up wires and points to take much notice of her. Round their necks flapped huge goggles, the kind First World War aces had been depicted wearing. When her eyes had got used to the black, she was surprised to find how light it was.

Back there, rolled up like an abandonded sea monster, was the rock outline of Antibes with Grimaldi Castle clearly recognisable on its promontory. With sharp eyesight (and Audrey Hopkirk's eyesight was exceedingly sharp), you could make out the life beginning to stir in the cafés along the quay, the concierges creeping out with their dustbins. And then her eyes followed the whole of that magnificent coastline dipping past Nice and swerving precipitously toward Cap Ferrat, towards Monte Carlo; and the sound of the Italian guns beyond.

The outer sea, now with the imminent bursting of dawn, the colour of very dark turquoise glass, was deserted. The only boat bobbing around was the one she was trying hard to balance herself in; for the rest, just the menace of those choppy layers of hard glass, banging almost metallically against one another.

And then her eyes took a nose-dive and she found herself once more down there by the black coils of the mackerel-stained sacking.

'She gets in the way,' complained Georges Bizet pettishly, groping with a fixture on his brand-new silver-screen quartersail.

'If she does it again, she goes overboard,' said a well-known voice, still with that well-remembered resonance which quite recently had sent other kinds of shivers down her backbone.

When she groped her hand round the gunwale and hauled herself up again she realised she must have shifted to the other side of the boat.

How had she ever imagined that this expanse of melting black glass was unpeopled? Something enormous was happening over there far to the left. A huge shadow was beginning to move out from its anchorings: *La Belle Bête.*

60

La Belle Bête was in full sail so as to catch any breezes that happened to be blowing. At the same time, the yacht's English Perkins engine was pumping out all the thrust it could generate. It was not exactly *bon ton* in Riviera yachting circles to use your engine power to supplement sail; but then Tenente Reggio of the Royal Italian Navy was unfamiliar with the traditions of Riviera yachting. By a desperate combination of crowded sail and a shuddering engine, *La Belle Bête's* new skipper was forcing the yacht through the water at a remarkable rate of knots.

But all the time the lumbering turbines of the old liner *La Fontaine* were building speed. It was gradually narrowing the gap between itself and the curiously-rigged night fishing boat. *La Belle Bête* was going to need an incredible gust of wind or a miraculous burst of power from its engine to get in between them.

'*Les yeux, les yeux, gardez les yeux!*' Dominick Craufurd was shouting through the yacht's loud-hailer as Tenente Reggio struggled to force *La Bête* to within easy hailing distance. Then he shouted in English, for what he hoped was his children's benefit, 'Lie down wherever you are and cover your eyes. Tell everyone to lie down and cover their eyes!'

Beside him on the deck, a grotesque figure was standing, which resembled nothing so much as the Walrus from *Alice in Wonderland.* It was dressed in a rubber suit, fully stretched particularly around the protruding stomach. Under the goggles strapped over the rubber head covering two human eyes and a nose peeped out, plus a moustache of near handlebar size. Centurione Pugno was not watching the crowded decks of the one-time luxury liner, his eyes were trained intently on the night fishing boat, and as he watched his thumb caressed the razor-sharp edge of a fishing knife. Jerome had guessed correctly; Centurione Pugno was eager to settle scores with the master-minds of *La Lumière Blanche.*

Georges Bizet had been too occupied with his preparations to notice that a new spectator was about to gatecrash the first full-scale demonstration of the White Light. Craufurd's loud-hailer alerted him. Once again, things were becoming perilously late for Michel André, but still not too late.

If anything, the yacht presented as curious a spectacle as his own eccentrically-rigged fishing boat and complement. André knew *La Belle Bête* of old. He knew its decks should by rights have been ornamented by elegant figures in blazers and white ducks and girls in fashions enabling them to show off bronzed shoulders and arms and even discreetly tanned bosoms. By rights, the sound of laughter and the tinkle of champagne glasses should have been audible on the decks. But the slowly spreading dawn illuminated a very different scene. The decks were packed with the dark silhouettes of men standing as rigidly as figures on a parade ground. He looked again, screwing up his eyes for better vision, and saw there was something even stranger about this crew. They were men dressed as fishes.

'Burn them!' he shouted at Georges Bizet. The sophisticate of Côte d'Azur society was losing much of his practised urbanity.

Dominick Craufurd saw the *Roi Oedipe* slowly wheel round to face them. As it did so, the silver sail which was mounted square-rigged where the jib ought to have been, shimmered with a dazzling reflection of the first sunlight of dawn. He took the loud-hailer from his lips. His mouth had totally dried.

Now he watched through binoculars, semi-hypnotised, as one of the night fishermen moved forward to swing the bogus acetylene lamp around until it was pointed upwards at the metallic sail. He tried to shout a warning but his tongue and lips were dehydrated.

And then the light went on.

Dominick did not understand why he was not blinded. The metallic sail had become a sheet of flame, as blinding as the sun seen through powerful binoculars. Why was he still able to blink at its obscene intensity?

The answer was that Georges Bizet was still range-finding. He had had to switch at short notice to a smaller target lying considerably lower in the water than the massive silhouette of the *La Fontaine*. As a result, a blistering white beam only brushed the triple mast tops of *La Belle Bête* and fastened on to the water about eighty yards away. Dominick looked behind him and saw a square patch of sea drained of all colour except white. Now this patch of terrifying radiance started to move, as Bizet adjusted his unique lamp and screen.

At last Dominick's mouth had moistened enough for him to be able to shout a warning. It was unnecessary. Centurione Pugno and several of his men were also watching the approaching carpet of snow-whiteness, and they were already experienced enough in Georges Bizet's special effects to know that frost was the last thing it would bring.

Even as Dominick started shouting in his fractured Italian, life-belts and rubber dinghies and anything else that would float were hurtling into the water, followed immediately by divers with thrashing fins.

And then the engine cut out.

For a vital few seconds Dominick hesitated. He had brushed aside Jerome's friendly suggestion that, like him, he should don one of these new-fangled frogman outfits. Now he wondered how long he would keep afloat wearing a blazer, a pair of trousers and suede shoes – there was only time to wonder, no time to strip. And perhaps, because the mind, if not the body, can move at incredible speed at such moments, he asked himself if he would somehow be deserting his children if he jumped. A split second later these questions became academic as the stern of *La Belle Bête* started to flow like the sun, and the decks turned into spreading rivulets of phosphorus. Dominick Craufurd had left himself no alternative but to hug the deck, with his hands clamped to his eyes.

'Now the liner,' Michel André called from the tiller. 'We musn't keep our German friends waiting.'

But Georges Bizet did not seem to be listening.

He was obsessed by the brilliant thing the tired old *Belle Bête* had become. He was almost tempted to pull off his goggles and examine minutely the full golden intensity of the miracle effects he had created, but of course he knew the experience could be blinding.

'Alors,' he muttered. *'Alors.'*

But the first full-scale experiment with *La Lumière Blanche* was by no means completed. The real test was still to come.

Impressive claims had been made in highly exclusive circles for the capability of *La Lumière Blanche.* A brief prospectus, of strictly limited circulation, promised the buyer that it was not only guaranteed to render a ship's crew sightless, it could also trap the ship itself in an irresistible cone of light from which it would be unable to escape. The principle of the 'Bounce' would ensure that a ship, or a fleet, or a convoy, glowed like beacons in the night until the submarines had done their work.

The precise technical specifications of the White Light awaited the cash deposit of the highest bidder. The highest bidder was Nazi Germany, and for this wealthy prospect the manufacturers had stretched a rule and agreed to mount a private demonstration.

Bizet waited with one thumb stuck into his mouth. In precisely three and a half more minutes the lamp would be generating enough heat to prove the point. The lamp would be switched off, but *La Belle Bête* would continue to glow like a beacon, trapped in a 'tennis ball' of light created between the yacht and Bizet's unique reflector sail. It had worked before, one revealing evening in his workshop. Would it work now, on the open seas at a range of over a thousand yards?

Of course it would. Of course it must.

'The ship of mercy,' Michel André snarled from the tiller, 'I have you on target for the ship of mercy. Please illuminate it for me.'

He loved the sombre genius Georges Bizet, as far as he could love anybody who did not talk. But his friend was beginning to tax this strictly limited amount of affection. His German clients were paying to see an ocean liner under the White Light and time was running out.

Reluctantly, Georges Bizet re-angled his reflector sail, then clambered into the cockpit in the bows to re-adjust his lantern. The final vindication of *La Lumière Blanche* would have to be delayed until the eyes went out on board the ocean liner.

61

They had the gun there (his memory of *Jane's Fighting Ships* said it was an 18-pounder), and it was pointed straight at them.

'Better keep here,' advised Niall, holding himself and his sister firm against the side-rail. 'It will give us a better chance of jumping clear before she finally scuppers.'

The surfaced submarine was so close you could see the Commander was watching through binoculars. You could see he was wearing a white polo-neck sweater. His cap was crammed jauntily down at an angle over his head. You could see his companions, too. When would he give the order to fire? Niall found he was biting hard on his lips, his sister's hot hand fluttered in his. Niall knew only one thing. The beliefs and certitudes of a short lifetime were on trial. His father had about sixty seconds left to make it. The scene was set for him, for Dad somehow to stroll in with one of his backhand rejoinders, with that quiet smile that assured them all would be well.

'It's too late,' said Oriana Craufurd, and every instinct in Niall's body echoed her pessimism.

'Funny goggles they've got,' he commented pointlessly, as, plain as a pikestaff, the small party on the U-boat conning tower handed round what looked like racing driver's heavy eye-shields.

The voice that came over the loud-hailer was at first too distant for the children to understand a thing it was saying.

'Shut up,' Niall screamed, 'stop that row.' Somebody out there was trying to warn them but he could not hear a thing thanks to the chanting going on all around them.

Then the voice came through nearer, clearing its throat, with a cough compounded of too many Player's Navy Cut cigarettes.

'Don't panic,' the gentleman, the English gentleman, at the loud-hailer urged them. 'Go downstairs, do it now. Don't panic, go downstairs, do it now.... Don't panic.... Cover your eyes.... Don't panic....'

Out of that curious ball of light to starboard, a yacht with flapping sails was drifting towards them. The decks were deserted except for one desperately gesticulating figure at the wheel. It was like something from a story Miss Hopkirk had read to them. They had forgotten who it was by.

62

The observers aboard the *U-436* were impressed. They had seen *La Belle Bête* lit up. They had seen ignominious ants diving into the sea. So far, so good. They were quite able to imagine the application of the principle to the dark waters of the Atlantic. Now they were impatient to observe the effect of *La Lumière Blanche* on a larger vessel, and, of course, they were anxious to examine the second and more stunning feature of the package – a ship stained permanently with radiant light.

63

They had refused to give her goggles, and they had tied her wrists behind her back. She had not dared to look at what had happened to *La Belle Bête* straight in the face; but she had been unable to resist peeping just once from under her bowed head. She supposed she was lucky she was not blind.

Audrey Hopkirk was glad she had come top of the class for gym. Otherwise she would almost certainly have reached the conclusion that her position was hopeless. As she had indicated to Dominick, her situation was real, not an episode of cinema where a girl with her wrists bound tightly behind her back inevitably came up against a jagged edge to cut her bonds with. 'Think of yourself as a ball, a tiny insignificant India rubber ball!' Audrey instructed herself as she drew her locked wrists across her trim bottom. Now came the difficult part. 'Imagine you are somebody with no legs,' she commanded her heart and soul, as with a suppressed scream of pain she drew her legs through the overstretched frame of her arms and bleeding wrists. 'Golly,' she thought, 'Miss Chelsfield was right. I *am* double-jointed!' Even so, what could a girl do with her wrists tied together in front of her? She could do one thing she had not been able to do before. She could raise her arms to the skies in outrage at the thing they wanted to do to the *La Fontaine.* In total darkness, they might have had some vestige of an excuse; but now it was grey pre-dawn and any woman, or any man, could see the pygmy figures packed on to the sun decks, like so many mice unable to leave a sinking ship. What else could she do? She could bring her bound hands down on the dark reverse side of the reflector sail, and pull and pull and pull until at last it started to separate from its fastenings.

It was unfortunate for the technician, Georges Bizet that this was the moment when his lamp beam hit his re-angled sail. Again the first principle of the White Light was triumphantly vindicated. Only it was a short circuit straight on to himself. He had time to pronounce a last word on this planet which was 'Mais .... ?' Then his whole face lit up like an electrocuted Guy Fawkes.

And then he was mercifully mantled by his own ingenious reflector sail, and Audrey opened her eyes to the spectacle of a shrouded, screaming figure pitching backwards into the water, a hooded shape trapped in a sudden inferno of light.

Michel André started to drag himself across the boat towards her. He had always moved with a slight limp, but previously this had been one of the attractive things about him. Certainly, the suave, interestingly crippled foreigner of the ice-cream parlour had mouthed nothing resembling the unrepeatable things he was telling her now. She was not in a mood to offer much resistance – she was still reeling from the astonishing thing she had done to Georges Bizet. Besides, her wrists were still tied. So she let him put his hands around her throat without too much of a struggle, and began to accept the idea of strangulation without too much heart-searching. After all, it had been on the cards since the evening began. So it was only the knife that came between her and immediate death. A blade suddenly thrust up between their feet and then started to work away like a shark at the woodwork of the fishing boat's hull. Perhaps Audrey Hopkirk had reached a greater degree of acceptance than had André. What was so extraordinary about one knife blade – no, two blades now – suddenly appearing at your feet on a bizarre night, or rather dawn, like this?

For Michel André, however, this upside-down intrusion of menace seemed to come as a genuine surprise. He looked away long enough to allow Audrey to get away to the cockpit, where the lamp was pointing at what remained of the stars.

Then he came on, despite the fact that the boat was now studded with knife thrusts (in one place a whole fist was showing through), despite the fact that the *Roi Oedipe* was springing water at all the incision points; and finally despite the fact that somebody was rocking the boat. He still had a few seconds to take evasive action. Bizet's lantern was still pointed at the stars. But he badly wanted to strangle her – this thing that had ultimately failed to arouse any emotion in him except red-hot hatred.

He kept on coming even when Audrey discovered the lamp's control lever and pulled it down out of the dimming stars. He kept on coming even when, with scorching finger-tips, she successfully angled the lantern into his face. His hatred seemed to have become his total motivation. And now it was a hatred that was literally blind.

He stumbled into her screaming with pain, but still totally intent on murder. She had to stand her ground. There was nowhere else she could fall back upon, except the sea. All she could do was to stand on tip-toe on the rocking prow of the *Roi Oedipe*. Later, she understood why he grappled her around her thigh, and started to exert maximum pressure with his thumbs. He had mistaken a thigh for a neck and all his hatred was directed towards the impossible effort of strangling a conventional area of desire. She did not struggle. She did not try to break free. A girl never took advantage of a blind man, especially when she happened to be the agent of his blindness. Besides, the boat was now rocking so violently it could only be a matter of time before she and her unseeing attacker were tumbled into the sea.

In fact, this is what happened next.

64

Someone had managed to get *La Belle Bête's* engines moving again, which was necessary because there was little wind, and the yacht had only one hand left on board.

But, under its sleek engine power, the craft was still formidable enough to convince an observer on the conning tower of the *U436* that this was not a vessel a submarine wanted to come into collision with. The observer tugged his superior's shoulder. The Commander of *U-436* unwillingly switched his attention from the ocean liner. Now he had to make a series of fast calculations. There was another factor, apart from the potential impact of stressed timber on exposed steel. His orders were that no U-boat was to be officially observed in Mediterranean waters. The Pact of Steel between Germany and Italy decreed that this was Mussolini's private sea. In the circumstances, the Commander had only one choice.

'Dive!'

The deck gunners had time to give *La Belle Bête* one spiteful shot before they had to scamper for the hatch, and the waters closed over *U-436.*

Blast. For one thing it was the first genuine dip he had taken for years in this melon-rind-ridden lake. Blast. The water was filthily cold, and he was in the act of shrinking a perfectly sound pair of trousers.

It was no time at night to go for a swim, and he had developed a hell of a headache. Also, he soon realised he was short of breath. It was not the thick black oil, clinging to his hands and arms. It was not the sea-weed clinging round his shoes and trousers. It was that blasted splitting headache, and the way that his eyes buzzed and gave him quadruple vision.

And then again it was not even that, as he splashed in a spirited imitation of a crawl towards that French launch straight ahead. It was what he had seen just a short time before.

That bloody grey silhouette welling down into the waters and his blasted yacht missing its damned conning tower by inches. Blast, bloody hell!

65

Audrey Hopkirk thought, I am drowning, but at least I'm not floating into the hereafter looking an absolute mess. She looked up to heaven, which was now a long way away and saw a brilliant shaft of light piercing the blue obscurity of the deep sea. She started to open her arms to it; but she found that her hands were still bound, and she recovered enough reason to decide this apparent sign from God was in fact the deadly beam of Georges Bizet's upturned lantern. The fish were not so percipient. They swayed towards it with all the stupidity of moths, and then as they hit the limelight started to rumba like animated creatures in a cartoon.

Audrey Hopkirk used her gymnastic legs to put a distance between herself and this light; but now she was unable to tell whether she was gaining height or losing altitude, surfacing or submerging. Everything suddenly became terribly muddled. She decided that she really was drowning.

And then she felt two firm hands around her waist. They were not the hands of God, unless God wore rubber sleeves, but slowly and surely they were bearing her up.

She was almost sorry when they surfaced.

'I love Constable,' her goggled partner panted, 'if you love him. If you say so, I will swear Sir Alfred Munnings is a better painter than Mantegna, because I adore you,' Jerome di Cavazza confessed, peeling off his goggles.

66

Dominick Craufurd could see the *La Fontaine* well over a mile away under full steam, for where? – it had to be French North Africa. Well, at least there was no U-boat visible any longer. Choking in yet another mouthful of sea water, he swivelled round, expecting to see the surface teeming with Italian frogmen, but not a ghost of one. He heard the quick throb of engines, loud enough, near enough, to penetrate beyond his colossal headache. He splashed round to see that black prow making straight for him. Then it swooshed past.

He grappled for a rope that seemed to be dangling somewhere above his head like a hangman's. At the second try, he managed to catch the bastard and cling to it. He stayed on *La Belle Bête,* but amazingly he could still see: bumping his way up the side, bouncing off its sides like a music hall marionette; emerging on to the deck to see in a haze that face which seemed to have been haunting him all these last few days; collapsing into Jerome's arms, whilst she (yes, *she*) bent over him to kiss him on the cheek, the loveliest girl in the world – for someone.

'My dear friend, you do look a sight,' said Jerome with a mixture of irony and concern.

'You saved her. I didn't know you could handle a pair of flippers.'

'And you saved them getting those engines coughing again, I didn't know you were a motor mechanic,' said Jerome wistfully.

He looked down at his hands. The old engines of the *Belle Bête* had coughed out their life blood on to his palms.

67

He had searched for it in every mooring place hidden along this rockily fragmented coast, he had slit a few leathery throats, inundated a sizeable number of Gauloise-infected lungs for it. And at least he had known it would be something he could wrap his huge hands around, something solid he could hug to his heart, a genuine contraption, not a puzzle in a picture.

But now it was slipping away from him, burrowing down into the recesses of the sea as if it had been a meteorite tumbling from heaven; turning the murky cavities below into something more startlingly aglow than daylight, whilst the multi-coloured fish spun off from its tumbling path in blinded shoals.

He slipped his knife out of the flaccid flesh of this drowning albino frog, his hair hanging like blond seaweed, adjusted his goggles and, closing his eyes tight, plunged down into the deep. A Pugno did not let things slip through his fingers, his only worry was that the thing's vicious luminosity might somehow cauterize and sizzle into shreds the black rubber of his suit.

An eel-like wriggle of his flippers, and the light was searing through eyelids and goggles, imprinting in his retina nightmarish silhouettes of blood-red fish, burning with an intensity that made them swim into his brain.

Now he knew that eyes are jelly and jelly melts, but to do this thing for Il Duce's fleet would be worth a white stick and a dark room in the naval hospital upon Capodimonte. The light held his brain, his eyes, from other matters. So Pugno did not notice a slimy presence lurking in his vicinity, blacker and more lethal, if similarly bodied, than a killer shark. And it did not notice him. With periscope down, it was effectively blinded. The U-boat commander felt the mildest of shudders coming from the prow end; it was the moment the cleaving front sliced through the frogman's backbone. Centurione Pugno died with his rubber-gauntleted hands actually around the circumference of *La Lumière Blanche,* pulling it in towards his heart.

The Catch

68

The police boat powered through the waves in hot pursuit of the *La Fontaine.*

'There's a saying currently going the rounds that may help you,' Dominick told Inspector Clément. 'Do not think – obey.'

'Do not think, obey . . . for a police officer that is impossible. You cannot stop him turning over evidence and wondering.'

'You are right of course,' agreed Dominick, finding a soaked Players packet in his trouser pocket and tossing it into the sea. 'At least we can be sure of one thing. That infernal Picasso's a red herring.'

'The most puzzling aspect . . . ' started Inspector Clément.

'Do not think. Obey,' as the police boat swung astern of the *La Fontaine* and Dominick raked it with his binoculars, trying to spot two young Craufurds.

69

Where the hell had they gone? What was the bloody Italian ponce up to? He had hurriedly changed his clothes. He had literally kicked his children into bed with orders never to wander out again without express permission or he would tan their backsides blue.

'Don't let me catch so much as one peep out of you,' he thundered as he splashed the dregs of a siphon of soda into his whisky. At what point had Audrey ceased to be the sort he could rely on? He expected at worst to see them canoodling on the sofa or rolling about on his bed. No such luck.

The only trace that they had ever been there was the ghastly grey police blanket that Audrey had folded and left on the chest in the hall.

So he slumped down in his favourite armchair and stared at the ceiling, reading the riddle of its yellow flaking paint.

'Not a dicky bird out of them,' he thought, the only messages which had been shoved through his letterbox being an account due from the Yachting Club, and a threat from the electricity people to disconnect unless money was parted with *tout de suite.*

And, because he had had one hell of a night and was not quite in tip-top physical condition, he closed his eyes and snoozed off there and then.

He had been out how long? Five minutes, half an hour?

There was the strong certainty that somebody else was in the room, close to him, that made him open his eyes.

'Well, Miss Hopkirk . . .' was what he was preparing to say. But the thing before him was singularly un-Hopkirkish.

It more resembled a gnome, somewhere between a gnome and a monkey with its merrily piercing eyes which seemed to be engaged in a subtle game of smirking at the antics of all humanity. He was something else too – a sorcerer, magician, conjuror.

'Monsieur Craufurd,' uttered the owner of the most enigmatic eyes in Europe. 'I wonder if we have. . . .'

'Never formally, Monsieur Picasso,' said Dominick, rising to his feet. 'I believe we have great friends in common, however. And in my small way I do dabble in the arts. Incidentally, I thought you were staying in Royan now, at least that's what the papers say.'

'In these times it pays to make a little smokescreen, no?' asked the painter. 'But you know why I come . . . I have mislaid a certain picture.'

'A picture?' Dominick suddenly reddened.

'It is only a painting, but it has somehow hung in my mind.' The older man turned his luminous eyes towards the mantelpiece where the hideously mutilated canvas was still placed. 'It was just a sketch, the germ of an idea I later developed on a somewhat larger scale. I was merely curious to see it again.'

'I don't know how I can begin to explain.' Dominick stammered. 'I can assure you I meant no disrespect. You see, I had a suspicion. . . .'

'That it wasn't one of my most satisfactory works?' the painter gave him what passed for a wink, a bit quizzical, a touch malevolent too.

'I'm not much of an expert, although, as I said, I deal in pictures a bit. It's all very difficult, very embarrassing. It wasn't the picture itself. I was interested in what was behind it.'

'As you see there was nothing behind it.' The painter cocked a mischievous eye towards the ravaged canvas.

'God knows what it cost. A million francs? In that case I'm afraid I can't pay you back. This war has cost me about the last bean I have. I suppose I'll have to go back to prison.'

'Do you think I might sit down for a moment? I seem to have been travelling for the past three days.' Five minutes later Picasso was sitting there, a glass of cooking brandy in his hand, fixing him with the look which had puzzled a generation.

'Tell me all, what you suspected about my picture,' he had asked.

And Dominick thought as a gentleman he was obliged to do just that.

When he had finished, Picasso got up, drained his glass and shook Craufurd cordially by the hand.

'Thank you, Captain Craufurd. You have done me a favour by destroying my picture. The thought gives me enormous pleasure. You have done me a great service. The sketch had all the crudity of the first draft. It was quite artless.'

It was as he escorted Picasso through the deserted restaurant and out onto the quay that the painter gave him some clue.

'You see, the real picture, *Night Fishing at Antibes,* is safe. Already it is a subject for discussion. Is it a premonition of this terrible war that has now overtaken us, a dialogue between predator and prey? Or is it a piece of sexual symbolism – two men, two idly watching women? Or is it yet again a perverse pastiche on that delightful picture by a seventeenth-century Dutch artist in the Louvre, Nicolas Maes I think his name is. All these are very engaging theories. But the picture wears a mask, as we all try to do, but not like the sketch. Please try and understand me, the picture *Night Fishing at Antibes,* which is now I gather safely in America, was a new departure for me. The art histories will say I was wandering with a certain lady after dark in the evening on this very quay in late summer. The thought came to me, I splashed it down straight away. Picasso had acquired spontaneity. No scratchings out, no fumbling sketches. Now that, Captain Craufurd, is a nice legend, it flatters an ageing man.

'There is another reason why I am grateful to you for anticipating what I proposed to do personally,' Picasso said, turning round to shake Dominick's hand. 'I painted the sketch at the suggestion of someone else, and that's never a sensible thing to do, particularly as the person in question was a young man whose judgment was sometimes questionable. You will notice I was particular not to sign the sketch.'

Dominick Craufurd watched the small figure shuffle off across the quay, off his stage.

Then he returned to his flat and his mantelpiece. No signature? No date? His distinguished visitor was right about the signature, but surely there had been a date! The blow-torch had left the bottom right-hand corner of the painting uncharred; he clearly remembered that the flame had not touched the date – whatever it had been. But someone had. A small, but significant rectangle had been cut clean out of the canvas where the date should have been. The incision looked as if it had been freshly made.

On the mantelpiece itself he found a scribbled note from Miss Hopkirk.

'Dear Captain Craufurd,

You must be beginning to despair of me. I'm sorry. All I can say is that this time I've been abducted quite voluntarily. Perhaps the events of the last few days have made us all a bit potty. Anyway, I'm afraid I'm mad about your friend the Tenente. He says he's keeping a souvenir of the picture just to remind him of what we've all been through. He asks you please not to follow him. It would bring us bad luck.

Your very apologetic servant,
Audrey

'A souvenir!' Dominick swore to himself. 'The girl's a bloody fool.' But on reflection he decided it was he who was the fool. He had never looked at the date on the picture.

70

'Good morning, Captain Craufurd,' Inspector Clément was calling cheerfully from the landing, 'it's a better morning today.'

'It's a bloody awful morning,' a hollow-eyed Dominick told him when he had released the chain on his apartment door. 'If you've come for Cavazza it's too late. The bird has flown.'

'It's a better morning for the alliance of our two countries,' Clément insisted. 'Haven't you heard the news. The Government is breaking off Armistice negotiations with the Germans. It is going to Africa to continue the fight. At least there is a spark of hope.'

There had been many sparks of hope for France during the disastrous last fortnight. There had been the hope that President Roosevelt would weigh in with the United States Army. There had been the hope that Churchill's dramatic offer of union between the two countries would bring the RAF back to France. There had been the hope that the replacement of Prime Minister Reynaud by Marshal Pétain would somehow work a miracle. Here was another vain hope.

'Quite so. *Vive la France*!' Dominick sighed.

'Once again we are allies.' Clément would not let the hopeless hope go. 'We will fight on together. You in England. We in Africa. There will be no surrender.'

'Like the Marne. Like the German offensives in 1918, these disasters could be a blessing in disguise, a prelude, perhaps, to victory,' Dominick repeated the most hackneyed thought of this disastrous summer. Clément noticed his lack of conviction and also his air of impatience.

'Are you going anywhere, Captain Craufurd?' he enquired with slightly narrowing eyes. Now he had noticed the packed Gladstone bag at Dominick's feet.

'Nowhere in particular, Inspector. But these days we all have to have our luggage ready.'

'He's going to the frontier, Inspector....'

'Shut up, will you!'

'He's going to the frontier to find Miss Hopkirk and Uncle Jerome,' a voice was piping behind Dominick's shoulder. 'It's not fair because he won't take us with him,' Oriana Craufurd obligingly gave the game away.

'You should have told me you were going to the frontier. I could have perhaps arranged to give you a lift.'

'Look, Inspector. Your people gave us a lot of help with Michel André, but I don't believe you're really in the business of catching Italians, are you? Yes, if you want to know, I'm going to find Signor Cavazza, but I don't think your Commissioner Lazzaron would approve of what I intend to do to him.'

'Commissioner Lazzaron does not represent France,' the young Inspector answered with a gleam in his eyes.

'So why not leave it to me, call it a personal vendetta,' Craufurd sighed, making an attempt to slam shut the door. He was not being subtle or tactful, it was difficult to be either in his state of fatigue. Inspector Clément was less fatigued. He inserted a substantial shoe between the door and its frame.

'What you are seeking is the property of the republic of France,' he said harshly. 'I will tell you something else, Captain Craufurd, I have seen enough of this light to know it could save France.'

'I am seeking my children's governess. It's really as simple as that,' Dominick evaded with all the English self-righteousness he could mobilise. 'I don't want to go through this war, if I can help it, constantly having to engage new governesses. Miss Hopkirk is a gem I would find very hard to replace in present circumstances.'

He liked Clément. He thought he was probably an honest and patriotic Frenchman. But, even so, he was convinced that the key to *La Lumière Blanche* was not for France. Conditional surrender was what the new Pétain government was all about, whatever today's news suggested. The key to *La Lumière Blanche* would come in very handy to a government looking to buy a little peace and quiet.

'The government is going to Africa to continue the fight,' the Inspector insisted. 'Mr Churchill will be pleased. You should be pleased. Like him you should show more trust in your ally.'

'I don't want to waste your time, that's all, Inspector,' Dominick lied.

'*La Lumière Blanche* is not wasting my time – or France's time. Would it interest you to know that the Italian Cavazza and his English female companion have been sighted on the coast road to the Italian frontier?'

Yes, it did interest Dominick.

'My car and my police siren are at your disposal,' Clément said. 'We will share the journey and we will share the discovery. As Mr Churchill has said, we are inseparable allies, are we not?'

71

At least the news that the Government was transferring to Africa had impressed the Prefect for the Province. On the off-chance that the war could be on again, he decided to act on the pile of confidential memoranda that Inspector Clément had created on his desk.

As Clément and Craufurd were driving eastwards through Cagnes-sur-Mer, a detachment of *Gardes Mobiles* was leaping from battleship-grey lorries outside a nearby villa.

They half-expected to be fired upon. So, when a pistol shot puffed at a window, they hit back with rifle fire, grenades and smoke bombs.

Commissioner Lazzaron was brought out on a stretcher. In fact he was only lightly wounded by a shrapnel splinter in the forearm, but his face was twisted in an agony of outrage.

'Idiots, fools, pigs,' he was shouting, 'don't you realise I'll be back in business in a couple of days and with a bigger stick. Do you know what I am going to do to you when my pals move in, I'm going to have you skinned alive!'

One group of aliens came out staggering from an earlier shock than the assault of the *Gardes Mobiles*. This was the little posse of men who had been sheltering at Commissioner Lazzaron's since their ordeal by blinding during the night-time attack on the villa of Les Ombres. In contrast to others of his comrades, Manipolo Battaglia was smiling. They had brought him out into the sunlight, and through the bandages he could see it was sunlight. He tugged off his bandages and to his astonishment he found he could see.

72

'Carina,' he lisped. *'Carinissima.'*

The words were prescribed magic. In fact they were just what a Latin lover should be saying at this particular milestone in a young girl's life, but they rang oddly wrong even to her ears.

The terrible truth of the matter was that, for all his china-blue eyes, fair hair and pale soft skin, the thing just had not been the roaring, raging success of the decade. In fact it had left her just about as empty as last year's sack of potatoes, and a shade disgusted with herself. All of which seemed to suggest something either wrong with her, or distinctly uncomplimentary about her Latin lover.

Audrey Hopkirk remained on the bed and pulled the thin coverlet high over her face, thus leaving her toes wriggling and exposed. Slumming had its advantages. There was a hole in the threadbare sheet big enough for one eye to peep through. Suddenly she had felt the need to keep Tenente Jerome di Cavazza under close scrutiny.

She had disguised it cleverly enough, fluttered her eyelids and closed them tight at the right moment, but Jerome was not deceived. He had added her to his list at the price of killing something in his soul.

Those fresh apples had tasted sourer than he had hoped. Even young apples could have maggots in them. Certainly this bed had; those slippery sheets, the pea-green lilies on the flaking wallpaper, the mattress that creaked under them; that live wire that vaguely connected to the table lamp.

And who was she to criticise with her amateurish fumblings? No make-up, nothing under the eyes, nothing much on the lips. Who was it who said all English girls were virgins at heart? And now she was pretending to sleep. All right, let her – he had other work to do. He left her on her bed and wandered on to the room's pathetic balcony.

He had a grandstand view this afternoon, all the way across Menton harbour from this ludicrous boarding-house on Cap Martin. At the extreme east, the port was clearly in Italian hands. Mussolini's army had managed to advance two hundred or so yards in ten days. But, by the *plage* and the Avenue Georges V in the middle of the town, the French against all odds were still holding out round that mausoleum of a Casino: the one with the twitchy croupier, a no luck place for Jerome. Well, today he had the combination *par excellence*, the unbeatable one, a postage stamp of scrappy canvas with a number scrawled on it. The morning that shuffling croupier would be forced to hand over the biggest winnings seen in Menton for years, that was something to look forward to. From there to final success was a mere scamper across a line not more than a few hundred yards away, and slowly advancing westwards to meet him.

Which left just one more thing . . . he turned to face the heap on the bed. The dark eye watching him through the hole in the counterpane had never seen exactly that expression on the face of Jerome di Cavazza. It was a cold look of intense dislike. The eye goggled as he moved stealthily towards the wardrobe where his jacket hung. She was off the bed and out of the room whilst he was still feeling for the Beretta in his pocket.

The shrilly cornering army truck almost overturned her. But then she was running wildly, her hands holding her skirt above her waist, her whole body intent on just that one thing.

Her eyes were like an animal's, a hunted animal's. She collapsed into the *poilu's* arms in a torrent of tears.

73

'You have an instinct about Menton,' Inspector Clément said, as they left Cagnes on the curving coast road to Nice. 'Or is it only an instinct?'

'Cavazza is making straight for his lines,' Craufurd answered tersely. 'That means he's bound to head for Menton.'

'Forgive me, Captain Craufurd,' the young policeman smiled earnestly, 'but we have all had an exhausting twenty-four hours, and you have been sleeping. Did you know you talk in your sleep, Captain Craufurd? In your sleep you were talking about the Casino at Menton. I wonder, why the Casino?'

How did you explain a hunch, or feeling, based largely on a hint Audrey had perhaps unwittingly let drop – Jerome's odd request not to follow him or it would bring him bad luck. Why should Jerome have bad luck on his mind when he seemed to have torn off with the clinching piece of the jigsaw, and the companionship of the girl into the bargain?

'Don't let's play the Casino at Menton,' Jerome had begged him once. 'It always brings me bad luck.' Well, how did you explain the ghost of a hunch like this to a practical Frenchman like Inspector Clément, assuming you wanted to explain it to him?

In a way he was relieved at the diversion.

A stream of Rolls, Daimlers and other unmistakably British cars was approaching them down the coast road. The convoy of British diplomats and expatriates from Menton, Nice and environs had finally got on the move. Now it was heading for its rendevous at La Croe where it would pick up a certain Royal Duke and his Duchess before proceeding to the Spanish frontier. The convoy was so vast that Inspector Clément had to slow into second to get past it.

Philip Hickson-Smith spotted Dominick from the driving seat of a Riley packed with elderly passengers and sea trunks.

'Where's that infernal picture, Craufurd?' his pink face spun round to scream. 'I left it all to you, but I gather it's my head that's on the chopping block. I understand there's going to be hell to pay when I get back to London!'

Further down the line of cars, a feathered maroon hat burst out of the rear window of a Daimler.

'Dominick, you cad, you deceived us all. You're going to Villefranche to welcome the Italians! Tootsy, Tootsy,' Dolly Orient pecked with her crimson fingernails on the glass partition that separated her from her general factotum. 'Tootsy Walpole, turn round at once. We're going to join Captain Craufurd at the victory celebrations in Villefranche.'

'Why don't you shut up, you grotesque old bean-pole,' Quintin Thorne suggested sourly. 'I don't want to be raped by the Italian army, even if you do.'

An era was passing.

74

All yesterday the Alps had been echoing with the noise of heavy artillery. Yesterday was 20 June, 1940, the day when the Prince of Piedmont, with the urgent promptings of Rome, opened his all-out offensive. The French were asking for an Armistice. There was no time to lose.

This morning the guns had started again dead on time at 5.30 a.m. The naval Commander was up early too. He was pacing the platform of Ventimiglia station, like a man waiting for a long overdue train.

He had other things on his mind than the Prince of Piedmont's offensive; but this trained ear could not help overhearing its fate. The sound of the big guns was coming from precisely the same direction as on the day before, which meant that the offensive was getting nowhere.

Well, let those fool soldiers play at their incompetent games, he thought to himself, the merciful thing is that it was still quiet on the Menton front.

The naval Commander had received a signal from Antibes. It indicated that Reserve Tenente Cavazza's mission had been successful. He had the key to *La Lumière Blanche,* and it was Italy's alone. There was only one fly in the balm, this message had applied to the naval Commander's mind. The message had also indicated that Cavazza would be attempting to come out through Menton. Didn't they understand that Menton was a battle zone? Had they never heard of the sea route?

By incompetence or good fortune, the guns on the Menton front had stayed silent. Here there was only the occasional cackle of machine-gun fire. The Commander was praying there would be no more activity until Cavazza was safely through the lines.

Another steam engine was sweating into the station. The Commander gave it only half a glance. For a week he had been watching troop trains steaming into Ventimiglia station with troops that were going nowhere. But now a cheery voice was calling to him by name. The Commander turned to see the Alpine-bronzed, moustachioed face of his friend Colonel Grimaldi. Behind him, stern-faced men in steel helmets and full packs were clambering down from the train. Colonel Grimaldi's regiment of Alpini had abandoned their feathers and casual mountain fighting gear. They were dressed for a full-scale shooting war.

'It's good to see you,' the affable Colonel greeted him. 'You must be in a pretty bad way if they have to pull the Second Alpini out of the mountain fighting and bring us all the way down here to the sea.'

'I have a man down there in Menton,' the Commander told him. 'You know him, I believe, a Lieutenant di Cavazza. I want him brought out in one piece. I will tell you why....'

The whistles of officers and NCO's started to blow and the finest body of men the Commander had seen on Ventimiglia station fell in and marched off in the direction of the frontier.

Then, as a mighty supplement of their tramping feet, the guns on the Menton front suddenly woke up.

What the Commander had been dreading had happened. The Prince of Piedmont's big guns had been switched to the Menton front.

75

'Yes,' they told them at the next roadblock, 'a car passed this way, a man and a girl. The man was a police officer on an urgent mission concerning the evacuation of gold deposits from Menton. He had all the required papers.'

'The man was an Italian agent!' Clément shouted furiously through the car window. They studied his papers with more than usual suspicion, and seemed reluctant to let them through.

At Pont-St Louis, a little town of major strategic significance in that it commanded access to both the Corniche and the coast road, they were waved down at a roadblock which had been reinforced by two Renault tanks.

No, they had not seen a man and a young girl. No, there was no question of proceeding further. Beyond was no-man's land. The sound of the Prince of Piedmont's artillery barrage was making conversation difficult.

Clément brandished his papers in the helmeted sergeant's face, swearing at him like a brothel-keeper. The sergeant answered back in unprintable argot. Both men had to shout to make themselves heard above the noise of the guns.

The only word that Dominick could understand – his public school French studies had at no point embraced these obscenities – was 'officer.' Clément was demanding to see the sergeant's superior officer, and the sergeant was not impressed. Finally, in a spasm of fury, Clément stepped out on to the road. Now he was engulfed by shouting enlisted men with rifles and fixed bayonets. It was at this moment that Dominick slid over into the driving seat.

Clément seemed to have made his point. Surrounded by a shouting escort of *poilus* of near platoon proportions, he was striding towards the command post about fifty yards off the road.

If he was ever going to lose the good Inspector Clément, this was the moment. Clément had left the engine running. All he had to do was to put the Citroën into second and step on it. In fact this was not quite all he had to do.

He had to drive the Citroën up on to the rocky shoulder of the road to by-pass a Renault tank, and then he had to get enough acceleration to smash through the barbed wired pole they had slung across the road behind the tanks. And then he had to keep his head down as the *poilus* opened up with their Lebels and a machine-gun started chattering in the turret of a tank. Difficult to tell whether it was a rifle or machine-gun bullet that shattered the rear window and snarled away through the roof. The important thing was that it was not the windscreen that shattered. He needed all the vision he could get to drive down into Menton on a road that was being blanketed by shellfire.

'What are you trying to do? What the hell are you trying to do, Craufurd!' he heard himself shouting at himself; but he did not hear the answer. Was it from love of country or love of a governess that he was driving straight into the Prince of Piedmont's three-corps offensive?

It really was not such a conincidence that he should see her walking along the Promenade Georges V. The town seemed to be deserted, except for the odd dog and the occasional party of French army demolition experts, scuttling away from their latest big bang. What was curious was the way she looked.

Her face was a mess but she was dressed in the height of fashion. She was wearing a sumptuous black picture hat that would undoubtedly have turned heads in the Bois de Boulogne and her dress was a lilac-coloured evening gown. As accessories, she was wearing elbow-length white gloves and in one hand she was twirling a silk parasol.

'I'm afraid I've been looting,' she confessed, when he had slammed on the brakes and joined her on the once-elegant pavement of the Promenade. 'Isn't it what a smart woman does when a love affair's turned sour – not looting, I mean, but dolling up? I mean, she doesn't sit around moping, she flounces off and buys herself a brand new wardrobe – glad rags. At least that's what I've read somewhere. Of course I didn't have any money to buy glad rags. But, honestly, you really can help yourself here.'

She swept off her black picture hat and made a little bow. 'From Mademoiselle Chanel's spring collection,' she explained. 'And this,' she gestured down to her lilac gown and struck a mannequin's pose, 'a Lanvin original! You ought to smell my scent, too,' she said, 'it's pretty *haute couture* as well.' And then she burst into tears.

There were shells bursting too, a mushroom of smoke was rising from the nearby Avenue Edouard VII. And, further along the seafront, a grand hotel was blazing. Italian shells and French demolition work were sending violent echoes ricocheting around the blue escarpments that surrounded the picturesque resort.

'The truth is I look awful and I feel awful,' Audrey Hopkirk sobbed, 'I think it's because I'm tired and I've had rather a rough time recently, and perhaps I hate myself for stealing, even though the window of that beastly chic little shop was smashed wide open. But also I do feel a little shop-soiled, a little fallen, if that's how a fallen woman is supposed to feel – the stinker! I must look a terrible fright.'

There was something in what she said. Audrey had been experimenting with cosmetics too. She had brushed her eye-lashes with mascara, tried to accent her eyelids with green shading, and daubed her cheeks with a random selection of powders and rouges. Her lips were garish with a new shade of lipstick. Now her tears were turning an untidy series of experiments into a bad water-colour painting.

'You look beautiful, absolutely top-notch.' Dominick thought he lied gallantly.

But, when she buried her face in his blazer and put a white-gloved hand on his shoulder, he realised he was telling the truth. The powder and the rouges, the mascara and the lipstick were ruining his blazer, but somehow he did not mind at all.

'You look completely bewitching, Miss Hopkirk,' he said with conviction this time. 'You look so marvellous I want to take you to the Casino – and show you off to everybody.'

76

Pierre, the head croupier of the Casino Municipal de Menton, emerged with his usual flattened Tibetan expression. He came up the marble stairs with his famous slouch, seeming to locomote his arms more than his legs.

He did not react to the earthquaking of this huge marble mausoleum dedicated to the newly discredited Goddess of Luck. He did not bat a dead eyelid at the flashes of gunfire or at the fact that, outside the security of this safe and poker-faced place, the graves of Hell were opening up all around.

He did not seem to react either to the fact that Jerome's revolver was shoved between two of the larger creases of his thick neck; or that the Tenente's hand was shaking on the trigger, whilst the safety mechanism had been clearly snapped off.

'This time you do not fix the wheel,' Jerome told him. 'This time you're opening up your safe. Tonight, Pierre, is my night.'

'If you want to play again, of course we can accommodate you,' Pierre mouthed in his famous hoarse whisper, which could still somehow carry right across a crowded Salle de Jeu. 'And who knows? maybe you lose again, eh?'

'Ah, that's good, my friend.' Jerome sank the revolver still tighter into these interlocking folds of skin. 'Your fangs are showing. But tonight I have a certain combination. Do you understand what I mean?'

'Of course this is a shade unusual,' wheezed Pierre. 'Normally there are other gentlemen, other players.'

'I play alone. Against the bank. Turn on the lights.'

'Electricity, it seems unnecessary.' Pierre gesticulated at the noisy daylight.

'On the contrary, we use the lights, and we draw the shutters,' Jerome told him, pushing his victim into the middle of the room whilst he edged back towards the huge shattered window at the end. 'It is important to see what we are doing.'

Dominick had never entered the Casino Municipal de Menton in quite the same way before. A flick of a smile to Louis the bewigged hall porter, a flick of a coin to his taxi driver, a slight pause before he ascended the staircase, a reassuring twist to his black bow tie – this was the normal way.

Today, it was a scuttling run across a street, straight across the arc of fire vision of a French machine-gun post, a smothered curse as a piece of barbed wire ripped a gash in his trousers, right hand pulling Audrey behind him. There was another way in, as Dominick knew very well, an alternative to the showy façade on the Avenue Carnot. It was an obscure back door where the evening Veuve Cliquot was wont to be delivered. This was not the way a gentleman would approach a gambling house, but Dominick Craufurd had no alternative.

Along the Avenue Carnot Fiat tanks were nosing forward, albeit cautiously. The battle for the Casino was assuming a certain ferocity, as though it was for the soul of France. The dust-sheet-covered gaming tables of the Salons de Jeu stood there silent and morose, for the moment decidedly *démodé.* The huge roulette wheel, pride and joy of Pierre, stood still. There was no one to be seen, but then they heard voices. And Dominick knew his journey had not been wasted.

For a split second he looked both startled and guilty, like a small boy caught in a neighbour's tomato shed. Then he was instantly Jerome di Cavazza again.

'My dear Dominick, this is unexpected. I thought you were taking a much-needed rest. And Miss Hopkirk....'

At the same time his revolver moved from the small of Pierre's back to look Dominick straight in the stomach.

'I don't know who invented it,' Craufurd drawled, 'but I do seem to remember some rule to the effect that a gentleman never brings firearms to the gaming table.'

'Perhaps I'm not quite a gentleman,' Jerome suggested, flicking a curious glance at Audrey.

'I'm sure the Craufurd blood is a bit mixed too,' the Englishman answered. 'I'm fully prepared to use this ungentlemanly bulge in my pocket if you want to play at cowboys. Seriously, Cavazza, why don't we both put our guns under the safe keeping of the excellent croupier I see you've conscripted. I've always found Pierre the soul of reliability.'

'What's the game, Craufurd?' asked Jerome with a shrug, strolling over to the green table and flicking his revolver like some *pourboire* towards the croupier.

'I thought you were going to tell me.' Dominick followed suit. 'But I wouldn't in the least mind a go at roulette....'

'Messieurs, les jeux sont faits,' wheezed Pierre.

'Vittoria,' yelled Colonel Grimaldi, standing there astride the Fiat tank in the Rue de la Republique, arms waving in the air like one of Garibaldi's redshirts. *'Vittoria.'*

The tank gunner grunted and shot a marble statue of Justice clean off its plinth on the Hôtel de Ville. Similar images of Trade, Prosperity and the Law crumbled too. Seizing his pistol, the Colonel urged his tank crew forward. Behind him followed a sprinkling of soldiers, cursing most colourfully beneath their steel helmets.

'Now we shall capture the Casino,' Grimaldi roared.

'You may be a madman, but you're nobody's fool,' Dominick Craufurd was saying. 'You didn't kick old Pierre out of his shelter just to have a flutter at roulette. So what's the game?'

He had played some pretty funny ones in his life; but this had to go on record as the most bizarre ever.

And one of the most bizarre things about it was that Menton had never been Jerome's course. In fact, the place had a decidedly jinxing effect on him. To his certain recollection he had never come out of the Menton Casino with a centime in his pocket. So why the Casino at Menton?

'He tore the date from the picture. He has it on him. It must be some kind of code,' Audrey whispered.

Of course it was some kind of code. He had been the biggest of chumps not to have thought of it before. But, if you were as clever and as perceptive as Jerome di Cavazza, why didn't you run like a hare for your own lines? Why did you stop to play roulette in an exploding no-man's land?

'The game is chance, as it always is,' Jerome told him with a brilliant smile.

For his first throw, Jerome had put his chips on 25. Then he stood up, put his hands in his pockets and, whistling through his teeth, gave Pierre a hard stare.

'And Captain Craufurd?' Pierre enquired.

'Why not,' he said, shuffling through his pockets. 'I tell you what, I'll go on nineteen.'

'What's so lucky about nineteen?'

'A bit private really,' Dominick told him. 'It concerns the birthday of a certain young lady. A rather charming young lady – and confidentially, Jerome, she thinks you're a bit of a rotter.'

'She's older now – a great deal older. And not so innocent,' Cavazza answered, shooting a malicious glance at the pathetically painted doll at Dominick's elbow.

The French had a machine-gunner on the roof of the Tribunal building. He was marking the entrance to the Avenue Carnot with sprouting fragments of tarmacadam and concrete. The leading Alpini were sheltering in doorways, as if from an unwelcome burst of rain. Then they were ducking from a much heavier downpour – the shattered masonry of the roof of the Tribunal.

'To the casino!' roared Colonel Grimaldi from the smoking turret of a Fiat tank. 'Find the coglione. We have a duty to gallant comrades.'

The Alpini troops tugged their helmets down on their foreheads, took a tighter hold on their Carcano rifles and made a dash up the Avenue Carnot for the ornate building where Dame Fortune dispensed her whimsical favours.

Dominick Craufurd collected another shovel-full of winnings, and frowned. It was not just that he was filling his threadbare wallet with the very dubious currency of the collapsing Third Republic. He had the unpleasant hunch that despite his winnings he was playing a desperately losing game.

'Why not spend it on a bridal gown for our Miss Hopkirk?' Jerome suggested with a half charming smile. 'This fancy dress you've put her in really doesn't suit her. She looks a mess! She's far too fresh and English for Chanel. Besides, what a picture she will make in white. I can see you both in Hereford Cathedral – a perfect couple, tailor-made for the pages of the *Tatler* and the *Sketch*. And afterwards, of course, you'll honeymoon in a quaint but damp hotel with Tudor beams. You're obviously made for each other – but I warn you, Dominick, old friend, and I speak from experience, you'll find this fresh apple of England is frankly a little green.'

'Perhaps you still haven't learned how to treat a lady,' Dominick fired back. But he knew he was only playing Jerome's game. Cavazza was playing for time.

Jerome had always been disastrously unlucky at Menton. Dominick had been luckier, as for that matter had Michel André. In fact it had been suggested by the town's more spiteful losers that André's friendship with Pierre went further than was strictly desirable between a gambler and his croupier. Michel, it was rumoured by the bad losers, had a secret understanding with Pierre. So was it André's game that Jerome was playing?

Jerome had moved back to the table and with a meaningful look at Pierre deposited his remaining chips on Numbers 30 and 9.

25.9.39. This had been the sequence of numbers that Jerome had backed. 25.5.39 was the date of the *Night Fishing* sketch.

It was so simple, but again he had been so slow!

And it was at this moment that Jerome di Cavazza made a lunge for his Beretta.

'Don't use your gun,' shouted Colonel Grimaldi to the Fiat driver. 'Just barge through.'

The Fiat tank swivelled round again and its tracks started to churn forward. The door trembled, then burst from its hinges. The tank had broken through, not into the inner sanctum of the Casino but into an outer room of play devoted to baccarat, blackjack and bridge. There was no resistance. The privileged who had idled by these tables had long since fled to more pacific climes. Grimaldi's Italian flag thrust forward like a lance and pointed to the next door.

'Put your foot down,' he screamed at his driver.

'Too slow,' Jerome breathed, 'too slow, my dear Dominick. Too slow on the uptake. Our Duce is right. You British have got a bit flabby.'

Dominick Craufurd stood there, one arm around Audrey Hopkirk, the other hand docked nonchalantly in his blazer pocket. He watched as Pierre shuffled back from the Manager's office and handed his enemy a large brown package. At the same time he gave Dominick a wry, half-apologetic shrug of the shoulders. 'These were Monsieur André's instructions, Captain Craufurd,' he wheezed. 'That was the combination agreed. The apologies of the House.'

A few doors away the advance guard of the Prince of Piedmont's army was bringing the massive Italian reinforcements – as if he needed any. Dominick Craufurd's shrewd guess was that his own allies were now in full retreat up the Avenue Carnot, through the Avenue Edouard VII and towards Monte Carlo.

'You're not seriously going to use that, are you?' Dominick asked, looking at the twitching muzzle of Jerome's Beretta. 'I would have thought there were enough Italians toting guns around this town without your adding your few halfpence-worth.'

A look of actual discomfort crossed the Italian's face.

'Your chances are small,' he said, 'but it's always on the cards you may get out of this town alive and back to England. In which case what you have seen this afternoon will be of value to your Government. You shouldn't have followed me, Dominick, and,' he looked venomously at Audrey, 'you shouldn't have picked up this lady in distress. I had finished with her, I had no further use for her.'

'You're a cool customer, Cavazza, but I don't believe there's a killer in you – not the kind of killer who shoots old friends.'

'For a friend, I don't think you know me very well. But then I don't think you know anyone very well. People, to you, are what you like to think they are. That's so English! You don't believe there is a killer in me? Why do you think our dear, dead friend Michel had an accident in the Alps? You see at that time I really adored Hélène. I didn't want to think of his hands on her.'

'But Michel André came back to life. You didn't do a very thorough job there.' Now it was Dominick who was playing for time.

'He was lucky. You are not so lucky. You had the picture on your mantelpiece and you looked only at the picture. You forget that Michel's little jokes were never obvious, there was always a joke within a joke. That was a bad mistake to make in wartime, Dominick. In wartime people die for mistakes like this.'

'You don't know whether to shoot me or run? Is that your difficulty?' Dominick asked solicitously. 'If you can't decide, why don't we play for it. But can we agree to leave Miss Hopkirk out of it?'

'No, if you lose you will die. It will be chance. And Miss Hopkirk. I have no use for her but no doubt I can find employment for her with our army. There is a call for sluts of this type behind our lines.'

'You've given me a lot to play for,' Craufurd murmured.

'Red against black. Or pair against impair, whichever you wish. Only if you don't mind I will keep my sidearms. I apologise, I am not after all a gentleman,' Jerome said with one of his most charming smiles.

'He's mad! He's playing games with you. Don't play his game!' Audrey cried, wrapping her bare arms around the one firm and steadying arm she had found in the South of France.

'I'm afraid he has no choice,' Jerome shot her a sly smile. 'Choose, Dominick.'

'Red, and be damned,' Craufurd answered.

Pierre turned the wheel.

The white ball slipped and slid, hopping over those tiny walls, going this way and that, misbehaving itself most frivolously beneath Pierre's hooded gaze; slipping, sliding, red, black, hoppity-hop, red, black, black, black.

Dominick was thinking – heads you win, tails you win. Red you win, black you win, pair you win, impair . . . you've got the gun.

It came from the other side of the room, a stentorian pounding as if a brontosaurus was at large in this normally quiet place. Colonel Grimaldi was riding roughshod straight into the heart of the Casino.

'Black,' shouted Jerome, 'I win.'

'It's still moving,' clipped back Dominick, as Audrey's hands tightened on his arm.

It *was* still moving, but the going was hard. And the wheel was changing colour, a snowstorm over the green baize, crazy flakes of Alpine snow falling in mid June. And this snow was no respecter of persons, it was falling lavishly over Jerome's curly hair, giving a much-needed covering to Pierre's bald cranium, flitting before Dominick's eyelids and causing him to blink, and choke.

Then with a whoosh the whole plaster ceiling collapsed, pancaking wildly to bury the game and gamesters alike.

He could see him through the cold smoke of the fallen plaster, a dim figure clasping a package to its breast, groping for an exit. A good old-fashioned straight right floored him, leaving the brown package free for Audrey to collect.

It was her stifled little scream that told Dominick he had overrated the power of his fist. There was more blood on Jerome's white shirt and sky-blue jacket than any honest punch could have drawn. Jerome di Cavazza had had the misfortune to stop a triumphal burst from the Fiat tank's machine-gun. Dominick had felled the virtual corpse of a friend who had never had any luck at Menton.

He took Audrey's hand and squeezed it, and did not let go. Hand in hand, they had a long way to run.

77

It had all the opulence, all the 'presence', of those lordly rivals, the Hôtel Normandie in Deauville or the Hôtel Negresco in Nice, even if it lacked something of their chic. Green lawns took you down by easy stages to Lac Léman where pretty boats cavorted without fear of mine or torpedo. The Hôtel Beau Rivage at Ouchy on the smart side of Lausanne was still as solid as the Bank of Switzerland, and about as unhurried.

'Well, that's blown it,' exclaimed Dominick, as he paid out his remaining Swiss francs on a ravishing evening gown in a swank shop in the hotel's shopping arcade. 'Now we sit tight and let that Hickson-Smith send us trunk-loads of money.'

'Shall I change now?' asked Audrey Hopkirk, her cheeks flushed with pleasure like a very ripe Cox's Orange Pippin.

'It's hardly cocktail time yet,' said Dominick Craufurd, consulting his half-hunter. 'On the other hand a traipse up to the room mightn't be a bad idea.'

'We really should have gone with the children to Geneva.'

'Methinks we've both had enough of aquatics,' said Dominick, grasping her arm tightly and steering her firmly towards the lift. 'And kids. Besides, you miss the whole point. In top circles, my love, before you dress up for cocktails, you've got to undress. It's what the gossip writers call gracious living, our friends the Windsors do it all the time.'

An hour later he was laying a playful pat on her bare bottom. 'Now then,' he urged, 'run along and help yourself to a bath. And try on that new dress. In a place like this it's not enough to look beautiful, you've got to look a billion francs to get served.'

She sat outside on the terrace drinking gin fizzes through a straw, making gurgling noises in the long highball glass. Dominick toyed with his whisky and soda but it was clear his mind was elsewhere. 'It will be damned embarrassing if that Hickson-Smith doesn't turn up with a handsome cheque. Hello....'

The figure that had come through the open windows and was hobbling towards them was not the stuffy attaché, however, although it appeared to be almost as prematurely aged, another case of *jeune vieux.* The heavy concentration lines in her lover's face caused Audrey Hopkirk to twist round, straw in mouth. What she saw caused her to freeze as fast as a well-shaken cocktail. He was traversing the long avenue that led through a series of small lawns down almost to the waterside. But his progress was slow because he walked with the aid of a white stick and the glasses were thick enough and black enough to suggest that they were there more for aesthetic than for optical reasons.

'Oh, God,' choked Dominick, when he had come close enough for unmistakable identification. 'Obviously no one ever taught you it was bad manners to tell the same poor joke twice.'

The man in question, who was wearing a quiet dark blue suit and the most anonymous of club ties, stopped and turned his ear in their direction as if trying to identify the voice against the sound of the wind and the sea and the distant hooting of boats. His white stick thrashed through the air quite close to them, knocking over a seat.

'Ah, there you are,' he stated in deep Charles Boyer tones. 'Ah, this is unexpected.'

Feeling with his hands, he found another seat and sat down in it.

'I'm sorry about your sight,' Craufurd grudgingly remarked. 'But you can't deny you asked for it.'

'There is a good English remark,' smiled Michel André behind his blacker-than-black goggles. 'Hoist with your own petard, eh? This is always very funny. However . . .' His long white fingers slid up to the glasses and with a conjuror's gesture snatched them off . . . *Voilà!*'

'Oh, God,' gasped Audrey in turn, staring into two burnt-out parchmenty pupils. 'That's horrible . . . !'

'Put those glasses back on,' barked Dominick. 'There are ladies present.'

'Alas,' said his old friend mournfully, 'there was a time, Nicky, when I thought you had flair, but I fear you've turned out as prosaic as the rest of your unutterable island race. You have many virtues, my dear Craufurd, but I fear you do not understand the science of *trompe l'oeil.*'

His beautiful hands were moving up with slow precision towards those sick eye-holes. Now they twisted sharply into and under the pupils.

'You're mad . . .' Craufurd began but did not finish.

Two ovals of membrane winking on the table, a discarded party joke. Two real eyes, triumphant, cruel and flecked with amusement and that infernal touch of salmon pink at the corner, also winked at them.

'Congratulations,' said Dominick.

'You see,' shrugged their owner, '*trompe l'oeil.* Or, to put it more simply for the benefit of the delightful Miss Hopkirk, you do not take to heart everything you see. That is the philosophy my dear friend, the innovator Bizet expounded and died for. That is the truth which our friends the Germans with their lavatory minds will never comprehend. That is what dear Pablo knew all the time. That is the dazzling nothingness behind *La Lumière Blanche.* A classic optical illusion, but then, what isn't?'

'You mean, those papers I sent our people . . . those notebooks full of algebra. . . .'

'A rabbit warren of false scents, a labyrinth of mirrored passages, a truth within a lie within a truth within a void. While the whole world's grunting and sweating it will be nice to keep a few of one's optical illusions.'

'Blast,' said Dominick Craufurd, worrying now about his credibility with his British masters and his future solvency. Instinctively he reached for the hand of Miss Audrey Hopkirk, girl, governess, and consolation supreme of a lifetime.

'Blast,' more gently now, as her hand responded to his. But her eyes were elsewhere, up there on the Hôtel Beau Rivage's massively bogus façade, pin-pointing a third-floor balcony where a figure stood in wafting cornflower-blue silk. It was fortunate Dominick Craufurd's eyesight was not that good because he had taken enough knocks for this particular moment. What Audrey Hopkirk saw was an outrageously beautiful woman in her prime with all the French elegance no English girl could ever match. What Dominick Craufurd would have perceived would have been something more: the triumphant shape and face of that murdered lady, Hélène Colmar.